I0818245

THE
STONE
SECRET

THE STONE SECRET

DEBBIE CASSIDY

Page & Vine
An Imprint of Meredith Wild LLC

This is a work of fiction. Names, characters, places, and incidents either are the product of the author's imagination or are used fictitiously, and any resemblance to actual persons, living or dead, business establishments, events, or locales is entirely coincidental. The publisher does not assume any responsibility for third-party websites or their content.

The author acknowledges the trademarked status and trademark owners of various products referenced in this work, which have been used without permission. The publication/use of these trademarks is not authorized, associated with, or sponsored by the trademark owners.

Copyright © 2023 Debbie Cassidy
Cover by Covers by Christian

All Rights Reserved.
No part of this book may be reproduced, scanned, or distributed in any printed or electronic format without permission. Please do not participate in or encourage piracy of copyrighted materials in violation of the author's rights. Purchase only authorized editions.

Paperback ISBN: 978-1-964264-74-5

CHAPTER 1

Cameron

The sun was making its way to midday position when I cracked open my dorm-room door to peer down the corridor.

All clear. Thank the gods.

"Cam?"

I jumped, hand flying to my chest. "Touron." I laughed weakly. "You startled me."

His eyes narrowed. "Startled you? Since when do you get startled so easily?"

A shadow moved at the bottom of my corridor. I dragged Touron into my room, slammed the door, and pressed my ear to the wood.

"Um...Cam? What in the world are you doing?"

"Shhh!"

Touron squeezed my shoulder. "You're freaking me out."

I hushed him again, listening for any sounds of movement outside my door. Long seconds ticked by, and finally satisfied that there was no one loitering outside my door, I turned to face him. "My ex is here."

"What?" His gaze flew to the door. "When? How?"

I'd been asking myself the "how" ever since Levi had shown up on my doorstep a few hours ago. "He turned up after you guys left this morning. I thought it was you. That you'd come back for your sweatshirt and then..." Levi's face filled my mind. His smile, the light in his eyes at seeing me and the answering lurch in my chest followed by a hollowing of my stomach because he couldn't be here. "This is fucked up."

"What happened? Tell me everything."

The hollow feeling returned. "He tried to kiss me, and I pushed him away. It was instinct, but the look on his face..." I squeezed my eyes shut. "Touron, he was so hurt." My stomach tightened recalling the look of pain in his beautiful sea-green eyes.

"What did he say?"

"Nothing. He didn't get a chance, because Mr. Raffi, the dorm master, showed up, asking him who he was. Levi went off with him, but he promised to speak to me later."

"And you thought later might be now?"

"I've barely slept. Touron, what am I going to do? If Levi is here, it means he came for me, because he loves me, but I..." Urgh.

"You're not in love with him anymore."

My heart ached beneath the weight of loss. "I can't be."

The pity in Touron's eyes made mine sting with the threat of tears.

He cupped my shoulder gently. "Cam, the mate bond is powerful and primal, and it *will* inevitably lead to love because your fated mate is your perfect match in every way, but the love you had for Levi was real too. You're allowed to mourn it."

Yes, that was what this feeling was. Grief. Loss for what could have been. "All I want now is Serath, and I know I can't have him, but—"

"He's your fated mate," Touron said. "Whether you can have him or not won't change the connection between you. Can you trust Levi?"

"Yes. Of course."

"Then you need to tell him the truth. About Serath being your fated mate, about you being a Basque, and about the fast track to elite and why. Bring him into the circle of trust."

He made it sound so simple. "I wish I'd come and talked to you earlier."

He shrugged. "What can I say? I have excellent problem-solving skills. Now, how about you shower and sort your hair out."

I reached for my hair, finger snagging in the tangles formed from all the tossing and turning I'd done. "That bad?"

"You look feral." He gave me half a smile. "On second thought, leave it. It's kinda adorable." He ruffled my already ruffled hair.

"Adorable?" I shuddered. "Hell no."

Compared to my frazzled state, Touron looked put together—fresh from the shower, sandy hair still damp, jaw clean-shaven. "You're up early, aren't you?"

He snorted softly. "You're not the only early riser in this dorm."

I usually was. My halfblood nature meant that I needed more sleep, so I usually went to bed earlier but woke before the other goyles. They didn't go to sleep until well after dawn and, even though they needed less sleep, weren't usually active till well after midday.

He patted my messy hair and headed for the door. "I'll put the coffee on."

"If you see a big guy with neck tats, tell him...tell him I need to speak to him."

"Neck tattoos?" His brows shot up. "Nice."

He closed the door softly behind him, and I grabbed a hairbrush and headed for the bathroom.

I'd broken up with Levi before coming to the academy, not because I'd wanted to but because I'd needed to let him go. I'd hoped to find him again, though, to rekindle things once my mission of finding out what happened to Romi was complete, and he'd probably realized that. He wouldn't be here otherwise.

But everything was different now. My wants, my goals...me.

Levi deserved the truth.

He deserved for me to let him go properly.

THIS EARLY IN the day the kitchen was free, allowing me and my friends to convene in private. I was on my second cup of coffee and all talked out. Sharniza, Palia, and Ginia were now also up to speed on Levi's arrival.

"I thought cadet intake was over," Sharniza said. "How did he get in?"

"Maybe his sire pulled some strings," Touron said. "Allowed him to take the entrance test late?"

"For a halfblood?" Palia looked skeptical. "His sire would have to have some serious clout to do that."

"What *did* he tell you about his sire?" Shar asked me.

I cast my mind back to the last time Levi and I had been together in the outside world. I'd told him the truth about what I was, and he'd been relieved because he was just like me. "He told me he was undeclared and in hiding, that his sire provided for him until he was eighteen, but that's all I know."

I'd walked out on him. Told him I didn't love him.

I guess my acting skills needed work.

Shar tapped the table with her blunt fingernails. Nails that would sprout talons when she shifted into her gargoyle form. "So, we know his sire has enough money and reach to hide his halfblood spawn." Like Basque had done for me. "Still, to get him into the academy...that takes the ability to pull some seriously powerful strings."

"Cadets have a high turnover," Touron said. "Only eighty percent survive cadet exams and make it to initiate or general training. We need all the goyles we can get, even halfblood ones."

"And now he's here..." Palia sounded speculative.

"Wow," Ginia said. "I can't believe he followed you. Took the entrance test just to be here with you." She covered her heart with her hand. "Swoon."

"You don't *say* swoon," Palia said. "You just do the action."

Ginia rolled her eyes. "Well, I say swoon. He's definitely in love with you." Palia elbowed her. "Ouch, what..." Her eyes went round. "Ah, yes, that's bad because you have Serath."

My stomach sank. "I don't *have* him. I can't have him." Having him would kill me and drive him insane. He was a sigma, and they were forbidden from consummating with a fated mate.

"It's so unfair," Ginia said. "On the one hand, you have Levi, who can be with you and who loves you, but you're off-limits because you're fated to Serath, who you can't have because..." She made a slitting throat motion with her finger.

"I think she's aware," Shar said dryly. "What we need to figure out is if we can trust this Levi to keep the fated mate information a secret."

Trust wasn't an issue when it came to Levi. "I've known him for almost a year. I trust him. He wouldn't do anything to hurt me."

"That may be so for the woman he loves and who he believes loves him back," Shar said. "But a goyle scorned is a vicious thing."

I couldn't imagine Levi being vicious to me. "He's a halfblood. He'll understand what it means to be fated." I glanced at Touron for support, and he nodded.

Shar sighed. "It's up to you. I still think we should err on the side of caution and wait to see how he reacts."

"To what?" Touron said. "To Cam telling him she no longer loves him?"

"Yes," Shar said.

"He didn't believe her the first time," Palia said. "What makes you think he'll believe her now?"

"Because *this* time, she'll be telling him she's in love with someone else." Shar fixed Touron with a pointed look.

Touron frowned. "What? You want me to..." He looked down at me in panic. "No. I can't."

Shar's shoulders sagged. "Right, there is *zero* chemistry between you two. He'd never buy it."

"You totally have the sibling vibe," Palia added.

"We need someone believable, someone..." She trailed off, gaze flicking over my head.

"What are you staring at?" Curi demanded with his signature lip-curl as he entered the room.

"Nothing." Shar's eyes gleamed wickedly.

Curi ambled over to the fridge and yanked open the door.

His blue hair was pulled back in a knot, and his feet were bare, giving him an almost vulnerable and approachable look. But there was nothing vulnerable and approachable about Curi. He'd been my most avid tormenter when I arrived, but somewhere along the way, he'd morphed into a silent protector. I didn't understand the goyle, and that left me wary around him.

Shar arched a brow at me.

I shook my head, mouthing, *Hell no.*

Curi drank straight from a carton of juice, crushed the empty box, then did a neat throw that dropped it in the trash can across the room.

"You can continue your pathetic conversation now," he said and left.

"Perfect!" Ginia said.

Palia looked horrified, but Touron seemed to be contemplating the concept.

What the heck? "You're crazy. Curi?"

"He saved you on the omega moon," Touron said. "And in the gym."

"He's an ass," Shar said. "But there's no denying the chemistry."

I stifled a gag. "Puh-lease." This was insane. "I don't need a fake boyfriend. I can tell Levi the truth." I looked to Touron for support again, but he had his gaze fixed on the table, chewing his cheeks in thought.

"You can," Shar said. "And you should, but only once we've seen what kind of jilted lover he makes."

"Shar's right," Touron conceded. "You've known the lover boy side of this guy. You have no idea how he'll react to finding out you can't be with him. I mean, if *I* was in love with someone, and she went with another goyle..." His chest rumbled in a low warning sound that made the hairs on the back of my neck stand at attention.

Palia nodded in agreement. "Goyle males are unpredictable when it comes to what they consider theirs, even halfbloods."

"If he takes it with grace, then you can tell him the truth," Ginia said. "You'll know that he won't go and spill your secret in a fit of jealous rage."

It looked like the team had made up their minds, and I had to agree that there was nothing wrong with caution. Telling Levi that I wasn't in love with him wouldn't be enough. Telling him I was with someone else might be, and, yes, I was curious to see how he'd take it. Curious to know if I could bring him into the circle of trust that had organically formed around me.

But our plan hinged on an angry blue-haired goyle's cooperation. "And what about Curi? You think he's going to just roll over and agree to play fake boyfriend?"

"I have a sneaky suspicion that Curi is more of a gentleman than he likes people to know," Shar said. "I think if you tell him you need help getting rid of Levi, then he'll do it."

"And Serath?"

The room went silent. Yeah, that shut them all up. My fated mate would not take kindly to any male playing happy family with me.

"If it keeps you safe..." Touron said. "You can tell Serath the plan. Get him on board."

I exhaled and dropped my head onto the table. "Fine. We'll do it your way. Test how Levi reacts and *only* tell him the truth if he doesn't go all psycho."

Shar patted my back. "Good girl."

Serath and I would be spending a lot of time together soon, seeing as my sire, Lionel Basque, had put him in charge of training me for the elite trial. My stomach trembled. Yeah, while my friends prepared for the initiation tests, I'd be training hard for the elite one, bypassing the initiation all together. I *had* to pass because without me the elite team wouldn't be able to get to Romi. Without me, there was no way to take down the graynite alpha.

I couldn't fail.

I wouldn't.

CHAPTER 2

CAMERON

Brown envelopes waited for each of us on the table by the exit.

"New timetables!" Palia said, way too excited about the fact.

Ginia smiled indulgently. "You are such a nerd."

Palia ignored her, too busy poring over the classes. "The new class is Supernatural Defense."

"I thought Arcana did that." Ginia looked confused.

"Aren't you going to open yours?" Shar asked. "We might still have some classes together."

"I doubt that. They'll probably have me in physical training every day." Basque wanted me fast-tracked to elite, and with the elite test happening in less than six weeks, I probably wasn't going to have much time for anything else. But I drew out the neat sheet of paper and studied the grid.

"You have Arcana and Supernatural Defense with us," Palia said, peering over my shoulder. "Herbology?" She made a what-the-fuck face.

"I asked Willowman to teach me how to make tinctures and stuff." The rest of my sessions were blocked out in red and blue. Blue for initiate training ground and red for instructor Halle. There was a lot of instructor Halle on the sheet, but then I was training to take the elite trial. A trial unique to the five bloodlines.

My stomach fluttered at the thought of the epic gargoyle. We'd be alone...touching, because you had to touch to practice hand-to-hand.

Fuck, what was I thinking? Nothing could matter but passing the test. I needed to be focused if I was going to learn anything, which meant that the mate bond between Serath and me couldn't be a distraction.

"We have extra training too," Touron said.

"Cadet exams are in three weeks," Sharniza said. "They'll be amping up the physicals."

"Then we'll join you in initiate training," Touron nudged, his forest-green eyes twinkling.

"You better." I swept my gaze over them all. "All of you need to make it." I wouldn't be taking the cadet exam. They'd skipped me over it and placed me with the initiates. My friends would join me soon, once they'd passed the cadet exams.

A solemn silence fell over us because we all knew that there was a strong possibility that not everyone would pass and make it to initiate training. "Does anyone know what it entails? The exam?"

"No," Palia said. "And believe me, I've tried to find out, but the cadets who make it through are sworn to secrecy."

And I'd be on the same training ground as those cadets. Cadets who'd survived. Who'd earned their place. Could I really be prepared for elite if I didn't earn it?

"Cam?" Touron nudged me. "Are you okay?"

"Yeah, I'm fine." But now that the thought was in my head, I couldn't shake it. I needed to speak to Serath.

"You should speak to Curi," Sharniza said.

"Huh?"

"About playing your lover. We could bump into Levi at any moment."

"I need to speak to Serath first and let him know what I've planned."

"The elites will probably still be asleep," Palia pointed out.

"Your initiate training is at five p.m., isn't it?"

She had a point. Levi was a halfblood like me and a new cadet. He might not be housed in this dorm, but he could be in the same class as us... "You're right. I'll speak to Curi now."

"We have class in an hour," Palia said. "Supernatural Defense, so be quick."

Speaking to Serath would have to wait. I had a blue-haired gargoyle to charm.

CURI YANKED OPEN his door on my third knock and then glared down his nose at me. "When someone doesn't answer their door, it usually means they don't want company," he growled.

"Well, you answered the door so..." I ducked under his arm and into the room.

A fresh linen scent hit me, clean and pleasing.

"What are you doing?" He sounded genuinely perplexed.

Wow, his room was neat as a pin.

"Walker!"

I spun to face him. "I need your help."

"No."

"No? You haven't even heard what I want."

"I don't need to." He crossed his arms and shook his head slightly. "I guess this is my own fault. I bail you out twice and you think we're friends."

"Ouch."

His eyes narrowed. "We are *not* friends, Walker. You're a liability. Likely to get yourself fucked, killed, or both. You don't belong here, and the sooner you take Mistress Carter up on her offer to bail, the better."

I guessed the news of my promotion to Basque heir hadn't gotten out yet. Perfect. I could use it to my advantage.

"Get out, Walker." He stepped away from the door and glared at me pointedly.

"Basque."

"What?"

"My name's not Walker, it's Basque." Was it wrong to enjoy the look of shock on his face? But in the next moment, his eyes narrowed to slits of disbelief.

"Bullshit."

"Nope. It'll be all over campus soon enough. I'm Lionel Basque's dirty little secret, and I'll be taking the elite trial in a few weeks."

He absorbed this information in silence. Then he closed the door. "You came here to find out about your brother, didn't you?"

"Yeah. I did."

"What did you find out?"

Curi wasn't in the circle of trust. "Nothing that wasn't already common knowledge, but my sire found out I was here. They need a Basque to complete the elite team, and I'm the only adult Basque they have."

"Well, that sucks for you. You won't survive to initiate, never mind elite."

No need to tell him that they planned to fast-track me because I planned to change that. "Maybe not, but I'm going to try. But that isn't what I came here to discuss. I need your help with something...unrelated."

He lifted his chin. "I'm listening."

Smart. I was a Basque, and even if I might only be one for a short time, he knew better than to burn his bridges. "My ex is here. I broke up with him before I came, but he's followed me, and I need him to understand that we're over."

His eyes narrowed. "Go on."

"I need a fake boyfriend." It sounded just as bad out loud as in my head.

His brows flicked up. "You want me to play your fake lover?"

Why did everyone keep saying lover? "*Boyfriend.* My fake *boyfriend.* Just for a week or so."

Curi dropped his arms and strolled toward me, stopping a

mere foot away. "And what's in it for me?"

I tensed at his proximity.

He let out a rough laugh. "Look at you. All wound tight. How do you expect your ex to believe we fuck on a regular basis if you can't relax around me?"

"I didn't realize this was a test." I forced my muscles to ease up and lifted my chin to look up at him. "I'm not afraid of you, Curi. I'm just particular about who I allow into my personal space. But I can make an exception for you...for a while."

He slow-blinked. "Fine. I'll do it. On one condition."

"What?"

"When it's time, *I* get to break up with *you*."

I bit back a smile. "Sure."

His lips curved in a wicked smile. "And when I do it, I want you to cry and beg me not to."

I grit my teeth. "Seriously?"

He shrugged a powerful shoulder. "Do you want me as your fake lover or not?"

Urgh. "Fine. I'll put on the waterworks."

He grinned down at me. "When do we start?"

"We have class in"—I glanced at my watch—"thirty minutes. You can walk me."

"Do I have to hold your hand?" He looked down at my hand as if it was a bear trap.

"It might help."

"Fine. I'll meet you in the foyer in ten minutes." He started pulling clothes out of his drawers. "Or you can stay and get comfortable with your lover's assets."

I was out the door in a flash with the sound of his low chuckle ringing in my ears.

Halfway down the stairs, my stomach sank. I was about to hurt the man I'd been in love with. It was the last thing I wanted to do, but Shar was right. We needed to know how he would react to know whether he could be trusted with the truth about Serath and me. I needed him in the circle of trust because I cared about him.

Hurting him was going to hurt me too.

CHAPTER 3

CAMERON

"Relax," Curi said under his breath. "Or do you want everyone to think I'm kidnapping you?"

I leaned into Curi, allowing our arms to touch, trying to ignore how large his hand was around mine. Levi and I had never held hands like this. Never had the chance to go out in public like this. We'd been together, but we'd never dated. Heck...*I'd* never dated.

Curi was the first male I'd held hands with.

"Why are you hyperventilating?" Curi asked, his voice a low growl of concern. "Is he here? Where?"

"No. I'm...I'm fine."

Goyles appeared on the path ahead of us, all headed to the main building for class. Several glances were thrown our way, but we were quickly dismissed. These cadets didn't know Curi's and my history.

"Relax," Shar said from behind us. "Unclench your ass."

"Sharniza!" Palia admonished.

Ginia snickered.

We approached the main building, where several goyles were gathered on the porch. I recognized Dayn's stocky form first. The gargoyle had been Curi's minion for a little while but had turned on him after Curi refused to fight the elite Selas. Bax, another one of Curi's ex-minions, stood with him. They fixed their stunned gazes on us as we strolled closer.

"What the actual fuck?" Dayn said. "You're banging the halfblood now?" He sneered at me. "If you spread your legs for him, you can spread them for us—"

Curi punched him in the mouth.

Blood sprayed, and Bax bellowed in shock.

Dayn wiped his lips and bared his bloody teeth. "What the fuck, Curi?"

"Don't talk about her. Don't think about her. She's mine!" His voice was a boom of authority that shook my insides.

Damn, he was good. But then, he was a Mason, one of the five elite bloodlines.

Dayn looked like he was about to throw down, but Saffe, one of the smaller goyles from our dorm, stepped forward. "Dammit, Dayn, haven't you heard? It's all over campus. She's a Basque."

Dayn stilled. "What?"

Curi smirked. "My Basque. Bitch." Then he took my hand and steered me around the group and into the building. Silence followed us, breaking only once we were inside.

"THAT WAS FUCKING awesome!" Ginia said as we made our way up the steps.

"Ginia!" Palia whisper-hissed.

Ginia ignored her. "The way you popped him in the mouth—fluid, fast. I need you to teach me how to move like that."

Curi slid a glance her way. "I'm not a fucking instructor."

Palia sucked in a sharp breath. All the cursing was probably giving her heart palpitations.

"How much longer do I need to hold your hand?" he asked me.

"Just till we get into class. If Levi is in there, then he needs to see us together."

"*Harrumph*."

We followed Palia up a flight of steps to the top of the building where the domed ceiling was situated.

"We're in the same room as Arcana," Palia said.

There was already a small line filing into the room, past all the plants that lined the corridor. No sign of Levi. Maybe he wasn't in this class.

Part of me was relieved, but the other part was disappointed, because the quicker we got this over with, the better.

I stepped into the room close behind Curi, my hand trapped in his, and froze at the sound of a familiar rumbling voice.

Levi stood at the front of the class, speaking to Yarrow. He was dressed, not in lastonflex, but in a shirt, sleeves rolled up to expose his forearms and top button undone revealing the intricate whorls of his tattoo.

My breath stalled.

"Cam?" Shar said behind me.

But I couldn't speak because Levi was looking right at me. His eyes warmed, then flicked to Curi and down to where our hands were joined. And there it was, the pain followed by the flash of anger.

"Everyone have a seat," Yarrow instructed. "I'd like to introduce you to our new instructor, Master Halle."

Halle? Serath was here? But no. Yarrow was looking at Levi.

Levi was the new instructor.

Levi was a Halle.

CHAPTER 4

CAMERON

Levi talked, but the rush of blood in my head made it impossible to focus on what he was saying. He stood in front of the class, looking like he belonged there. Like he had wisdom and skill to impart.

He cut a powerful and beautiful figure, and my heart ached for the pain I'd put into the lines of his face. He didn't look at me as he spoke, and after a few moments, the buzzing in my head subsided.

"You could have told me your ex was the new instructor," Curi said under his breath.

My head reeled. "I didn't know."

"Hunters come in two kinds," Levi said. "Those that are born into it and those that choose to take up the mantle." He tapped the tattoo on his neck. "This is my hunter's mark. A sign of the grove I was born into."

"What are groves?" Saffe asked.

Levi's gaze flicked my way, and my heart climbed up into my mouth because this was stuff we'd never talked about. Stuff he hadn't told me.

"A grove is a group of druids. There are several, all descended from a different druid bloodline. All with their own mark. We help to protect the natural order of things by eliminating anything that threatens it."

"Like graynites?"

His mouth slanted down. "Hunters, in general, don't have the ability to harm a graynite. We work on keeping the other threats in control to allow the gargoyles to focus on the graynite threat."

"You're a halfblood, though, aren't you?" Dayn said. "Are you saying you're part druid?"

"Yes. My mother is the leader of our grove." He looked at me. "But I left that life to fly solo a long time ago. I wanted to hunt on my own terms not be bound by heritage."

But he'd come back to it. To this place. Into the thick of it. For me. I hated that I was doing this to him.

"I can't teach you how to bring down a graynite," Levi continued, "but you won't always be fighting graynites. There will be other threats. Mutts, fangs, and lesser-known malevolent creatures that lurk in the shadows. I'll teach you about their weaknesses, and along with Master Yarrow, I'll show you how to shield yourself against the negative energy they exude while harnessing the positive energy of nature that's all around us. My technique will also help you learn to activate and reinforce your shields, should you come across a graynite."

Yarrow stepped forward. "This is very exciting. The arrival of Master Halle means we can hone your shields in practical tests against real threats in a controlled environment."

"What do you mean?" Waxen asked.

Yarrow's smile was thin and wicked. "It means that in a couple of weeks, you'll be testing your shields against a real threat."

Murmurs broke out among the cadets. I tried to catch Levi's eye, but he had his gaze fixed studiously on Yarrow.

"Master Halle will teach you how to feel for and call to the power of nature to assist you." He looked at Levi, handing the floor back to him.

"Pureblood druids can manipulate the elements of nature. Druid hunters use nature to fight against threats; however, as a halfblood, I don't have such a direct line. To compensate, I've learned how to coax my goyle shields to merge with the elemental power around me so they are enhanced. I can teach you."

"With Master Halle on board, we will make this class the strongest defense," Yarrow said, his golden eyes bright with excitement.

Levi was druid born. He was a Halle, one of the big five gargoyle families just like me, but the biggest thing, the thing that twisted my stomach into knots was that being a Halle meant he was related to Serath.

THE CLASS PASSED quickly with a Q&A mainly centered around Levi's past, things that I didn't know about the man I'd been in love with. Things that made me see him in a different light. Not as an equal, but as someone who was above me—a mentor, a warrior.

My attraction to him made sense now. My gargoyle nature had recognized his and been drawn to his strength. We were kindred in so many ways but not an ultimate match, according to the cosmos. Serath was my match. My mate. And now, with Levi's association to him, it would be even harder to hide it.

"I need to tell him the truth."

Shar looked torn but then nodded.

"Okay," Levi said from the front of the class. "If there are no more questions..."

"I have one," Dayn said. "What branch of Halle do you come from?"

"Mr. Lowther, that is hardly relevant," Yarrow snapped.

"No." Levi's throat bobbed. "It'll come out eventually, and I have nothing to hide." His neck tensed as if he was stopping himself from turning his head to look my way. "My sire is Ulrickson Halle."

The room fell into pin-drop silence.

What the fuck? Was that bad? Shar's face had drained of color.

"If that's all, then class dismissed," Yarrow said.

Yarrow led Levi to the back of the room while everyone began gathering their things to leave.

I had to talk to him. To tell him how sorry I was and apologize. To tell him the truth. I made to get out of my seat, but Shar grabbed my hand, her eyes wide with panic.

"Don't," she said.

"Shar, he's related to Serath. It'll be nearly impossible to keep him in the dark about us so—"

"His father is Ulrickson Halle." She said it as if it should mean something to me, but the blank look on my face must have reminded her how little I knew about this world. "Ulrickson is no ordinary Goyle. He's head councilman."

I shook my head. "Okay...so?"

"Dammit, Cam. When it comes to Stone law, he *is* the law."

Needles of ice pricked my skin. "Levi wouldn't tell him."

"Can you be certain of that?" Shar asked.

I wanted to say, yes, that of course I knew Levi, but the last thirty minutes had taught me how little I knew about the man I'd shared a bed with.

"Miss Basque," Levi said. "A word, please."

Fuck.

There was warning in Shar's eyes as she let go of me.

Curi stood with me, playing the dutiful boyfriend.

Levi gave him a cool smile. "You can wait for her outside the room, Mr. Mason. I won't keep her long."

Curi looked to me. "You okay, babe?"

I bit back a wince. "Of course. I'll meet you in the foyer downstairs."

He shrugged and followed the others out of the room.

Silence settled around us.

The door closed.

We were alone.

It hurt to look at him. Familiar. Comfortable. Mine. But not any longer. That thrum, that connection that had existed between us was gone. At least for me, and it left a hollowness inside me.

"You moved on fast," Levi said finally.

The words *I'm sorry* sprang to my lips, but if I was going to do this, then I needed to be confident in my decisions. "Curi is a good match for me."

Bitterness turned his smile upside down. "And I wasn't?" He shook his head. "I don't believe that, just like I didn't believe you when you told me you didn't love me."

"I don't love you."

His eyes narrowed. "No. What we had. What I felt. What *we* felt was...*is* real."

"You're wrong, and if you came here based on that, then you made a mistake."

He flinched. "You're lying. You're hiding something. I know you, Cam."

"I wish I could say the same about you."

He exhaled. "I was going to tell you everything that night, but you left. You didn't answer my calls, and I knew...I knew you'd gone."

"So, you decided not to take no for an answer." I forced my lips into a wry smile. "Typical arrogant male behavior."

"Dammit, Cam, this isn't you. What's going on here? I find out you're a Basque, that you've been fast-tracked to take your brother's place as an elite? Do you even know what the elite trial entails?"

"It doesn't matter. I'm doing it either way." He didn't know about Romi being alive and how this was the only way to save him, and I couldn't trust him enough to tell him. His father might be head councilman, but I had no clue if Ulrickson knew about guardian activity and Romi's predicament.

"Listen, I get it. The next Basque is still a child. They need an adult Basque, and they're probably pressuring you into this. I can help. I can speak to my father and fix this."

His father. Not his sire. My heart sank. "You two are close?"

Levi shrugged a shoulder. "He's always been there for me."

"I thought...I thought you said he kept you a secret. Provided for you but kept you a secret."

"Yes, he did, but only because my mother wanted it that way. She didn't want her indiscretion getting out. The fact that she lay with a gargoyle..."

"I don't understand."

"Gargoyles are outside of nature because they're not from this world. It's heavily frowned upon for a druid to have relations with such creatures. My father would have been proud to claim me, halfblood or not."

"So, what changed? How come he went back on his word to your mother?"

"I didn't give him a choice. Look, Cam, up until now, I didn't care either way, but when you left..." His throat bobbed. "I knew I had to be a part of this world. That I had to be with you." His voice cracked with emotion, and guilt crushed my lungs.

He'd come here for me. He'd left his life behind and convinced his sire to get him a position here so he could be with me. The Levi I knew prized his independence, his freedom. He reveled in the hunt, in getting his hands dirty, but...but he'd given it up for me. He loved me...truly loved me, and I...

I hated myself.

My eyes heated with the threat of tears, but I blinked them back, pushing out the words that needed to be said. "Levi, I'm sorry, but it's over. You and I are over. I'm with Curi now. I'm happy. You should...You should go back to your life."

He studied me for several beats, his sea-green gaze intense and probing. "This *is* my life now, Cam. I'm not going anywhere, and if you're determined to take this elite trial, then I'm going to make sure you have the strongest shields imaginable."

My throat pinched because fuck him for being so amazing. Maybe I could trust him. Maybe—

"But I still think you need to reconsider. I can speak to my father and—"

"No. If you do that, I'll never speak to you again."

He blinked sharply. "I'm trying to help you."

"And you can do that in your classes. Other than that, I'm fine. I've made friends and found my place here."

"You mean you found Curi."

There it was—the bitter edge of jealousy. "Yes. I have. Now if you'll excuse me, I don't want to keep him waiting any longer."

I headed for the door.

"I'm not a fool, Cam," Levi said to my back. "Like I said, I know you. I know when you're hiding something."

"Yet you didn't know I was hiding what I was."

"No, but I knew you were hiding something."

I hurried out of the door and down the corridor, his words ringing in my ears because, yes, he'd suspected I was hiding something. He'd probed for information enough times.

Hiding my connection to Serath from him was going to be harder than expected.

All I could do was hope it didn't prove impossible.

CHAPTER 5

CAMERON

Curi had waited for me in the foyer. It was strange to see him hanging with my friends. We hurried outside, away from all the other goyles.

"Oh. My. God," Ginia said. "An instructor? And he's gorgeous."

"If you swoon, I'll slap you," Palia said.

My heart rate slowed from its pounding pace of fight or flight. "I didn't know he was an instructor."

"Did he buy it?" Touron asked.

"He thinks I'm hiding something."

"Dammit," Sharniza said. She fixed a glare on Curi. "You need to play the part better."

Curi gave her a filthy look. "What do you want me to do? Stick my tongue down her throat in front of him?"

"If that's what it takes," Shar said.

"No!" I stared at her in horror. "Hell no."

Curi yawned and stretched. "You have no idea what you're missing." He stepped close and put his arm around my shoulder. I made to pull away on instinct, but he gripped me tight, leaning in to whisper, "He's on the porch, watching us."

Shit. I turned my head toward Curi so our faces were inches

apart, and I could feel his warm breath on my lips. "Thanks, I—"

"Miss Basque!" The booming voice shot straight to my core.

I didn't need to look to know who it belonged to, but I did anyway.

Serath bore down on us, his huge frame taut with tension, husky-like pale eyes stark and bright in his beautiful face, which was all angles of rage right now.

"Oh shit," Touron said.

"We have training. Now," he snapped.

Bullshit. Training wasn't for a couple of hours, but the fire in his eyes warned me to put distance between Curi and me immediately. But Curi had other ideas.

"See you later, babe." He pressed his lips to mine in a soft kiss that turned my blood to ice, because he might well have sealed his own death warrant.

But there was no roar. No bellow of rage. Nothing.

And the reason stood beside Serath with her hand on his arm. Selas watched us with milky eyes, her lips tight as if she were in pain.

"Meet us in training room two, Miss Basque," she said, her voice strained.

Serath's jaw was tight. Was he grinding his teeth?

I took a step toward him, and Selas shook her head, the motion so slight that if I hadn't been looking for it, I'd have missed it.

They turned and walked away.

"Your ex has gone," Curi said, but his attention was on Serath's and Selas's retreating forms. "I need to hit the gym. When do you need me next?"

"I'll let you know."

He ambled off, and Sharniza let out a low whistle. "That was too close. You need to fill Serath in. Now."

"How come your ex didn't speak to Serath? They're both Halles," Palia asked.

"I doubt they know each other. Levi didn't grow up around

the goyles."

"Still," Touron said. "They're family, and he must know who Serath is, even if Serath doesn't know who he is."

"I don't know." And right now, it didn't matter. "I'll catch you guys later."

I had a raging gargoyle to placate.

So far, we'd only used training room one and the outdoor training fields but never room two. My insides felt like jelly as I made my way down a flight of steps and pushed through the double doors that led into a room lined with workout equipment and mats. The center of the room was clear of all equipment, though. Strange.

Serath stood on the far side of the room with his back to me. His shoulders bunched at my entrance, but he didn't turn to face me.

Selas patted his back, whispering something to him. He growled low and menacing, and Selas stepped back, shaking her head.

"What were you thinking?" she said to me.

"Look, I was going to come see you and tell you—"

"Tell me what?" Serath said, his tone low and rumbling. "That you've taken up with the Mason boy? Is that how you intend to manage your urges?" His shoulders heaved. "By giving to him what is rightfully mine?"

"Serath!" Selas admonished. "Cam, you can't have a lover. Not while you're here. Not while *he's* here." She jerked her head toward Serath.

"Neither of us gets to fuck anyone else," Serath growled. "Ever. You're my fucking mate."

The way he said it, the possessive ownership, made the beast simmering under my skin sit up and purr. But I wasn't allowed to have this. Enjoy this. Him. Us. It was forbidden, and now he was standing with his back to me, ordering me to suffer. To eat up the pain and deal with it.

Rage bubbled up from the dark place inside me where all my pain and disappointment resided and spilled out of my mouth in a series of harsh words.

"So, I'm not allowed to have a life? Date? Have sex?"

"Cam!" Selas stared at me in shock.

I didn't mean it. I didn't care about any of it, but I couldn't stop. I was pissed. Eye-burning, pulse-thumping pissed. Pissed at how unfair this was. How much it hurt to be standing in the same room as him and not be able to claim him. Not be able to hold his hand like I'd held Curi's.

It wasn't his fault, but, "Fuck you, Serath. You don't want me, so no one gets me. I have to be a fucking nun for the rest of my life? Is that it? Is that what you—"

He moved in a blur, grabbed me, and hauled me to his body, crashing his lips to mine and turning my angry, stiff frame into putty. I melted against him, fingers sinking into his hair as I kissed him back with bruising intensity. There was no need for oxygen, no need for thought, just the pressure of his teeth and the rasp of his tongue, and I was drowning in him.

"Serath, Serath, stop!" Selas's voice penetrated the fog of desire and need clouding my mind.

The kiss softened and broke, but Serath didn't let go. Instead, he gripped my nape and locked gazes with me.

"Let's get something straight, Cam. I want you. I want you so fucking much it's like fire ants beneath my skin. But I can't have you. Not without losing you. Believe me, if this was just about my sanity, I'd happily give it up just to know..." His throat bobbed. "To know what it's like to be complete, even if it's only for one night."

His visage blurred, and I blinked back tears. "I'm sorry. I didn't mean what I said, I'm just..." I lightly touched his face. "This is just so hard."

"I know." He cupped my cheek. "I understand why you think having another male will make it easier, but I'll kill him if he touches you like that again." He said it calmly and matter-of-fact.

I believed him, because if another female kissed him, I'd have to kill her too.

It was the nature of our beasts.

It was who we were.

"Curi isn't my lover. I asked him to pretend."

"What?" Selas said, reminding me she was in the room. "Why?"

"Because my ex followed me here."

Serath's eyes narrowed to slits, and his grip on me grew tighter. When he spoke, his tone promised pain. "He followed you?"

"I broke up with him before coming here. I told him I didn't love him."

He exhaled sharply. "But you did. You loved him."

A dull ache bloomed in my chest at the bereft tone in his voice. Knowing my heart had belonged to another was causing him pain, and my instinct was to take that pain away. "I was falling for him. But now..." I dropped my forehead to Serath's jaw and closed my eyes. "Now there's only you."

He wrapped his powerful arms around me in a hug that made me feel small and safe. "You believe showing him you've moved on will work?"

"Yes. It'll prove I meant what I said before I left him, so I asked Curi to be my fake boyfriend."

"Because you can't tell him about Serath." Selas nodded. "I understand. You want to keep him at a distance." She frowned. "And Curi agreed to do this for you?"

"I guess my being a Basque helped with his decision."

She pressed her lips in a thin line. "Hmmm."

I sighed. "Look, I would have told Levi the truth. I was going to. I always trusted him, but..."

"But what?" Serath asked softly.

"He's not a cadet, Serath. He's the new instructor."

"We have a new instructor?" Selas looked surprised.

"Yes." I peered up at Serath. "And his father is Ulrickson Halle."

CHAPTER 6

SERATH

The sound of Ulrickson's name on her lips spawns lava in my gut as long-buried emotions threaten to rise, but I bury them expertly. I've had years of practice.

Ulrickson has a halfblood son and yet kept him a secret. On the one hand, I'm not surprised. Ulrickson is all about appearances, but on the other hand, goyles love to boast about their virility, and there are many halfbloods outside of our world who carry their sire's name proudly, working on the outskirts in admin positions.

But this goyle, Levi, is here as an instructor. What makes him so special? "What is this Levi teaching the cadets?"

"Supernatural defense. His mother is a druid, and he's a hunter."

She sounds proud of that fact, and my beast doesn't like it. "You can't trust him. If he's anything like his father, then you must keep your guard up."

"What do you mean?"

"Serath..." Selas nods at me. "Tell her. She should know."

Most everyone knows my story, but only my team knows of my suspicions, and the fact that Selas is encouraging me to share them with Cameron shows that she already sees her as part of our team.

A gentle warmth fills my chest, and I shoot her a smile.

She nods, milky eyes soft with encouragement.

"Ulrickson is my father's older brother, and I'm certain he orchestrated my parents' death."

Cam stares at me in stunned silence. "Serath...what the... How?"

Memories of that time rise, bringing the very emotions I've suppressed for so long with them. This time, I allow them to wash over me, letting them breathe before pushing them back down.

"My father was an elite, and my mother was a medic." I can see them in my mind's eye, smiling at one another or holding hands and kissing. There was so much love in my life back then. So much hope. "My father was an alpha, and my mother chose him as her only mate, even though as an omega she could have taken several. But then, my mother was always headstrong. She even joined an alpha team as a medic. They used to argue good-naturedly about it all the time, how an omega's place wasn't on the front lines, but my mother had a gift for healing, and she wouldn't be denied. They were so close. The love they shared...Sometimes it was as if I wasn't there." Fuck. I'm oversharing. "Anyway, elite teams are allowed time off every six months, even though they're still on call. While on leave, my father got a call that an outer rim settlement was under attack. My parents left late in the night but never returned. I found out later that the call never went out to the other elites or the alpha team. My parents walked into danger alone. Their bodies were never recovered among the charred remains of that settlement, but they found my mother's medic bag and my father's broken watch."

"Oh, Serath..." Cam's eyes are wide with horror and compassion, and my throat pinches. "How old were you?"

"Ten years."

Shadows dance in her eyes. "I'm so sorry for your loss."

The sincerity in her words acts like a balm on wounds that will likely never heal. "Thank you."

"What happened to you once they were...gone? Did Ulrickson

take you in?"

A bitter smile tugs at my lips. "Ulrickson didn't even come to see me. Not once. I was taken to a group home for orphaned goyles." My jaw tightens at the memory of that place. The hunger, the constant need to be vigilant. "Farnell took me in a few years later. He caught me pummeling one of the other goyles in the yard. Told me there were better outlets for my aggression. He was shocked to find out I was a Halle. Apparently, that information had been left off my records."

"Ulrickson was trying to hide you?"

I love how her mind makes connections. Love how smart she is. "I think so. Together, Farnell and I found out that Ulrickson had made the dispatch calls the night of the attack. There'd been an inquiry where he claimed something must have gone wrong with the comms units. The reports confirm a technical issue, but I know...I know he created that issue."

"But why? Why kill his brother?"

I've wondered this very thing for so many years. "Ulrickson wasn't always head councilman. He failed the academy and was forced into admin while my father passed and became an elite. Ulrickson was responsible for dispatch for years, but after my father died, he clawed his way up to councilman and now...Now he's one of the most powerful gargoyles in Arcadia, and I know...I just know the death of my parents paved his way. I simply don't know how."

She wraps her arms around my waist and squeezes. "I'm sorry, Serath. So sorry."

How can this contact be so soothing? How can her holding me like this take the edge off a pain that's acted like a thorn in my side for decades?

I hug her back, reveling in her scent and her body, which fits perfectly against me. This female is made for me but denied to me. Her hair is silken against my lips as I drop a kiss to her head and breathe her in. Mine.

My chest vibrates as my beast stirs.

"We should train now," Selas says. "We only have a few weeks until the elite trials and a few days before she trains alongside the initiates prepping for their final exams. She needs to be on par with them."

My heart sinks. She'll be in danger. So much danger.

Cam wriggles in my arms, body rubbing against me and inflaming me. I release her with a soft growl, and she looks up at me, cheeks flushed.

Fuck, she is so beautiful. If Selas wasn't in the room right now—

"I'm not skipping the cadet exam," Cameron says.

Her words are ice water.

"What?" Selas draws her away from me. "What do you mean? Your father said—"

"I know what he said, but hear me out. If I have to wait to take the elite trial till *after* the cadet exam, then why can't I just take the cadet exam like everyone else?" Selas looks like she's about to speak, but Cameron forges on. "I don't feel comfortable training alongside the initiates if I haven't earned the right to be there."

"You're a Basque," Selas replies. "The only Basque that can take up the mantle and—"

"You think I might die in the cadet exams and never make it to elite."

Selas snaps her mouth closed and breathes through her nose. "I don't think that. I believe in you."

And so do I. "Cameron's right." Selas looks at me in surprise, but I forge on. "The elite trial can only take place on a sidhe moon, which is six weeks from now. She could take the cadet exams if she wants. It will be good preparation. It's not like we can fail her. When she makes it through, she can join the initiates and take the elite trial."

Cameron is looking at me with an indecipherable expression.

"What is it?"

"You didn't say if. You said when." She beams at me, and my head feels light with euphoria. "Thank you."

"I think she needs to know about the elite trial," Selas says softly.

The warm, fuzzy feeling vanishes.

"I know it'll be dangerous," Cameron says. "But I'll be ready. I'm willing to work hard, and I have you guys to prepare me for it."

Selas arches a brow my way, handing me the floor.

I cup Cam's shoulders. "The other exams are pass or fail. Yes, some cadets die during them, but there is no penalty for failing to score. You can score low and still survive and end up in an administration position. The elite trials are pass or die. There is no in between."

"What...what do you mean?"

"You either pass the tests and live, or you fail and don't come out at all. There is no scoring low in the elite trial. No body to be returned to a family if you fail."

"What happens? What is the trial?"

My scalp tightens as my subconscious recalls the trial, but the memory is gone, wiped by the council.

Selas answers for me. "We don't remember. Our memories of the trial have been wiped."

Cameron's disquiet is loud in the silence that follows. When she speaks, her tone is firm, and her eyes flash with determination. "My brother is in the clutches of the enemy. Failure isn't an option for me, and neither is death. Speak to Lionel and tell him I'm taking the cadet exams. I need to do them, for my own confidence and peace of mind."

"I'll speak to Lionel," Selas says.

Cameron nods curtly, her expression fierce. "Now let's train."

Not falling in love with her is going to be impossible.

CHAPTER 7

CAMERON

Selas demonstrated how to evade, how to get under Serath's defenses and attack, but I was struggling to nail it. Serath's scent and proximity scrambled my mind.

I landed on my back for the umpteenth time with him on top of me, huge frame hovering over mine. He was beautiful and sexy. Yes, so fucking sexy. My skin flushed, heat focused like a firm grip on my throat and a pulsing need between my thighs. Every point of contact was fire, every breath shared was aching need.

I wanted his mouth on mine. His naked skin against mine.

His pupils swallowed his irises, and a rumbling vibration thrummed between us. He dipped his head, lips drawn to mine.

"Focus!" Selas snapped.

Shit.

Serath blinked sharply and, in the next moment, was shoved off me by Selas. She stood over us, hands on hips like a superhero facing off against a villain. "This isn't going to work."

Serath groaned and pulled himself to his feet, walking away from us, his hands fisting at his sides.

I closed my eyes and breathed, forcing his scent out of my head. "I can't concentrate."

"I know," Selas said. "We need to rethink this training

method. You two together are a bad combination."

"We need to figure this out," Serath said. "Once she's an elite, we'll be on the same team. In the same building." Another groan.

Yes, we'd be under the same roof with our rooms close together. Rooms with beds and...Oh God, this was insane. "I need to be able to focus with him around, or I'll be a liability."

"It won't come to that," Selas said. "We'll bring in the others to help next session. Orix can take Serath's place in hand-to-hand, but Serath will stay in the room so you can get used to his scent being present during battle." She offered me her hand to help me up. "We will figure this out."

My hair was a mess, most of it having come out of the tie. I yanked off the elastic and gathered it up into a high pony, then rolled my shoulders. "I'm not done for the day. Selas, can we spar? Like, really spar, no holding back on your part."

Selas smiled wickedly. "With pleasure."

SELAS KICKED MY ass.

Nothing surprising there, but it gave me a chance to study her technique and to fight with Serath's scent hanging in the air. It spiked every time Selas landed a blow, every time I hit the mat. His low growls accompanied every hit I took, as if he felt the pain of it.

Selas called it after twenty minutes. "Take a seat, Cam." Then to Serath, "You did well. I was expecting you to tackle me to the ground at one point."

Serath looked sheepish. "I can't say it didn't cross my mind." He bridged the distance between us and gently pinched my chin, tipping my head up so he could study my face. "No bruises. Good."

"Her stone skin activated every time I landed a blow," Selas said. "Unlike with Curi. You're getting more in touch with your gargoyle self," she said to me. "We can work on that more too."

I'd only had a couple of sessions with Selas, but her methods worked. "Thank you."

"Now take a seat and observe."

Serath was still holding my chin, his thumb sweeping back and forth against my skin.

"Um...Serath?" Selas said.

He released me reluctantly and headed to the mats with her.

For the next few minutes, I watched Selas use her smaller frame to her advantage, slipping past Serath's defenses several times to land a hit, managing to evade his grasp over and over. She didn't have the height and bulk of the elite leader, but she was faster and lighter on her feet, her moves like a mesmerizing dance, and wait...It was a dance. Her moves were the kata she'd shown me but amped up. Damn...

Selas did a flip and landed in a crouch just as the door at the back of the room opened.

"Looks like time's up," Selas said as Farnell strode in.

"You're not booked in for another hour," he said to Serath.

"It was empty," Serath said. "Don't worry. We still have enough energy for the initiates."

Goyles started to file into the room.

Farnell's jaw ticked as his gaze fell on me, raking me over as if he couldn't quite believe what he was seeing. "You've got some big shoes to fill." He shook his head. "If you even survive."

"She can do it," Selas said firmly.

Farnell exhaled through his nose. "If she makes it, all she needs to do is hold the position until a full-blooded goyle comes of age. Just in case the alpha emerges. With your help, she might just do it."

It was obvious he didn't know about Romi and the real reason I was being pushed into elite.

"I'll walk you out," Selas said to me. "Serath is on initiate training today."

Serath avoided my gaze now that Farnell was in the room, outwardly aloof and disconnected from me. He was protecting me, of course, hiding our connection, but it still stung.

It was only when we were outside and past the group of

initiates heading into the room that a thought hit me. "I'm the only Basque who can take an elite spot and get Romi back, right?"

"Right."

"So, if they find out I'm Serath's fated mate, won't that stop them from killing me? They need me now."

"Yes, they need you, but Serath can be replaced. There are other Halles who can take his spot."

"Wait...what...They'd send him away?"

"No. Cam, they'd probably just kill him. Rather him than you. After all, you're the valuable one now."

My blood ran cold, ice pricking at my nape. The threat of my own demise was nothing compared to the threat of Serath's.

Our secret could never come out.

Levi could never know, which meant any kind of friendship, any connection we'd ever had would have to end.

CHAPTER 8

CAMERON

The gang were in the kitchen, making food, when I got back. Touron fried steaks while Palia pulled baked potatoes out of the oven, and Shar tossed a salad. Ginia was busy setting the table.

A cadet popped his head in the door, took one look at the scene, and backed out again.

Shar chuckled. "It looks like we've claimed the kitchen for the evening."

"Oh no." Palia looked up guiltily from the potatoes. "There's plenty for everyone."

She hurried to the door and almost walked right into Curi.

His blue hair was damp and tucked behind his ears, and his cheeks were slightly flushed. His dark eyes brightened for a moment at the sight of us all, then a shutter came down, dimming that light.

He snorted and turned away.

"Hey." I leaned back on my seat. "Where do you think you're going, *lover*?"

Shar choked on a carrot stick, and Ginia snickered.

Curi stilled.

I pulled out the chair beside me. "If we're going to play a couple, we should learn to share meals. You know, be seen together."

Curi turned to face us, his expression tight. "I said I'd help you. You don't have to bribe me with food."

"This isn't bribery, Mason, it's an invitation to hang out."

Silence filled the room, pregnant with expectation. If someone had said to me a week ago that I'd be asking Curi Mason to hang out with me, I'd have laughed in their face, but the goyle had proven not to be a total dick. He'd saved my ass on more than one occasion, and I'd seen a reflection of my own loneliness in his eyes. I knew what it was like to be an outsider, and for all his bluster and aggression, Curi was just a male who wanted to belong.

Maybe he could belong with us. Maybe I was overthinking, but fuck it. This felt right.

Touron broke the silence by slapping a steak on a plate and holding it out to Curi. "Hope you like it medium rare."

Curi's shoulders relaxed. "Yeah, I do."

He took the seat beside me, and Palia slid a couple of jacket potatoes onto his plate.

"You can help yourself to salad," Shar said. "I don't serve."

We dug into our food, and for a little while, the only sound in the room was the scrape of forks and knives on plates.

"What did you season this with?" Curi asked after polishing off his steak.

Touron tapped the side of his nose. "Secret recipe."

"Well, I'll have to figure it out myself, then." He took another steak off the skillet and rejoined us.

"You won't be able to," Touron challenged, looking smug.

Curi ate slowly this time, savoring each bite, and Touron watched him, the smug smile still in place.

"Salt, pepper, garlic," Curi said.

"Of course," Touron said. "Standard practice."

"A hint of lemongrass."

Touron's smile dropped slightly. "Right..."

"And..." Curi chewed slowly, then swallowed. "Ginger and...a hint of chili."

"Fuck! How did you guess?" Touron shook his head. "Impressive."

"My mother always said I had a clever palate. We used to cook together before..." He popped another bite of steak into his mouth, the sentence unfinished.

"What do we have here?" Dayn entered the kitchen, trailed by Bax and Saffe. "You slumming it with the losers now, Mason?" He smirked. "You think having a Basque in your bed makes you better than us, makes this group of losers suddenly worth something?" He sneered at me. "I heard about you taking the elite trial. You'll be dead before then. You might be a Basque, but you're still a halfblood. And you..." Dayn turned his sneer onto Curi. "I paid my mother a visit. It's been a while since she's seen me, so she was more than willing to tell me exactly what happened between you and Selas."

Curi went as still as stone beside me.

Dayn smirked. "You're nothing, Mason. Not anymore." He spun on his heel, but his exit was ruined when he bumped into Bax, who then knocked into Saffe.

"Fucking out of the way!" He shoved past them both, and they followed him out of the room.

"What was he talking about?" Sharniza asked Curi. "What happened between you and Selas?"

Curi shoved his chair back and left.

Touron shrugged, mumbling something incoherent around a mouthful of food.

"I sense a backstory here," Ginia said.

Palia just stared at the doorway in concern. "He's hurting." She looked over at me. "Maybe you should—"

I was already on my feet. "Keep my plate hot for me, would you?"

I CAUGHT UP to Curi just outside his room.

"Go away, Basque," he drawled. "I don't need to share my feelings." He stepped into his room and made to close the door, but I slipped inside on impulse, regretting it as soon as I caught the flash of anger on his face. "You have serious boundary issues, you know that?"

I crossed my arms. "Maybe. But sometimes you need to cross boundaries to reach someone."

He rolled his eyes. "I don't need your sympathy or an ear, or a shoulder, but if you want to offer me your cunt for the night, I'll take it. I could do with a little stress relief."

My cheeks flushed, but I held his gaze. He was trying to push me away with his crude talk, but I was beginning to understand him. This was his defense mechanism. His shield.

"Is that what you really want, Curi?" I took a step closer, and lo and behold, he took one back.

"Dammit, woman."

"Look, you don't have to tell me what happened between you and Selas. It's none of my business, but don't hide from us. Dayn and his cronies are assholes, but we're not. I think...I think you might like being friends with us." I shrugged. "I think you belong with us." Fuck, had I said that out loud?

He ducked his head and snorted. "You're a pest, you know that?"

"I've been called worse."

He nodded. "Fine. Tell me the real reason you want to keep Levi Halle at arm's length, and I'll tell you about Selas."

Damn, he was more perceptive than I'd given him credit for. "I told you. He won't take no for an answer, obviously, because he's here."

Curi gave me a closed-lip smile, then grabbed his gym bag. "I'll speak to you later, Basque."

"Wait, you said you'd tell me about Selas."

"I did. But only when you tell me the *truth* about Levi." He held open the door for me, watching me with dark, knowing eyes.

There was no way I was going to spill the beans about Serath to him. Curi might have an invite to the friend group, but he didn't have one to the circle of trust.

Not yet.

I shrugged and strolled past him.

"Whatever. Knowing Dayn, he'll blab about it eventually."

"Yeah? And if you want to believe the bullshit that'll come out of his mouth, then be my guest."

He stepped out after me, slammed the door, and stormed off.

I'd pulled him close only to shove him away.

Urgh. I needed to learn to keep my mouth shut.

THE STEAK DIDN'T taste as nice after my chat with Curi. I'd messed up, and it bothered me. I'd had no right to push him into revealing information that was obviously painful for him, but my knee-jerk reaction to his probing about Levi had been defensive.

Back in my room, I kicked off my shoes and carefully cracked open the wardrobe, searching the shadows for the mournful eyes that always made me feel better.

Derek emerged, blinking up at me as if waking from a sleep.

"Hey, buddy, how you doing?"

"Unngg arga."

"Really? I didn't know that you slept."

"Ummm jagad."

Yep, he didn't usually, so this was strange. "Maybe it's this place. There are strong wards here, and we're in some kind of hidden part of the rim." I pulled the door wider. "You want to come and hang out for a while?"

"Mmmm gah."

I stepped back, and he spilled out of the wardrobe, tall and wide, and what the actual fuck? When had he gotten so big?

He looked down at himself, shadow hands patting his shadow chest. "Huh?"

It would have been comical if not for the fact that it was

downright abnormal. "You've grown."

"Hung ha grag."

"We'll have to figure out how." But who to talk to? Derek was a tulpa. My tulpa. But there was obviously more to him than simply being a boogeyman. He'd protected me when Ignus, the new breed of graynite, had attacked me. Derek was special, and I couldn't risk him being taken away by the instructors here. Gargoyles extinguished tulpas, so I needed to be careful who I trusted with this...this development.

Willowman might be a good choice. He worked directly with the elite, and I'd be on that team soon...

Made sense to speak to him about this.

"Wait a second, Derek." I pulled my timetable out of my pack and studied it. Herbology was on there, second period after Arcana on Friday. Two days away. I'd ask him then. "I'm going to figure out what's happening to you, buddy. Don't worry."

Derek groaned and sat on the edge of my bed, head bowed, staring at his large hands. "Karik agoo."

"You're not a monster." I sat beside him and put my arm around him. It was weird how he could be shadow but also have physical form. "You're my buddy, and I love you no matter how big or small you are, okay?"

He looked at me with eyes that gleamed with gratitude and smiled with his razor teeth. "Huugg uuu ooo." He yawned, and his eyelids drooped. "Gubba sleep."

"Yeah, get some more rest."

I tucked him back into the closet and closed the door, then jumped at the sight of Melanie by the window. "Shit! You scared me."

Melanie stared blankly at me, her mouth moving without sound.

"Melanie?" I took a step toward her, and she vanished.

This was my fault. I'd roped her into helping me find out what happened to Romi, and she'd broken into the filing room where all the classified information was kept to get to his file. She hadn't been the same since. And the information she'd come back with...

Wait a minute...She'd told us that Romi had died in a cave-in after going against orders, but that was a lie. Would the gargoyles have planted false information in a classified file? Would Lionel have ensured that? Or did she find out the truth that day and get caught? Oh...wait...Flora had been found unconscious close to the office.

Could it all be related?

I'd speak to the others about my thoughts tomorrow, but right now, I needed a shower and bed.

I WOKE TO whispering and the gray light of dawn. Melanie stood by the window again, but this time she was holding out her arms, as if waiting to be given something.

"Please. Let me. Please, let me hold...I won't...You can't do that...I...Please...She's mine."

"Melanie?" I sat up, and she turned her head to look right at me. Her eyes went wide with recognition, then she vanished.

I slumped back onto my pillow. Yep, I was definitely going to have to fix my ghostly roommate.

CHAPTER 9

SELAS

Serath shadows me up the steps into the main building. He's managed to stay away from Cam all day, aside from the training, but I can sense his agitation. It isn't normal for fated mates to be apart for long periods of time. I know of two such pairings, and both goyles were relieved from active guardian duty because they needed to be close to their omegas. It's a physical and emotional need. A soul bond. And my friend is fighting hard against it.

I can't begin to imagine how hard this is for them, but for him in particular, because he's full goyle, and his beast is stronger, able to exert more control, which heightens his primal instincts.

Still, staying away from Cam means he's been stuck to me like glue all day. "You don't need to come with me to speak to Carter. I can pass on the plan myself."

"I know, but just in case Lionel pushes back..."

"Cam will get her wish to do the cadet exams, Serath. I'll make sure of it." But maybe this isn't just about seeing Carter or staying clear of Cam. Maybe this is about bumping into Levi, the male that had Cameron's heart before she came here. "You could just go see him."

"No."

He knows exactly who I'm talking about. "He's your cousin."

"He's nothing to me. Insignificant."

Aside from the fact that he's blood and was once the object of Cam's affection. "That doesn't change the facts. And he might be nothing like Ulrickson—heck, he can't be, not if Cameron fell in love with him."

He growls, a warning not to continue this line of thought.

"Fine, but I think you're being ridiculous."

"I don't care."

Damn, he's a stubborn beast at times. "So, if you bump into him, then you'll speak to him?"

"I'll be polite."

I bite back my smile. "Of course you will."

But the journey to Carter's office is uneventful—the halls quiet because classes are done for the evening. Most goyles will be in the gym or in their dorm, and Levi will probably be in the instructors' quarters.

We climb the stairs to the administration floor, taking them two at a time.

"Wait up!" Willowman calls out from behind us. "You headed to see Carter?"

"Yes, why?" Serath asks.

"I need to see her too."

"About?"

"The attack. The orb that was switched." His tone takes a slightly sibilant tone that tells me he's clenching his jaw. "They're trying to pin it on me. Say I messed up. I didn't."

"I know you didn't," Serath says. "I have your back."

Willowman is too meticulous to fuck up. "Let's go get this sorted, then."

Someone deliberately gave the omega nest mother the wrong transportation orb, and it took her to the outer eastern settlement where they were attacked by grotesque. Evelyn fought to protect her charges, but the grotesque and the new breed of graynite who calls himself Ignus weren't after the omegas. They wanted Cameron because she's the last adult Basque. The council are aware of this.

"We need to look into what happened," Willowman says. "A proper investigation needs to take place."

Travani is coming out of Carter's office when we get there, and I'm hit with a sense of the lethargy that follows sexual gratification. "Well, this is an entourage." She goes back into the room, and we follow.

Carter is at her desk, seemingly at work, but the air around her is tinged orange, the color of sexual energy.

I guess the rumors about these two are true. They're lovers. But why hide it? It's not like anyone here cares.

"What is this?" Carter asks.

"We need to speak to Lionel," Serath says.

"Is this about Miss Basque?"

"Yes."

"And I want to know what's being done about the orb investigation," Willowman adds.

"The mistake you made?" Travani says.

The air crackles with tension that comes from Willowman's direction. "I didn't make a mistake. Someone switched the orbs."

"But you handed the return orb to Bodi, and he delivered it to Evelyn," Travani says. "Are you insinuating that he switched them?"

Tension is tinged with exasperation now. "No, I trust him completely. But someone else must have made the switch."

"Yes, so you keep saying, but you must understand, Mr. Willowman, for that to be the case, we are to believe that someone tampered not only with Bodi's pack but also broke into your cottage—not once, but twice. The first time to retrieve the orb to the outer eastern settlement and the second to return the correct orb, the one that was meant to bring the party home, into your special orb box."

"Yes. I understand that." Willowman bites out the words. "There is a mole here at the academy, and we need to find him or her."

"You're unwilling to consider the possibility that you made an error?" She sounds irritated.

"Are you willing to consider the possibility that I didn't?" He takes a frustrated breath. "Are you willing to take the risk and ignore the possibility that I'm right and that there's danger within these walls?"

"Travani?" Carter sounds strained. "Maybe we should alert the council and—"

"I've filed a report," Travani says. "It's been lodged as a mistake."

Silence falls heavy around me.

"Why would you do that without consulting with me first?" Carter asks.

"Retract it," Serath says. "Willowman doesn't make mistakes. Not of this magnitude."

Travani sighs. "Look, if you're right and if there is a mole here, then calling in the alchemists will only push them underground. We may never find them."

Serath tenses beside me, and I can sense his panic because alchemists are known to have the ability to read minds or memories. If they came here...If they read our minds... "You're right. We should conduct our own investigation."

The mood in the room is immediately one of relief. I guess we all have secrets we wish to keep hidden.

Carter speaks, her voice filled with authority. "We'll begin by upping security on classified material and tighten our wards both in and out of the academy. All exits and entrances, all correspondence, will be monitored. They want Miss Basque, so we must protect her; however, putting a security detail on her will draw too much attention. So instead, we move her to the elite residences."

Oh shit. "I don't think that's a good idea."

"Why not?" Travani asks.

Think, Selas, think. "The other cadets might call it favoritism." It's a lame excuse, and Travani blows it out of the water.

"She's a Basque, our *only* Basque, and she's bound for elite, so it makes sense."

I look to Serath, expecting him to put forward an argument, but he simply nods.

"She's safest with us," he says. "But she should be allowed to keep her dorm rooms until after the cadet exams."

"What have the cadet exams to do with this?" Carter asks.

"Because she wishes to take them, and I agree that it would be good for her to do so. Part of the success of any cadet is mental health. I believe the relationships she has formed in the dorm will be beneficial. Cutting her off from those so soon could prove detrimental."

He's minimizing the amount of time she might spend at the observatory tower. Clever.

"And this is why you needed to speak to Lionel?" Carter asks.

I nod. "Yes."

"I'll speak to him for you," she says. "Travani, please make sure Miss Basque gets a new timetable that includes full cadet exam training classes as well as her sessions with the elites. Prepare a room for her in the observatory and make sure she sleeps there even if she spends her days at the dorm with her cadet group. We want her protected from dawn to midday when we are the most vulnerable."

The tension in the room ebbs, but my stomach is in knots because although I knew Cam would be coming to the observatory at some point, I thought we had time to prepare, to use the training sessions to acclimatize her to Serath's scent and vice versa, but now...I doubt any of us will be getting much sleep.

CHAPTER 10

CAMERON

Touron didn't answer his door when I knocked for him at one in the afternoon, but Shar yelled a slurred, "*I'm up,*" and, "*Meet you downstairs.*"

I'd slept longer than usual and felt better for it. Derek was sleeping too. A shadowy mass in the back of my closet—I hadn't had the heart to wake him.

Willowman would have answers, and if I didn't see him before Friday's lessons, I'd ask him then.

The kitchen was empty, but it wouldn't be long before the goyles were up and about; classes started in a couple of hours. I set the coffee pot bubbling and cracked eggs for an omelet.

Sure enough, Waxen and Saffe shuffled into the room a few minutes later and grabbed coffee. Goyles were not morning people. They weren't day people. But let the sun set, and they came to life, filled with energy and power. Right now, these two huge males looked as if they were sleepwalking.

"You want some eggs?" I held up the spatula.

Waxen raised his mug my way. "Let me help."

"You could pop some bread in the toaster."

"On it."

Saffe sipped his coffee, flicking glances my way. "Dayn isn't here. You can talk to me if you want."

"I...It's not like that."

"Then what is it like?" I flipped an omelet onto a plate and placed it on the table. "You do what he says, right?"

Saffe dropped his gaze. "We do what we have to in order to survive."

"You don't need to hang out with a turd, though," Waxen said.

"Easy for you to say. Your father's on the council."

Waxen had a council member father? "Does your father know Ulrickson?"

Waxen snorted. "My father is an admin on the lower floors of the Stone Council HQ. He knows the basement well, but that's about it."

"But still..." Saffe rubbed the back of his neck. "Dayn won't mess with you."

"He can't mess with you, either, if you don't let him," Waxen said.

I flipped another omelet onto another plate and held it out to Saffe.

"He doesn't want it," Dayn said from the doorway. "We're eating at Stone Comfort." He jerked his chin at Saffe. "Move."

Saffe hurried over to the larger goyle.

Dayn gave me a smug look and threw a lip curl Waxen's way before heading off, Saffe in tow.

Yep, he was a total turd. "What is his problem?"

"Small dick," Waxen said. "It's got to be."

I bit back a snort and put Saffe's omelet onto his plate.

"I smell omelets!" Ginia entered followed by Palia. "Ham and cheese?"

"Of course."

Shar joined us a few minutes later, and Waxen excused himself in favor of the gym. It wasn't until we were polishing off our food that Touron emerged, freshly showered, sandy-colored hair slicked back from his handsome face, but his eyes were bloodshot, as if from lack of sleep.

"What happened to you?" Ginia asked. "You went to bed early last night."

He poured coffee and stifled a yawn. "I didn't sleep well, though."

He grabbed some toast and the remaining omelet, then joined us at the table. "What did I miss?"

"Waxen confirmed to Cam that Dayn has a small dick," Ginia said.

Palia shot her sister a lethal look, mumbling admonishment through a mouthful of food.

Ginia giggled. "Dick."

Palia swallowed her mouthful. "Ginia!"

Now that everyone was here, and we were alone... "There is something I wanted to speak to you about."

"Go on," Shar said.

"There's something wrong with Melanie."

"The ghost?" Palia looked confused. "I mean, she's dead, so..."

"Yeah, but she's gone all weird since she broke into the office."

"What do you mean?" Touron asked.

I filled them in on Melanie's strange behavior. "Forgetfulness is normal in ghosts when they've been stuck on this plane for long enough, but I'm thinking that maybe something happened to her. I mean, Flora was found unconscious on the office floor the same night that Melanie did her snooping, right?"

"And the information she came back with was wrong..." Shar added, jumping straight onto my train of thought.

"Or maybe that's what they put in the file?" Palia suggested.

"You think someone caught Melanie and did something to her?" Touron asked. "You think they planted the lie in her head about what was in Romi's file?"

"Maybe."

"But who would do that?" Palia said. "Oh...do you think the same person who messed with Melanie messed with Flora?"

We sat in silence.

"That coupled with the orb being switched..." Shar said.

I'd almost forgotten about that. "We have a spy. A mole. A fucking rat at the academy."

"Which means we need to be extra careful," Shar said. "That Ignus creature was after you, and no doubt the traitor in our midst is working for the graynites, so we need to—"

"Oi! You. Basque." Bodi, the academy messenger, stood in the doorway. "For you." He held out an envelope.

Palia was closest and took it. But Bodi lingered, his gaze flicking to the coffee pot, then to me.

I knew what he wanted.

I took another travel mug off the shelf and filled it for him. "Bring the cup back next time you pop over to see me." I passed him the coffee, and he took it with a derisive sniff, but the gleam in his eyes was all gratitude.

"What the heck?" Ginia said.

I shrugged. "Coffee is a universal language."

"What are we going to do about the mole?" Palia asked, taking us back to the main topic.

"I'll speak to Serath when I see him at training later." I took the envelope from Palia and tore it open to find two sheets of paper. The first was another timetable, this one with all the cadet training classes added to it, which had to mean... "I think...I think I get to take the cadet exams with you guys!" I flipped over the second sheet of paper to find Serath's beautiful script. My cheeks warmed, expecting a romantic note, but the words on the page were instructions that spawned contradictory emotions in my belly.

"What's wrong?" Shar asked.

"You look like you're about to throw up," Touron added.

I swallowed against the sudden dryness in my mouth. "It's from Serath. It says that as of tonight, I'll be sleeping at the observatory for my own safety."

Touron's face fell. "They're moving you?"

"She was going to have to move once she became elite anyways," Palia pointed out.

"But so soon?" Touron pouted. "Who's going to bring me coffee in the morning?"

"I'll still do that. I can still be here, stay here during waking hours. I get to keep my room for now, I just...I have to sleep there."

"Oh..." Shar's eyes went round as the implications sank in. "Let's hope they put you on a different floor to Serath."

"Of course they will," Touron said.

But even if they did, would it stop us from finding each other?

I wasn't so sure, and that...that worried the hell out of me.

THERE WERE A few surprised faces when I strolled into cadet training, but Farnell didn't give me a second glance. He ordered us to pick a sparring partner to warm up and then retreated to the other end of the training room with his clipboard and a frown.

"You want to partner?" Shar asked.

"Only if you promise not to take it easy on me."

"You have my word."

I spotted Curi's blue head as he entered the room, but he wasn't alone today. He had Waxen with him. He scanned the room, zeroed in on me, and headed over.

I forced my body to relax as he put his arm around me and dropped a kiss on my head. "You didn't save me an omelet," he said, voice low. "Waxen's been bragging about how delicious they were."

"You didn't come down for breakfast."

"I'll make sure to join you guys tomorrow."

I looked up at him in surprise. He sounded softer, his gaze less angry. It suited him.

"We're here to fight, not canoodle!" Farnell growled. He walked off, muttering something about goyle males and sex drives.

The next twenty minutes passed quickly. Shar didn't hold back, attacking with purpose, but my sessions with Selas had obviously done something because I was able to evade and even landed a couple of blows. Still, we ended with me in a headlock, patting her arm to indicate surrender.

"You did good," she said. "Training with the elite is paying off."

"I still have a way to go."

She ducked her head. "I'm sorry for doubting you when you got here. I truly didn't believe you'd make it, but now I know you will."

Her words were like warm molasses filling the crevices of doubt in my psyche. "Thank you, Shar, that means a lot."

"Now that you're all warmed up, it's time for a little field work."

My ears perked up.

"You'll be sent off campus in pairs to one of five locations," Farnell continued. "You'll have a map and some supplies and an hour to reach extraction point. You'll need to work together to make it back on time. There'll be points to the team who makes it back first and deductions for the team who makes it back last."

"Do we get to pick our teammate?"

"In a manner of speaking." He held up a bag. "You pick a name. If it's your own name, you pick another. That will be your teammate. You won't get to pick and choose your unit if you qualify. Out there, every guardian is your friend."

Shar shot a worried glance my way, but I shrugged. Farnell was right. We were training for guardian, and in my case elite. There was no room for prejudice on the field.

Shar was called first and picked Waxen. Ginia got Saffe, and Palia got Curi. That left Dayn, Bax, Touron, and me. An awful sense of déjà vu came over me.

If I got stuck with Dayn...

Touron went up next, took a deep breath, and pulled out his own name.

"Again, Lomax," Farnell drawled.

Touron glanced my way, the pressure visible on his face. I lifted my chin and smiled to let him know it was okay, no matter what.

He drew again, his shoulders tensing. My pulse stalled.

"Lowther," he said.

He'd drawn Dayn, leaving me with Bax, which was fine by me. Bax was all talk around Dayn, but having some alone time with him might give us a chance to get to know each other. I wasn't expecting to make friends, but we could be civil, which certainly wouldn't have happened with Dayn.

"That leaves Bax with Basque," Farnell confirmed.

Bax glanced my way, but Dayn grabbed his arm to draw his attention away.

The goyle was a bully. I couldn't believe I'd overlooked his attitude, thinking Curi was the asshole all this time. Curi, who now happened to be watching Dayn and Bax with narrowed, suspicious eyes.

"Everyone, move," Farnell said. "To the gates. You'll find packs and maps waiting there."

Excitement mingled with anxiety because this was a chance for me to test myself. A challenge to push me up a rung toward taking the cadet exams, but the last time I'd left campus, we'd been attacked by grotesque, and I'd almost been kidnapped by Ignus. Was he a graynite? Lionel hadn't confirmed it, saying it was intel for elite only.

Curi and Touron flanked me as we headed outside.

"You need to be careful with Bax," Curi said. "Watch your back."

"And punch him in the nuts if he fucks with you," Touron added.

"She'll be fine," Shar said from behind us. "She's a fucking Basque."

I just hoped I could live up to the name. Not for myself or for anyone here but for Romi.

CHAPTER 11

CAMERON

Willowman waited at the main gates, greeting Farnell with a nod before turning his attention on us.

"Each pair grab a pack." Farnell indicated several backpacks lined up on the side of the gravel path.

Bax moved fast and picked a pack, shooting me a quick glance as he did so.

"Mason and Lambert, you're up first," Farnell said.

Willowman clicked his fingers, and a scroll appeared in his hands. He handed it to Curi. "The extraction point is clearly marked, and you have a compass in your pack. You have two hours to get to the exit point, or you'll be stranded."

I leaned in to speak to Shar. "They'd leave us out there?"

"You sound surprised," Farnell said. Shit, he had sharp ears. "The cadet exams are in less than three weeks, and I will weed out any weak links before then. Navigation and survival are essential skills for a guardian. This is a cakewalk. You have partners, after all, but next time you'll be going solo, and the time after that... Well, not all of you will make it back, and I'm okay with that." His eyes narrowed. "Being a guardian is about more than having the right name or the right bloodline. It's about fortitude, strength, and skill. Those aren't always genetic."

Ouch. Looked like he had zero confidence in my ability to make it to elite. I'd just have to prove him wrong. There was no way I'd be left stranded, even if I missed the extraction point. They needed me for elite. But the same couldn't be said for my partner, and I wouldn't be the reason he failed.

Farnell turned his attention to Shar. "Aziza, you're up." Willowman produced another scroll out of thin air, then another until each pairing had one, then he asked us to line up. "Your scrolls are keys, and today, the gate will act as a port. Each pairing must be touching the scroll as they pass through and be transported to the designated location. Remember, you have two hours from entrance to get to your extraction point."

"Don't we need to *open* the gates?" Dayn asked.

"No."

Curi and Palia went first, holding the scroll between them. There was a flash of blue light as they neared the iron bars, then they were gone. Shar and Waxen went next, followed by Ginia and Saffe, and then it was my turn. Bax held out the scroll, and I grasped one end.

I'd been through a warping and traveled by orb and felt sick both times. What was this going to—

Light seared my vision, and when it ebbed, the gates were gone, and we were on a nature trail bordered by woodland. The sun above was tinged orange, signaling late afternoon, and a sniff of the air told me there was water nearby.

Bax's expression was tight. He was clearly not a fan of partnering with me, but like hell would I let his personal feelings ruin our chances of passing this test.

"We're on a clock here, and there's no time for bullshit."

He blinked sharply, then nodded, relinquishing the map to me.

I unfurled it, studying the carefully drawn lay of the land. Trees, rivers, mountains. A red dot for extraction and a blue one for drop-off. "I need the compass." Bax rummaged in the pack and found it for me. "We've got to head northeast. Looks pretty straightforward. But there's a river to cross. No way around it without missing our extraction window."

Bax reached for the map. "Let me see that." He studied it for several long seconds. "We could head west to this bridge over here." He pointed at the bridge, which was at least a mile and a half in the wrong direction.

"We have two hours to get to the extraction point. If we head for the bridge, we won't make it."

"There has to be some other way."

He studied the map with stubborn intensity as if he expected the line on the map to shift and reveal an alternate route.

"What is your problem?"

He shoved the map at me. "There'll be another way." He stomped off.

He had a problem with rivers? Or maybe water. Wait... Couldn't he swim? Was that it? Sunset was a couple of hours away, about the time we'd make it to extraction, and no doubt Farnell had timed it as such to stop the goyles shifting and simply flying to their destination, but if Bax couldn't swim, we had a huge problem.

The woods were filled with the sounds of nature, the atmosphere peaceful and tranquil, but Bax radiated anxiety like a furnace.

Ten minutes passed in silence, and nothing eventful happened. I checked the compass, the map, and the terrain. We were headed in the right direction, and there hadn't been any obstacles so far.

Was this deliberate? Had Willowman given us an easy path? Did Serath have something to do with this? No. He wouldn't do that. He wanted me to pass the elite trial, knew that I needed the training. He wouldn't interfere in the process.

The sound of running water washed over the chirp and chitter of the woodland wildlife.

Bax slowed his pace, but I picked mine up, walking around him to take the lead to the wide river, the water moving fast, as if in a hurry to get to its destination. Beyond was more woodland,

and beyond that were blue and gray mountains, their tops tinged orange by a late afternoon sun.

The mountains were our destination. We'd find our extraction point there.

Bax walked off along the riverbank, searching for a way across.

He wouldn't find one. "The only way across is to swim, Bax."

His shoulders bunched and then drooped. "I can't," he growled finally. "I can't go in there."

I knew it. "You can't swim."

He turned to face me, and the pallor of his skin told a different story. This wasn't about not having the skill. This was about fear. He was *afraid* of the water.

His lip curled. "If you say a word, I'll hurt you bad."

I arched my brow and crossed my arms. "You'll have to get *out* of this place to do that, Bax."

He looked at the water, his eyes darkening, breath coming faster. "I'll wait for sunset."

"It'll be too late. Extraction is fifteen minutes before sunset."

He dropped his chin to his chest. "I'll wait. Just go."

I knew enough about fear to know it couldn't be conquered in a few minutes and enough about goyles to know he'd probably fought with this weakness for as long as he'd been afflicted. There was no point trying to talk him into getting into the river, but I couldn't leave without him either.

There had to be something we could do. Some other way across. My gaze fell on the trees on the edge of the woods. These trees had slender trunks.

I held out my hand. "Let me see the pack."

Bax looked confused but handed it to me.

There was a bottle of water, some energy bars, a penknife, and some rope. Not thick rope but the slender, strong kind you could use for rappelling.

"You think you can pull up that tree?" I pointed at the smallest one.

Bax's frown deepened. "What? Why?"

"Can you do it or not?"

"Yes, but—"

"Get to it. You'll need two at least."

"What are you going to do?"

"*We're* going to make you a raft."

CHAPTER 12

CAMERON

It didn't take long to use the rope to tie the two tree trunks together. It was large enough for Bax to kneel on. But I wouldn't be riding the thing. I'd be pulling it across the river using what was left of the rope. I kicked off my shoes and handed them to Bax.

"Do *not* lose those."

He looked at me strangely, as if he wasn't sure if this whole thing was some kind of trick or not. I didn't have time for his insecurities and doubts. We had maybe an hour and a half left to get to extraction.

I hauled the makeshift raft to the riverbank and shoved it partially into the water. "Get on."

He hesitated. "You're sure you can do this?"

"Have I swum across a river lugging a makeshift raft behind me before? No. But I'm confident I can do it. You just need to stay onboard, okay?"

He swallowed hard and nodded. "Okay."

Two minutes later and I was submerged and swimming for the other side of the river. Thankfully, the current wasn't too strong, and I was able to move quickly because, damn, the water was icy.

"You keep an eye out for any critters in the water."

"It's clear so far," Bax said. "We're good." He sounded strained, but that was to be expected if he was afraid of water.

I picked up the pace, alert to potential threats. My dip in the rushing river a couple of weeks ago played on my mind. There'd been creatures in the water. I'd almost drowned. But today we reached the other side without incident. Bax quickly crawled off the raft, eager to be away from the water's edge.

My lastonflex was soaked, my skin icy, but by the time I'd reached for my shoes, I was dry. "What the fuck?" I patted my clothes. "Don't tell me, another awesome feature?"

Bax merely nodded, his expression wary and conflicted.

He'd exposed his weakness to me, which was probably a huge no-no in the goyle world, and considering he was Dayn's bitch, I was also the last person he'd want to share it with. "Look, it's no big deal. I'm not going to tell anyone, okay? That's not who I am. We're a team, right?"

A little of the unease melted off his face. "Right."

I didn't have time to pacify him any further; we had an extraction point to get to.

I took a moment to study the map again, then headed into the woodland onto a trail that should lead us to the mountains.

Bax followed.

Silence reigned for several minutes before Bax broke it. "This hardly seems like survival training. Aside from the river, which... They couldn't know about my aversion, and there was nothing dangerous in the water, so..."

"I don't know. We still have an hour left to get to extraction. A lot can happen in that time, so stay sharp."

The steady symphony of woodland sounds told me that all was well. The buzz was a base marker, and if it stopped, then I'd know something was wrong. Smell was another thing for me. Danger didn't have a specific scent, but the particles in the air seemed to become charged when there was a threat nearby.

Years of hunting had primed me to pick up on these things, and the assessment was constantly running in background mode.

"So, tell me about you. You got any siblings?"

He was silent for so long I was beginning to think he wasn't going to respond, but then he spoke, his voice low and gruff.

"A sister. She's an omega. She'll be coming here next year."

The ground was getting softer, almost mushy, and the air was beginning to get humid. The trees gave way to large, leafy bushes that had an almost tropical vibe. "What is this place?"

"One of the academy training grounds. They've got several," Bax said.

"And they really just abandon cadets here?"

"Yes." He looked away.

"What is it? What are you not telling me?"

"You didn't have to help me back there, you know," he growled.

"No. I didn't have to."

I didn't get why this goyle would ally himself with Dayn, of all people. It couldn't just be about family name and status, surely, because if that were the case, then Bax would be sucking up to Curi, Sharniza, or even me. So, why was he so tied up with Dayn?

There was only one way to find out. "Why do you hang out with Dayn?"

He pressed his lips together. "That's none of your business."

"I didn't say it was. I'm just curious, because you don't seem like an asshole."

He made a sound that sounded suspiciously like a laugh. "You shouldn't go around saying things like that."

"I'm not afraid of him."

"Yes, you can afford not to be."

"What's that supposed to—"

The world around us was suddenly silent.

Beside me, tension rippled off Bax. He felt it too. Danger. But we continued to walk, to act unaware, even though we were no longer alone.

There was something in the woods to our left. Something stalking us. I caught a shift of shadows in my periphery, and ice gripped my spine and pooled low in my belly.

Whatever was out there was lethal, deadly, and sentient.

I wasn't sure how I knew that, but the conviction blared in my mind. As long as it thought we were unaware of its presence, it might hold off attacking.

But it *would* attack.

We'd have to fight it, and the farther we went, the softer the ground got, to the point where it was almost muddy. This terrain would make it harder to stay upright in a tussle.

"Bax, the ground's getting too soft."

"I know."

The path widened up ahead. We couldn't be far from exiting the forestland. The map showed rocky terrain leading into the mountains.

"It has to be now," Bax said.

He was right. We couldn't risk taking the fight deeper into mushy ground.

We both came to halt.

The tension in the air spiked.

"Where is it?" Bax said.

I could feel the presence pressing in on us—close, watching, assessing. "We know you're there." Silence, pregnant with expectation, followed. The hairs on my arms stood at attention, fear clawing at my insides, chased closely by rage because whatever was out there was powerful, and we had no weapons except a penknife, tucked in the pack, and our fists.

Why would the academy do this to us? Why throw us into this situation so unprepared? There was no way we would have gone on a mission unarmed.

The shadows beyond the tree line moved, sliding back and forth. The mass was huge.

"Fuck..." Bax fell into a crouch.

I caught the flash of red eyes and the low rumble of a growl. It was toying with us. Scaring us.

Rage burned away my fear, and I took a step forward. "I'm

not afraid of you. You want a bite of me, then come try to take it." My body vibrated with tension, muscles bunched, ready for action.

The shadow stopped moving, and the low rumble rolled over us again...not a growl but something that sounded suspiciously like a chuckle, and then the shadow vanished.

Long seconds passed, and the sounds of nature filled the air once more.

"What the fuck?" Bax said.

It was gone. "Let's get the fuck out of here before it comes back."

CHAPTER 13

TOURON

"Where's Cam?" There's less than forty minutes left on the clock, and she isn't back yet.

"There's plenty of time," Shar says. "She'll make it back."

Shar and Waxen were already here when Dayn and I got back. I think part of the reason we made it through to extraction so quickly is because we couldn't wait to get away from each another. That and my excellent sense of direction. The catacombs we had to go through to find our extraction point were creepy as fuck, though.

There's no sign of Farnell, and Willowman is busy cleaning his nails with a pen knife, nails he's painted purple and black.

Where is Cam?

The port lights up, and my heart leaps with hope. Ginia appears, trailed by Saffe. They high-five one another, shaking water from their hair. Even though their lastonflex suits are dry.

"River?" Shar asks.

"Extraction was at the bottom of a damn lake," Saffe says.

"Luckily, I can hold my breath for ages," Ginia says with a dirty smirk.

Is Saffe blushing?

Curi appears next, with Palia clinging to his back.

"Palia!" Ginia rushes forward to take her sister from Curi. Palia is pale, but other than that she looks exhilarated.

"What happened?" Shar asked.

"The extraction point was via a zipline," Curi says. "Just the one. We had to take it together or risk one of us getting stranded. The mechanism for calling it back was busted."

"Lucky you checked," Saffe says.

"Palia checked," Curi says. "I wouldn't have otherwise." He looks annoyed at himself.

We're all here except Cam and Bax. "What's taking them so long?"

"Shouldn't Mason be the one worrying?" Dayn sneers. "Or have you got a hard-on for the halfblood too?"

"Fuck you, Dayn," Curi says flatly.

"No," Dayn says. "How about I fuck you?"

Ginia snorts.

Dayn frowns and shakes his head. "I mean...I didn't mean..."

"We know what you meant," Palia says primly. "But there is no need to be vulgar."

Dayn flinches, then catches himself. "Whatever. I don't have to listen to you." He turns his attention back to Curi. "I can make your life here very uncomfortable, Mason. You know it."

Curi's shoulders heave, and when he raises his head, his eyes are like chips of obsidian. "Go for it, Dayn. I don't give a shit. But the other parties involved in your story might."

Dayn's eyes narrow. "You think that'll stop me?"

"I don't care."

Dayn's jaw flexes. "Of course you don't. Your reputation is already in the mud now that you're fucking a halfblood."

"Shut up, Lowther," Willowman drawls from his position by the gate.

Dayn snaps his mouth closed, but I can tell he wants to make a retort. Maybe put Willowman in his place. Lowther might not be one of the big five, but it's still a prestigious bloodline, and to Dayn, Willowman is just the help, but he's also a witch with the kind of power that Dayn can only ever dream about.

So, the goyle does the wise thing and shuts the hell up.

The crunch of gravel signals Farnell's return. He counts heads, eyes crinkling at the corners when he realizes we're missing two. "How much longer?" he asks Willowman.

Is that a flash of concern on the witch's face? "Not too much longer."

Come on, Cam. Where the fuck are you?

CHAPTER 14

CAMERON

The forest opened onto boggy land. There was a body of water to our right, bordered with reeds and buzzing with dragonflies, but my attention flew to the rockface ahead. The ground sucked at our boots as we made our way across to the last leg of our trek, but my heart sank as we got closer because the rock face was smooth—no notches or footholds for us to climb.

"There's an iron hook!" Bax pointed.

The rusty-looking hook winked at us in the sun, high up and perfect to loop a rope onto. But we'd used our rope to build a raft, cutting it into smaller sections in the process to tie together the trunks. If we'd saved it, then I could have tied the penknife to it and slung it up there. The piece we had left wasn't long enough to use for this.

Bax cursed softly, too, realizing our predicament. But all wasn't lost.

"We can still do this. If you lift me up, I might be able to grab the lip and pull myself over."

"So, you can run off and leave me?"

"If I wanted to leave you behind, I'd have done it at the river."

He looked sheepish. "Point."

"I'll use what rope we have left to haul you up once I'm there.

It should be long enough for you to get a grip on the end." I pointed to an outcrop of rock above. "I can brace myself on that."

He nodded. "Okay."

The ledge was so high up that I had to stand on Bax's shoulders to get a grip on it, but thanks to my upper body workouts, I was able to pull myself up and over.

I pulled the rope from the pack and wrapped one end around my arm. Hopefully, there was enough to reach Bax. I threw the other end down to him, then used the outcrop of stone to brace myself. "I'm ready."

The tug on the rope was tentative. "Are you sure?"

"Yes."

His full weight had me straining, rope cutting into my arm, but to give him credit, he made it over fast, swinging his huge body over the ledge to join me.

I unwound the rope, rubbing my arm to get the circulation going again.

"There's another ledge," Bax said.

I hadn't bothered to check, but yep, there was. This one had no hook, but it wasn't as high as the first one either. Still, it was too high for me to climb. Bax, on the other hand, would just about be able to make it.

I passed him the rope. "Your turn."

He tucked the rope in his pocket, then leaped up to grab the ledge. His fingers slipped, and his boots hit the ground.

"Let me help." I moved behind him. "Try again."

I stepped forward to brace his ass with my shoulder as he dragged himself up and over the edge. "Whoop! We've got this. Now throw me the rope." Several beats of silence followed. "Bax?"

His face appeared over the ledge. "I'm sorry, Cam. I like you, I really do. But I've got to do this."

Ice filled my veins. "What are you talking about?"

"Dayn said to make sure you got left behind."

He wanted to leave me stranded? What the... "The elite need me. They won't leave me here."

"Not if I tell them you're dead."

Ice gripped my nape. "What?"

"I'm sorry, Cameron."

"Dammit, Bax, I'm the only Basque able to complete the team and take down the graynite alpha. You need me."

"Dayn says the alpha isn't a threat. Hasn't been seen in years, and I...I have to do what he wants."

"Why?"

"My sister...He...knows things. I have to protect her. I'm sorry. So sorry. Please forgive me."

"No, Bax, wait!"

But he was gone. "I helped you! You bastard!"

Fuck, fuck, fuck!

I clawed at the ledge with blunt fingernails, panic taking over because every second spent stuck on this ledge was another second lost getting to extraction. I couldn't get left behind. I wouldn't.

My fingers burned and morphed into granite-colored talons.

What the fuck?

They melted away a moment later.

Wait...what had just happened?

I stared at my hands, willing the talons to appear, but nothing happened. Was this some kind of partial shift? Was that even a thing?

There was no time to dwell on it right now. I needed to get up this rockface and over this mountain.

If Bax told them I was dead, would they believe him? No. Serath would come looking for me regardless. He'd find me, right?

But then what? I'd be the goyle that needed rescuing. Fuck that.

No way.

Think, Cam. I had the pack which contained the compass, map, and pen knife, none of which would help me over the ledge. But...maybe the ledge wasn't the only way up. The platform I was on extended beyond the outcrop of rocks to the right. I squeezed past, my back to the wall, to peer along the mountainside. The ledge I was on led to a small cave. I had no idea where that cave went, but it was better than leaping off this ledge and breaking a leg.

I shuffled toward it, and in a matter of moments, the ledge shrank to a space so narrow one slip would have me in free fall.

Breathe. You can do this.

The tips of my boots hung off the ledge that was suspended over the body of water. Muddy water that was almost viscous in places, bubbling here and there as if breathing. There were creatures below the surface, no doubt, hiding in the reeds. If I fell, I was fucked.

Nope. Not happening.

Keep moving.

The cave got closer. Only a few feet away now. What if something was inside it? A creature of some kind. The thing from the forest?

No. Stop it.

I bridged the final distance, feeling for the cave edge with desperate fingers. The rock face was jagged here, making it easier to grip.

I took another step, leaving my shoulder exposed to whatever was inside the dark aperture. If something *was* lurking, now would be the time for it to make itself known, but there was no prickle of fear, no warning alarms in my body. I took a deep breath and swung myself into the darkness. But wait...it wasn't pitch black. There was gray light in here and air flow.

I dragged the map from my pack. "Okay, mountain here. Ledges are a direct route, but..." There was a silver dotted line that cut across the mountains, tracing the path I'd just taken. This was another way to the extraction point, not over the mountain but through it.

Five minutes later and it was clear I was coming to an exit because the gray light had turned orange.

I picked up the pace and exited onto a wide ledge. Rough stone steps to my right lead to a rope bridge that stretched across a chasm. The bridge would get me to extraction, and if my calculations were correct, I had less than fifteen minutes to make it across the bridge to the port, which would be on the other side.

The stone steps were steep, leaving me with a sting in my glutes, but with victory so close, I barely felt the pain. The bridge rocked as I stepped onto it. The thing was old, the rope frayed in places, and some of the planks of wood looked rotten.

I took it slowly, careful to step over the rotted planks. Halfway across, I could see the glow of the port built into a lone tree directly opposite.

Three quarters of the way across and the energy from the port kissed my skin.

Almost there.

The bridge rocked violently. I cried out, grabbing hold of the rope and crouching for balance.

Shit. Bax was on the bridge behind me, moving fast, no doubt to stop me. I swung my body forward, focus sharpened by the threat as I picked up my pace, faster and faster.

The whole thing swayed violently.

"Stop!" Bax cried.

He shook the bridge on purpose, trying to throw me off. Like hell. "Fuck you, Bax!" I held fast, moving forward steadily.

The bridge jerked to the left, and I dropped into a crouch to keep my balance. I glanced back to find Bax advancing slowly. I needed to move faster. I picked up the pace, heart in my mouth and an iron grip on the bridge. The other side inched closer, but there was a gap ahead where the wooden planks had fallen away. I'd have to jump.

Shit.

"I don't want to hurt you, Cam," Bax called out. "Just stop and come back."

The gap grew closer.

Bax shook the bridge again. I cried out, bracing myself, rope burning my palms. The gap was a couple of feet away. I could leap it, but to do that, I'd have to create momentum. I'd have to run, and to be able to run, I'd have to let go of the ropes on either side of me.

My heart pulsed erratically in my chest as panic threatened to take over and the urge to look down gripped my neck.

I fought it, keeping my focus on the bridge ahead. On the spot beyond the gap. The rush of blood in my head muted Bax's urgent bellows.

You can do this, Cam.

I released the ropes and pushed off into a run.

The gap rushed to meet me, and I was airborne, sailing over it and landing on the other side of the gap.

Yes!

The bridge shook, throwing me forward a step. I grabbed the ropes just as the plank beneath me gave way with a crack. My stomach shot up into my chest and my heart into my mouth as I dropped.

My grip on the rope bridge was the only thing keeping me from death. Hands burning, arms screaming, I hung there like a prize pig.

Don't look down.

Don't look down.

I looked down into the mist, spotting a hint of gray jagged rocks.

My bowels turned liquid, and dark panic clouded my mind. Like hell was I giving in to the dread. I hauled my body up, arms straining with the effort.

"No!" Bax shook the bridge again. "I didn't want to hurt you. I just...I'm sorry."

It took every ounce of power I had to keep hold of the rope as my bones rattled, hips slamming against the planks around me.

I didn't have the energy to yell back. Everything was focused on staying attached to the bridge.

"I can't let you go back." Bax's voice was louder.

He was getting closer.

I wouldn't go out like this. Not here. Not today. "Argh!" I

pulled myself up and out of the gap, enough to swing my body forward. If the next plank was rotten, I was fucked.

Please, please, please.

My boots connected with solid wood, and relief threatened to weaken my knees.

"Cam, no!"

I let out a curse and pushed forward, moving faster but staying light on my feet so as not to put too much weight on any single plank.

I hit the other side a moment later and turned to look back.

"No!" Bax broke into a sprint, uncaring of the planks.

The idiot was going to get himself killed. "Stop! Bax, don't—"

A sharp crack cut through the air, and Bax's eyes went round with horror, then he fell through the bridge, his bellow of horror echoing in my ears while my own scream remained trapped in my throat.

He was gone.

He was fucking gone.

My chest ached with the horror of it, my throat pinching with the threat of tears. But that part of me determined to live dragged itself to the surface and forced me backward toward the port. Toward the tree.

I hit the light, and needles of fire erupted across my skin, raking over my senses as I pushed through the pain and past the strange resistance.

What was this? Why couldn't I get through? Did we have to be in teams, holding the map and—

The resistance vanished, and the light swallowed me.

CHAPTER 15

CAMERON

I stumbled onto gravel, heart punching my rib cage, eyes hot with the threat of tears, and slammed into a hard wall of muscle. Familiar forest-green eyes looked down on me in concern.

"Cam, thank fuck." Touron wrapped his arms around me. "You made it. We were so worried."

"I told you she'd be fine," Shar said, but her smug smile dropped at the sight of my face. "What happened?"

"You're shaking," Touron said.

"Where's Bax?" a male voice demanded.

Dayn...

Behind me, the port winked out.

"What did you do to him, you bitch?" Dayn demanded.

A tide of rage swept over me, pulling me from Touron's arms and propelling me across the path toward the goyle responsible for Bax's demise.

My fist connected with his jaw hard enough to jar, hard enough to draw blood, because the bastard didn't see me as a threat, and his stone skin hadn't activated.

Good.

I hit him again, but this time, bone met stone with a crunch.

I barely felt the pain through the fire of fury coursing through me.

"Enough!" Farnell dragged me away from Dayn. "Where is Bonet?"

My hot gaze remained on Dayn. "Dead. Because of you!" I jabbed a finger at him. "You told him to leave me behind. You blackmailed him, and he died because of it. Because he was so desperate to stop me crossing the bridge, and he..." My throat closed up, cutting off my words. I swallowed past the lump. "He fell. He fucking fell off the bridge."

Dayn's eyes flared, then his expression smoothed out. "I don't know what you're talking about."

"You lying piece of shi—"

"Basque, stand down." Serath's voice wrapped around my rage, wrangling it into submission against my will.

He was here. Oh gods, he was here, and my body was torn between throwing itself at him and wailing or attacking Dayn again. But beating on the goyle wouldn't bring Bax back. It wouldn't reveal Dayn's dark soul. All it would do was make me look like a hysterical female.

I exhaled through my nose and sucked in a deep breath, stepping away from Dayn. My back hit a solid chest, and Serath's scent filled my head. He didn't touch me. Didn't need to. This contact, this was enough to ground me.

"Are you taking on insane elites now?" Dayn sneered. "She probably murdered Bax. Pushed him off this bridge she's yelling about."

Serath's chest vibrated against my back, a warning to Dayn that the stupid goyle couldn't hear. I pressed against him, letting him know I had this under control now.

A moment ago, I'd have happily launched myself at Dayn and clawed out his eyes, but now, with Serath here, my senses were clear and my emotions cold and calm.

I injected that ice into my tone now. "You're a worm, Dayn—digging up information on your fellow cadets and using it to control them. Bax died to protect a secret you were threatening to spread. He died because he was protecting someone he loved, and that...that's on you." I allowed the corner of my mouth to turn up. "I hope you sleep well at night."

I turned on my heel and strode away. No direction in mind, just away, because if I didn't, I might lose my grip on this cold, calm façade and break his nose after all.

SHAR AND THE others caught up with me by the dorms. My feet had taken me toward what my brain obviously considered home now, except...tonight I'd be sleeping in the observatory under the same roof as Serath. I wasn't sure I had the emotional strength to fight my instincts tonight. The primal need to seek the comfort in his company would be too great.

We trooped into the kitchen together, taking our regular seats on autopilot. Curi joined us a moment later and put the coffee machine on. His dark eyes glittered with anger, and there was a tic in his jaw as he grabbed mugs off the shelf. He didn't ask if we wanted a drink, just made them.

I slumped in my seat. "He fell into the chasm. He fell right in front of me. He fucking died because he was so focused on stopping me from getting back."

"And he told you Dayn asked him to do that?" Palia asked.

"Yeah. He did. I told him it wouldn't matter. Someone would come for me because of the elite thing, but he said he'd tell them I died."

I filled them in on what happened at the river, the ledge, and then the bridge. "He didn't need to die. We would have made it back together. He just kept shaking that bridge, wanting to throw me off it, and then when I made it to the other side, he lost focus and..." I shook my head. "He was a decent guy."

"Dayn doesn't deserve to be a guardian," Ginia said. "He has no honor."

"It doesn't matter." Curi placed a cup of coffee in front of me. "The Stone Council want the fastest, the strongest, the most ruthless guardians. Dayn is all of those things. But he's also a worm." He slid a glance my way. "You said Bax was protecting someone?"

"His sister. She'll be coming here as an omega next year, and he said Dayn had information about her..."

Curi's eyes narrowed in thought. "Then maybe it's time we played him at his own game."

"Get intel on him," Touron said. "Something he's hiding."

The two males shared a silent look of communication.

"In the meantime," Shar said, "stay away from the creep. He put us all in danger by trying to tell Bax to leave you behind."

"Even if he told us you were dead, no way would we have believed it," Palia said.

"I know that. But I guess he just wanted to please Dayn."

"Dayn has an issue with halfbloods," Curi said. "Always has. The Lowther family pride themselves on having sired none. Their bloodline is pure goyle, and—" Curi broke off, his attention on the doorway.

Selas stepped into the kitchen, her milky gaze tracking over the space to settle on me. "It's getting late. We should go."

My heart sank. "I want to stay here tonight."

She sighed. "I'm sorry, Cam, but that's not possible. Now more than ever."

Now that they knew that other cadets were out to get me. I wanted to argue, but it was better to save my energy for resisting Serath.

"I'll get my things."

"They've already been moved."

"Great." My tone was dry. I pushed back my seat and stood. "I'll see you guys at breakfast tomorrow."

I followed Selas out of the room but paused at the steps to the upper floors. "I need to check something in my room."

"You mean your boogeyman?" She arched a brow.

Only my friends and Serath knew about Derek. But even

Serath didn't know that Derek had saved me from Ignus. "What did you do to him?"

"Nothing. But he can't be here. The wards should have kept him out."

"I figured as much, and I was going to speak to Willowman about him. Derek saved me from Ignus."

Her gaze sharpened. "Interesting. Willowman will be joining us for supper. You can speak to him then. In the meantime, the tulpa can stay in your dorm room. You can check on him tomorrow."

I usually ate with my friends, but it looked like I'd be sitting down to an evening meal with the elites tonight.

With Serath.

I wasn't sure how I felt about that.

No. That was a lie. I knew exactly how I felt, and it was wholly too good.

CHAPTER 16

CAMERON

We were halfway to the observatory when Levi stepped into our path. "Cam...I heard what happened earlier." He walked up to me, his sea-green eyes filled with concern. "Are you all right?"

My body leaned toward him out of habit, but I stopped myself and took a step back. "I'm fine." My smile felt stiff.

He tutted softly. "Can we have a moment please?"

It took me a second to realize he was speaking to Selas because he hadn't taken his magnetic gaze off me.

I swallowed past the sudden dryness in my mouth and broke contact to look at Selas.

The elite's milky gaze held warning, but she shrugged a shoulder. "That's up to Cam. But you should know that we don't encourage tutor-cadet *fraternization*." The emphasis made her meaning clear.

"I'm not just her tutor. I'm her friend," Levi said.

My heart ached at his words because he was right. We'd been friends first, always friends, but I wasn't sure we could be that any longer, not when his sire was Ulrickson.

Still, I owed him my time. I owed him decency. "I'll join you at the observatory in a few minutes, Selas."

"I'll wait. It's not safe for you to be out alone."

"I'll walk her over," Levi said.

Once again, Selas looked to me for confirmation.

I nodded. "I'll be fine."

"I'll see you in a few minutes then. Buzz to be let in." She walked off into the night, and Levi and I were suddenly alone in the moonlight.

The darkness pressed in around us like a shroud of intimacy, and my feet ached to take a step closer to him. To hold him and say, *sorry, so sorry, Levi. I never wanted to hurt you.* I hated being this aloof person. Hated the distance between us.

"Did the cadet hurt you?" Levi asked softly.

"No. He was a good guy, just...under the influence of a bad one. He didn't deserve to die."

"I'm sorry you had to see it happen."

His tone was warm with sincerity, inviting me to let down my guard and get comfortable, but I kept mine cool and short. "I'm no stranger to death, Levi. I'm fine. Honestly. You don't need to check on me."

"No...I suppose I don't. You have the Mason boy, after all." There was no bitterness in his tone, which told me he was probing, not having a dig.

I wouldn't bite. "He's not a boy. He's a grown male."

Levi gave me a half smile and reached up to gently pinch my chin. "Is he?"

My cheeks flushed, a familiar heat climbing up my body to hug my neck and sting my lips, forcing them to part. Fuck this shit.

"What are you doing with him, Cam? You don't love him, not the way you love me."

A lump formed in my throat, and a heavy feeling settled in my chest because it was still there. My feelings for him were muted against my connection to Serath but not dead. Being around him, seeing him, letting him touch me...all bad.

I jerked my head, tugging my chin from his grip. "I didn't take you for the kind of guy who can't take no for an answer."

He stood taller, looking down his nose at me. "I know you,

Cam. I know when you're lying to me, and back in Old Town I let it slide, but not here. You're hiding something, and I'm going to find out what it is."

Damn his insight. "I'm not hiding anything, but if it helps you to believe that me not wanting to be with you is all due to some secret, then go ahead. Whatever helps you to get over me. But *I* am over you. I love Curi. I'm happy. Just...let me be."

He let out a rough bark of laughter. "Pretty lies from your pretty mouth."

I forced my lips into a thin smile. "Delusional doesn't suit you." I began to walk away. "I'll see you in class."

He caught up to me in two strides. "I promised the elite I'd walk you to the observatory, and unlike some people, I don't break my promises."

"I didn't promise you anything, Levi."

"No...I guess you didn't."

CHAPTER 17

SERATH

I can't believe what Selas is saying to me right now. "You left her with him?"

Selas sighs. "She's perfectly safe."

"With *him*." I take the steps to the observatory watchtower three at a time. I don't bother to turn on the lights. I don't need them. Besides, I need to be incognito while I spy on Cam and her ex-lover.

I spot them on the gravel path that leads to the tower. He looms over her like a dark cloud, his large frame blocking most of her smaller one from view, but I can see the oval of her face turned up to his. It's impossible to read her expression from this distance, but I'm hoping it's one of indifference. Disgust even.

Dammit, I need the telescope, but my feet remain rooted to the spot as the male reaches up to touch her face. Why is he touching her? What the actual fuck?

"Serath, calm down." Selas places a hand on my shoulder.

"Stop that!" I shrug her off. "I don't need calming down. I need that impudent wretch to get his hands off my woman."

"What are we looking at?" Orix drawls from behind us.

"Serath is spying on Cam and the Ulrickson male," Selas says.

"Without the telescope?" Orix sounds genuinely confused.

I take a step toward the contraption, but Selas blocks me.

"Don't," she says. "You'll just make yourself feel worse."

Orix's adopted cat pads closer and meows as if in agreement.

But I need to see. "I have to see her face." Need to see how she looks at him.

"She deserves her privacy," Selas says.

Bullshit. "If she wanted privacy, she wouldn't be on the path in plain view."

"You *want* her to have privacy with him?" Orix asks.

My chest rumbles, the beast inside waking up.

"Will you stop goading him?" Selas snaps at Orix.

Far below us, Cam pulls away from Levi and puts distance between them.

The knot in my belly eases. "That's my girl."

"Oh boy," Selas groans.

I don't need an audience while I act like a lovesick youngling. "Don't you have somewhere to be?"

"You mean aside from watching you spy on your mate?" Orix retorts.

They're both right. This is ridiculous. What am I doing?

Something soft rubs against my ankles, and I look down to see two peridot eyes staring up at me. Taz meows and bumps his head against my leg as if to say, *It's okay. We understand.*

I exhale and step away from the window.

"You need to give her as much space as you can," Selas says. "It'll be hard enough having her under this roof every night. Hard seeing her every day. Hard for both of you."

I grit my teeth. "Stop. Saying. Hard."

Orix snorts, and I shoot him a dark look. He holds up his hands. "Hey, I'm just thinking what you're thinking."

"Cam deserves to have someone in her life. A real lover."

Her words slice into me, tugging a low growl from my lips. "Stop."

"No. You need to accept that," Selas says. "You can't expect her to be chaste all her life. And you can't be either. I know what I said to her in the training room the other day, but it isn't sustainable, not if she ends up as part of our team permanently."

"You mean if Romi isn't...If he can't be an elite anymore," Orix says.

"Yes," Selas replies. "We need to be prepared for the worst, in which case, Cameron will stay on as elite for years. You'll both have to learn to lead separate lives while under the same roof."

"You're saying I should encourage her to fuck other males?" Even saying the words makes me furious. "I'll kill anyone who touches her."

"So, you want her to suffer? To need relief all the time?" Selas asks.

Fuck. "Stop it."

"That sexual tension will need to be relieved or else—"

"Enough!"

Silence fills the space between us. "I can't think about it. I can't know. But I won't...I won't intervene." Fuck, it hurts to even say it.

But she's right. She's my mate and my beast wants only her. But until a fated pair have consummated, they can control their beasts enough to take their pleasures elsewhere. At least, that's the theory. But I don't know of any fated pair that have tested it. Cam and I will be the first.

I feel sick.

"Giving her permission to take a lover doesn't mean she will," Selas says. "The woman is about as stubborn as you are."

"But she can't have Levi," Orix says, joining us at the windows. "The spawn of Ulrickson is too much of a risk. The Mason boy, however...He's a safe choice."

The inferno in my chest rages on, logic fighting primal nature. Beast fighting the goyle.

"She's on her way here now," Selas says. "I'll let her in, and you..." She shakes her head at me. "Go take a cold shower and calm down."

Cold showers are about to become my best friend.

CHAPTER 18

CAMERON

Selas and I took a lift to the sixth floor and into a lounge with four doors leading off it.

"That's my room." Selas pointed to the right. "Shared bathroom." She pointed straight ahead. "And this one is yours." She pushed open the door to the left of the bathroom and stepped back to let me inside.

The room smelled like fresh linen. The king-size bed took up most of the space, the rest occupied by a dresser and wardrobe. My things sat neatly on the rug at the foot of the bed. There was only one window, fitted with blinds.

"I know it's small," Selas said. "But you can make it your own. We'll go into Asteria and grab some throws and cushions if you like."

"No. It's fine the way it is. Easier to keep tidy."

"You sound just like Romi." She bit her lip. "I'm sorry...I shouldn't have—"

"No. I want to talk about him. I need to." I scanned the room. "Was this...Was this his room?"

"Yes. Is that okay?"

I blinked against the gathering heat behind my eyes. "It's more than okay. Thank you."

She cleared her throat. "Okay, well. I'll leave you to unpack. Supper will be ready in thirty minutes." She closed the door, shutting me into what had once been Romi's space.

There was nothing left of him in here now, but the fact that he'd been here, occupied this room, meant that he'd left an imprint. I pressed my palm to the wall and closed my eyes. "I will find you, Romi. I'll find you, and I'll bring you back."

THE OBSERVATORY WAS a tower, housing seven floors. I was on the sixth with Selas, two floors above Serath, with Orix and Prasan a floor below us.

Each floor had a lounge, but there was a huge communal space on floor three and a kitchen on floor two. A state-of-the-art gymnasium filled the first floor, which explained why I'd never seen the elites in the training room.

My stomach trembled with nerves as I took the lift to the second floor. So far, the other elites had stayed out of sight, but now I'd be thrown into their midst, forced to get to know them and be a part of this group. Would I fit in here? I couldn't imagine feeling at home, not like I did in the dorms with my friends.

The doors to the elevator opened, and a delicious meaty smell hit me, nudging my stomach to rumble in appreciation.

This room was a huge open-plan space with support beams cleverly hung with interesting prints. A long table sat in the center of the space, lit by low-hanging overhead lights, and a modern functional kitchen made up the back of the room, complete with breakfast bar and stools.

The elite moved between table and kitchen with practiced synchronization, carrying plates and cutlery, huge bowls of stew, and plates of fragrant bread, but they all stopped to look at me as I stepped into the room.

My attention zeroed in on Serath like a homing beacon, and the nervous flutter in my belly turned into a different kind of flutter. The kind that spawned beneath heated touches. My breath hitched as our gazes snapped and locked.

He swallowed hard, and my stomach flipped in response.

"Welcome!" Prasan, the scholarly elite, approached me with a warm smile. "You can sit here with me." He pulled out a chair at the opposite end of the table from Serath, and I noted how Serath's eyes narrowed slightly. He didn't protest, though; instead, he broke eye contact to place the tray of bread on the table before taking extra time to adjust it.

"Here you go." Selas popped a plate in front of me. "Help yourself to food."

It wasn't the easiest thing to focus on the food with Serath in the room, but I did my best. There was stew, bread, salad, and some round dumpling-type things. "Everything looks and smells delicious."

"Consider it a welcome meal," Orix said. "We don't always cook like this."

"There's a rota on the fridge," Prasan said. "You'll be cooking with me tomorrow."

"We cook in pairs," Selas explained. "For the team."

"Makes sense."

"Can you cook?" Prasan asked.

"I get by."

"Prasan's a great cook," Orix said, "but a nightmare to cook with. So fucking precise."

Prasan sniffed and lifted his chin. "The final product is worth the care and effort."

"Everyone, take your seats," Serath said. "Let's eat."

"Without me?" Willowman entered via a door on the far side of the room. Probably the stairwell.

His dark hair was windswept, kohl-rimmed eyes brightening as they took in the spread. He rubbed his hands together. "Smells delicious. I'm starving."

"Take a seat," Serath said.

Willowman shrugged his jacket off and flung it onto the

breakfast bar before parking himself on the opposite side of the table to me. Everyone left one seat between them, which was kind of needed because goyles weren't exactly tiny. I was cocooned between Prasan and Orix while Selas sat directly opposite me, between Serath and Willowman.

We loaded our plates, and the scarfing of food commenced. The stew was thick with a tomato base and just enough spice to give it a kick. The bread was soft on the inside and crusty on the outside, the perfect accompaniment to the stew. The salad was crisp and fresh, and the dumpling things were delicious when dipped in the stew.

Plates scraped clean, we all loaded up a second time.

"How are you feeling now after the extraction run?" Willowman asked me.

"I'm fine. Bax, on the other hand..."

Willowman's expression hardened. "The administration will be keeping an eye on Mr. Lowther."

"He should be kicked out," Serath said.

"There's no evidence of his blackmail. All we have is Miss Basque's word."

"Which should be enough," Serath growled.

"You know that's not how it works," Selas said evenly.

"*Hmmmmm...*" Serath took a sip of his water, and our gazes clashed over the rim. My heart lurched, and I tore my attention away, dropping it to my plate. My pulse raced, and it took a moment for it to slow.

Focus on other things, Cam. Anything else but him.

But my mind was blank, my body thrumming with awareness of the male sitting opposite me.

"Cameron, didn't you want to speak to Willowman about your tulpa?" Selas said.

Her words were a lifeline. "Yes. Um, I have a tulpa."

Willowman swallowed his mouthful. "Right. It's not usual for a goyle to have one, but you're a halfblood, so—"

"No. I mean I have one. Here. At the academy."

"Oh?" He set down his spoon, suddenly interested. "You created it here?"

"No. He's been with me since I was a child, but he came here a couple of days ago. After Ignus tried to compel me to go with him, Derek appeared and protected me. He helped me to break free of Ignus's control. I wouldn't have escaped otherwise. And after that, Derek was here, in my dorm room closet."

Willowman leaned forward, elbows on the table. "And what kind of creature is Derek? What kind of tulpa?"

"A boogeyman."

"Why didn't you tell me he saved you?" Serath asked.

"I'd just found out my brother was alive. Derek kinda slipped my mind, but there's something wrong with him. He's...growing."

Willowman frowned. "Growing?"

"His form is expanding, and he's scared."

"Your boogeyman is scared." Willowman looked skeptical.

"Look, Derek isn't like other boogeymen. He's sweet and kind, and I love him. I need you to help me fix him."

Willowman plucked at his napkin. "Standard protocol dictates we extinguish any tulpas born on campus."

"What? No!" I sat up straighter in panic. "You can't hurt him. I won't let you."

"He won't." Serath snarled.

If Willowman was threatened by Serath's snarl, he didn't show it. In fact, he didn't even look his way, keeping his attention on me. "No. I won't. Because your tulpa *wasn't* born on campus. He somehow found his way in. I need to figure out how. These wards are impregnable."

"Obviously not," Orix said. "Your orb was tampered with."

Willowman grimaced. "Which means we have a mole. An insider playing us. Nothing to do with the wards and everything to do with loyalty."

Finding the traitor was up to administration. But Derek was my responsibility. "I don't want you to hurt him. I just need him to be okay. He's family to me."

"I won't intentionally hurt him," Willowman said. "I swear it."

I believed him. "There's something else. Melanie, the ghost in my room, has been acting...odd."

"Odd? In what way?"

I explained Melanie's spaced-out behavior. "Ever since she broke into the confidential file room to get Romi's file and—"

"What?" everyone said at the same time.

Ooops. Okay, they didn't know about that escapade. "Yeah, I did a thing..."

I filled them in on Melanie's file room break-in and what she said she found, along with her weird behavior ever since. "And that was the same night that Flora Yarrow was found unconscious on the same floor."

Willowman chewed on his cheeks. "I don't believe in coincidences."

"Surely, Romi's file would have contained the truth about what happened to him," Selas said.

"It would have been logged for sure," Prasan said. "But someone obviously didn't want Melanie passing on that information."

"Someone must have messed with her memories," Willowman said. "Fed her a false one and sent her back to you."

"Someone who didn't want the truth about Romi getting out," Prasan said. "But that's everyone high up."

"They couldn't have known who Melanie was getting the information for," Serath said. "They were protecting it."

All this conjecture didn't help Melanie. "We need to fix her."

"She's dead, Cam," Selas said. "There is no fixing her."

It was the first time I'd felt irritated with the elite female. "Her body is gone, but her soul is here, and it's in pain. That matters."

Selas tucked her chin in. "I didn't mean to sound callous. But we're guardians, and our responsibilities lie with protecting the living. It's where our focus needs to be. Looking into your tulpa's evolution is enough of a stretch on our resources."

"By resources, you mean me, I assume," Willowman said coolly, sitting back in his seat. "And I can speak for myself." His golden eyes warmed as his gaze settled on me. "I'll do what I can to help her. I have some contacts in the rim I can speak to. Which reminds me, the blood sample I took from you was ruined. In the hubbub of finding out the orbs had been switched, I must have forgotten to properly store it. We'll need to take another."

I'd completely forgotten about my mission to find out how I'd bypassed the ward to the forest on the omega moon. The strange flushes and itchy skin were gone, but it didn't mean they wouldn't come back.

"Can you take a sample later this week when we do herbology?"

"Herbology?" Serath was looking at me again, and it was hard to breathe.

I nodded. "I can't fly or shift, but I can be useful with tinctures and potions."

"My little apprentice," Willowman said with a small smile. "I do have a lot of knowledge to pass on. It'll be fun."

I caught movement in the corner of my eye—Selas's hand on Serath's arm.

My stomach cramped, and annoyance gnawed at my chest. Did she have to touch him *all* the time?

But when I lifted my gaze, his attention was on me, intense and hungry, and damn if I wasn't suddenly starving for the feel of his thick cock between my thighs and—

"Dessert, anyone?" Selas asked, her tone higher pitched than usual.

"Not for me," Serath said. "I need some air."

He pushed back his seat and left, and it took everything I had not to follow him.

"You did well," Prasan said.

I let out a rough chuckle. "That obvious?"

"The pheromones in here are thick," Orix said. "Even Taz can't stomach them."

A tiny meow alerted me to the little feline hiding under the table. He popped his head out and peered up at me inquisitively.

"Hey, my name's Cam. It's nice to meet you, Taz."

Taz bumped his head against my leg and purred loudly.

"Cats are great judges of character," Orix said. "The fact he likes you means you'll fit into the team just fine."

"Are you glad you didn't kill me now?"

Orix rolled his eyes. "Are you ever going to let that slide?"

"Probably not."

"I'll get dessert," Selas said. "Cam, would you like to help?"

"Sure."

I joined her in the kitchen, where she retrieved a large cheesecake from the fridge. "I'm sorry if I upset you earlier."

"Don't be. You're a guardian. An elite. You have a job to do, and I get that. But I wasn't born into this. I'm a hunter at heart. We kill the bad shit, but we also do our best to save the good."

"But it's more than that with this ghost, isn't it? You've grown attached."

"Impossible not to. She's a sweetheart...at least she was. Besides, if we fix her, we can find out who messed with her in the first place."

"You think that person might be our mole?"

I shrugged. "I don't know, but we can look into that once we have his or her identity."

"I should have thought of that." A small smile lifted her lips. "A little hard to focus with all the phero—"

"Please. Don't." I groaned. "I hate that word."

She chuckled. "If anyone can fix Melanie, it's Willowman." She paused in her slicing. "He's a great guy too. Attentive. Caring. Powerful. You'll enjoy your time with him, *and* he's *not* a tutor, so the official no fraternization rule doesn't apply."

Wait...was she... "Are you trying to set me up?"

She sighed and turned to face me. "You don't have to be a nun just because you can't act on your fated bond with Serath."

"That's not what you said the other day."

"I know, but I was wrong. You could be stuck with us here for a long time."

"But when Romi gets back, then..." The look on her face made my stomach hurt. "You don't think we'll get him back."

"It's not that, Cam. I'm more worried about what state he'll be in when we do."

She thought he'd be messed up like Varsa. Heck, I'd be lying if I said the thought hadn't crossed my mind; I'd just buried it, though.

"We're going to do everything in our power to save him," Selas said. "But to do that, we need you and Serath to be focused."

And she thought all the ungratified sexual tension would cause a problem. Her logic was sound, but the thought of being intimate with any male other than Serath made me feel ill. "I don't want anyone else."

"I know. But there will be times when you *need* someone else. Both of you."

Serath with another woman. Serath fucking someone else? My fingers ached and burned, and a low, menacing growl vibrated in my throat.

Selas's gaze dropped to my hands. "Cam..."

My fingers were elongated and tipped with granite-colored talons. "Shit." I shook them as if that would get rid of them. "Shit, shit."

The talons melted away.

"What was that?" Orix hurried to join us from across the room.

I had no idea. "It happened on the extraction run but only for a moment. It's never happened before, though."

"A partial shift?" Willowman joined us too. "May I?" He took my hand and studied my fingers. "Partial shifts are impossible for halfbloods and incredibly rare for gargoyles. We need to get that blood sample looked at by my contact as soon as possible."

"Why not HQ?" Orix asked. "They have alchemists that could look deep and find..." He trailed off. "Right, got it."

They might find out I was Serath's fated mate if they cross-referenced samples. My original sample would have been screened at the intake center. According to Lionel, the same samples would have been sent to another lab, and that was maybe where my identity as Basque blood could have been discovered, as deeper screenings were done there. The sample had never made it to HQ.

"We *will* figure this out," Willowman said with confidence.

And I believed him.

"Let's enjoy this dessert, then you can get some sleep," Selas said kindly. "The next few weeks are going to be intense."

Sleep with Serath under the same roof?

That was going to take some training of its own.

CHAPTER 19

CAMERON

Being under the same roof as Serath was harder than I expected. Knowing he was only a couple of floors down, knowing I could simply head out of my room and take the stairs down to him was a simmering temptation in my lower abdomen.

He hadn't returned by the time we finished dessert and Selas had walked me back to our floor with instructions to stay on it.

They weren't taking any chances, and I was glad they were keeping watch because, honestly, I didn't trust myself when it came to my mate.

Back at the dorms, I'd have fallen asleep by now, but tonight, sleep eluded me. After an hour of staring at the ceiling. I shoved my feet into slippers and headed into the lounge. Serath was two floors below, so that was a no-go, but I could go up. The observatory watchtower was supposed to have an amazing view.

I entered the moonlit space silently and froze at the sight of the large figure silhouetted by the windows.

Even in the gloom, it was impossible for me not to recognize my mate. My feet took me a couple of steps toward him before I regained control.

His shoulders rose and fell as if he were taking a deep breath. Was he inhaling my scent? "It's all right, Cam. Willowman reinforced my anklet."

An invitation. I wanted to take it. "You might have an anklet, but I don't."

"Are you afraid you'll throw yourself at me?"

"Yes."

He let out a soft groan, and the air spiked with his scent.

My throat went dry, my pussy clenching.

"Maybe you *should* go." His tone was low and gruff.

"Right." I needed to leave this room. This unbuffered space where it was just him and me and the primal call of whatever mystical shit lived in our blood.

I crossed the room toward him instead.

"Cam..." He turned his head, offering me his beautiful profile. Straight nose, hard jaw, and those lips. Those full, luscious—

I stopped a couple of feet from him, chest heaving like I'd done a sprint. "This is insane."

He turned to face me in the moonlight, pale eyes darkening as they swept over me. His hands curled to fists, his breath coming short and shallow as he finally locked gazes with me.

A jolt passed through me—our connection, strong and steady, even though we were denying it.

"Being alone is dangerous." His nostrils flared. "I can smell your arousal. Your need."

And I could smell him—a thick, cloying scent that was his arousal. The pulse between my thighs beat hard and deep. I was wet for him, and he hadn't even touched me.

"I should go." My tone held a plea.

He reached up to tentatively cup my cheek. "*Hmmmm...*" He swept his thumb over my bottom lip, then pressed down slightly, parting my mouth.

I licked the tip of his thumb, tasty salt, then closed my mouth around it, drawing it in and suckling.

"Fuck." He tried to pull free, but I gripped his wrist, locked gazes with him, and slowly, carefully withdrew his thumb from my mouth.

"Cam..." His chest heaved.

But I was hungry for him. Desperate to taste him like he'd tasted me that night on the tower. I took a step forward, and he took one back.

"Cam, you need to go before I lose control."

"You have the cuff." My voice was deeper now. "I just need a taste." I pressed my hand to his chest and ran it down slowly to cup his crotch. Fuck, he was huge and hard. "Serath, please." I rubbed and squeezed.

His eyes rolled back as he angled his hips, pushing his cock into my hand. "Cam...I can't. We fucking can't."

"You want someone else to have this?" I squeezed again, and he groaned. I grabbed his wrist and guided his hand to my crotch, to the sleep shorts that burned with heat. "Do you want someone else to have this?"

His eyes snapped open, burning with possessive heat, the signature of his beast. "Mine."

"Yes!" my beast growled.

I pushed against his fingers, opening my thighs so he could touch me through the wet fabric of my pants. Fuck, his fingers were so thick. I stroked him, rubbing the ridged length of cock and pushing down on the head through his lastonflex to elicit delicious moans and pants.

I'd wanted to taste him, but this...fuck this had to happen now. We leaned against each other, chasing our climax.

"Need to feel you..." His deep voice rumbled against my senses.

My beast pressed against my skin, stronger than ever before. "Yes."

He adjusted his grip to push his hand into my panties, cupping my throbbing pussy with his palm.

"Need it." My voice was thick with desire.

"Take it." His thick fingers parted my swollen flesh, the abrasion of his calloused digits firing sensations through me that fucked with my sanity. My knees buckled, but he caught me. He pressed his thumb to my clit and entered me with two fingers, curling deep to hit the magic spot.

Stars filled my head as my body convulsed, releasing the orgasm it had been holding for what felt like forever.

I bit down on his bicep to stifle my cry, hot juices spilling all over his hand, thighs trembling with the force of my climax.

"Cam..." He nuzzled my ear, his lips ghosting across my cheek toward my mouth. "My Cam..."

Our mouths met in soft, needy kisses that tasted of mint and coffee.

His fingers pumped inside me, mimicking the act we so desperately wanted. I came again, sobbing into his mouth at the almost painful release.

I needed to give him this too. Needed him to have the same release.

I lifted myself off his hand, thighs quivering and wet, and began to peel down his lastonflex.

He leaned back against the window ledge, bringing his fingers to his mouth and sucking them clean of my cum.

My pussy throbbed, because fuck, that was hot.

The lastonflex snagged on his arousal, and I worked him free. Oh gods...he was epic—thick, long and ridged, the head slick and glistening with precum. I gripped him, fingers unable to wrap all the way around him. He swelled even more, jerking in my hand, begging for release. There was no way I'd be able to take it all in my pussy, let alone my mouth, but I needed this. I needed to make him come.

I kept my gaze locked with his as I knelt and wrapped my lips around him. Flavor exploded on my tongue, salty like caramel.

His moan edged on a growl as his fingers sank into my hair, holding me to him as I worked him.

He pulsed as I took him as deep as I could.

"Cam...Fuck." He tried to push me off, but I took him deeper. "Fuck!" He came hard and hot, and I swallowed every drop, greedy for the taste of him.

We remained locked for long seconds, his hands flexing in my hair, his hips rolling as the orgasm trailed off. He stroked my cheek and carefully drew himself out of my mouth with a soft pop.

I licked my lips, heart aching with loss as he tucked himself away.

"Oh, Cameron..."

Was that regret in his tone?

Ice pricked at my senses as the beast retreated.

He steered me to my feet, the husky pale irises of his eyes almost silver in the moonlight as they tracked lovingly over my face, but a moment later, those beautiful eyes were filled with pain.

He dropped his forehead to mine. "This was a mistake."

His words hurt, even though I knew he was referring to our lapse in judgment, not the beauty of what had happened. "We'll do better."

He rolled his forehead against mine "We can't be alone together." He pulled away, his large hands settling on my shoulders. "We can *never* be alone together. We might be able to fight the bond, but our beasts don't want to. They can't. To them, the bond is everything and must be consummated."

He was right. I'd felt the surge a moment ago. The demand from the beast within to claim. To take and own. To seal the bond. Yes...he was right: being alone together was tempting fate.

I stepped away from him, and the distance between us opened like a wound.

"Go." His voice was gruff and broken. "Go before I stop you from leaving."

This time, my feet listened to my command.

I turned and ran.

CHAPTER 20

CAMERON

"So, what was it like at the elite tower?" Palia asked as soon as I joined them at breakfast.

"I miss the dorm." I parked my butt and took the coffee mug Touron passed me. "But I get to stay in Romi's old room." The coffee was sweet with just the right amount of milk. "I think I love you."

Touron looked horrified. "Never say that around you-know-who."

"Why? Don't you love me too?" I gave him my best cutesy grin.

He rolled his eyes. "Shut up and drink your coffee."

Shar plopped a plate of crispy bacon in the middle of the table, and we all descended on it. The next few minutes were spent in happy munching.

Saffe and Waxen joined us as Touron was doing refills, and the mood in the room immediately dipped.

They'd been friends with Bax.

Bax was dead.

"Where's your boss?" Shar asked Saffe. "He not joining you for breakfast?"

Saffe hung his head, and it was Waxen who spoke for him.

"Saffe isn't hanging with the turd any longer."

"I told him he could say what he liked. That I didn't care anymore," Saffe said.

"What did he have on you?" Ginia asked.

"Ginia!" Palia frowned. "That's none of our business."

Saffe shot her a grateful smile. "Dayn was called in to see Carter this morning."

"I hope he gets kicked out," Ginia said.

"He won't." Curi entered the room, running a hand through his bed-head hair. "They'll warn him, maybe, but guardians are too important to throw away without evidence." He rounded the table to drop a kiss on my head and then took the seat beside me, throwing his arm along the back of my chair.

This time, my body didn't tense up at his proximity. Instead, I played the part and leaned into him.

"A warning won't bring Bax back," Touron said stiffly.

"No. It won't," Saffe said. "He was my friend." His throat worked as he wrangled his emotions. "I'll miss him."

A lump formed in my throat. "I'm so sorry, Saffe. But you're not alone. You have us." He looked up at me in surprise. "Look, I came here knowing I'd be a target. Knowing I would be treated like crap for being weaker, but I found friends that feel like family. We're stronger together. We have the same goal. It makes sense to have each other's backs."

"Hear, hear!" Curi picked up my coffee mug in a toast. "To not being wankers."

Palia winced but didn't protest as we all echoed the sentiment.

"Shit, we need to get to class," Waxen said. "I got to grab my bag." He hurried from the room.

I drained my coffee, stomach in knots because the first class of the day was Supernatural Defense.

I'd be seeing Levi again.

I POPPED INTO my dorm room and checked on Derek. He was huddled in a corner breathing softly but didn't wake when I called to him. If I wasn't mistaken, his form had expanded. Again.

Melanie didn't make an appearance when I called, so I headed back down to join the others on the walk to the main building.

Curi held my hand, demonstrating our "togetherness" for all to see.

The campus was teeming with activity, training grounds filled with initiates battling it out under Farnell's watchful eye. I caught a glimpse of Orix running between the masses, barking orders, but there was no sign of Serath.

My pulse spiked as memories from last night flooded me. The way we'd touched, his lips on mine. His cock in my mouth. A rush of heat left me momentarily breathless.

Curi leaned in to sniff me. "Fuck. You smell good."

The hot, itchy feeling was back. "I don't feel great."

His dark eyes sharpened in concern. "Do you need to sit down?"

The heat dissipated, leaving me cold. "I'm okay. It's gone. Weird."

"The weird feeling from the omega moon?" Touron asked.

I nodded.

Curi's grip on my hand tightened. "In that case, you better stay close." He tucked me under his arm and dropped another kiss on my head.

Shar arched a brow. "You're really getting into this, aren't you, Mason?"

"I don't do anything by halves, Aziza."

The main building came into view where Blake and Flora Yarrow stood on the steps, chatting with Levi.

"What are they doing out here?" Palia said. "It's time for class."

Several goyles from the other dorm trooped out of the building to pool at the bottom of the steps. Our group of goyles might have entered the academy together, but the classes were for all cadets preparing for the cadet exam. The faces were familiar now, but the names still eluded me.

Levi's attention zeroed in on me as we approached, completely ignoring Curi. He half smiled, that cocky smile of his that used to make my insides melt with heat. There was no denying the flutter in my belly, but it was muted by my beast.

"Gather 'round!" Yarrow waved us all over. "We'll be taking our lesson outdoors this afternoon."

My heart dipped. Were we going off campus? So far, leaving had resulted in death and danger. My apprehension must have shown on my face because Levi's eyes narrowed.

He stepped forward. "We'll be staying on campus. We simply need a little more space."

He was reassuring me. Being there for me just like he'd been for the past year. I was an ass for hurting him. Everything would be so much easier if I could tell him.

I pressed closer to Curi, and he dipped his head and grazed my temple with his lips, sending a shiver through me. "You okay?" His voice was a gruff whisper.

"Peachy."

"Everyone, follow Miss Yarrow. We'll make up the rear. Head to Greenwood Forest."

"What do you think we'll be doing that needs space?" Palia asked.

"We'll find out soon enough," Sharniza replied.

THIS DAMN CLEARING. How many times had I been here now? I'd lost count. We stood against the tree line facing our tutors for the day. It looked like Supernatural Defense and Arcana were going to be working together. Flora stood to one side, clipboard and pen in hand. I caught her eye, and she smiled shyly.

We'd meant to have one-on-one lessons, but she was no longer on my timetable. I'd have to ask about that because my arcana was weak and my shields non-existent. If I was going to be an elite and pass that exam, surely I needed to have the best shields possible.

"Today, we'll be testing your shields against a manifested threat," Yarrow said. "But first, Mr. Halle, will show you how to harness the power of nature to fuel your natural shields."

Levi took the floor, hands tucked into his pockets. His sleeves were rolled up, exposing more intricate tattoos—markings I'd spent hours tracing. Kissing. I swallowed the nostalgia that clogged my throat and focused on his words.

"I explained to you that pureblood druids can manipulate the elements of nature. Druid hunters can use nature to fight against threats. But as a halfblood, I never had that direct line. I learned to merge my shields with the elemental power around me and thus enhance them. You can do this, too, not by taking from nature but by asking it for help. There's power all around us. Nature is imbued with spirit, and you can speak to it. Today, we'll work on making that connection." He nodded at Yarrow.

"I tested your shields in our last lesson," Yarrow said. "Today, I'll be testing them again after you've attempted to connect with the elements around you."

"As gargoyles, the earth is our strongest connection, followed by air," Levi said. "We'll test them both." He lowered himself to the ground and sat cross-legged. "Everyone, sit and close your eyes."

I parked my ass between Curi and Shar and closed my eyes.

"Feel the wind on your skin," Levi said. "Hear the whispers of woodland life around you, and smell the aroma of fresh earth and the hint of rain to come. Open your senses to the world and allow your beast to rise to the surface."

Long seconds passed where I was hyperaware of everyone breathing around me, but eventually those sounds faded, leaving me alone with the kiss of a breeze and the scent of nature. My breathing deepened until it felt as if I were floating. My blood warmed, and my beast pushed against my skin, wanting to touch the world.

Levi's voice sounded dream-like and far away. "Let your beast rise and touch the world. Let it swim in the spirit that is all around you."

Something tugged at my chest, and I was floating. No...not me. Her. The goyle part of me that I'd been disconnected from for so long was outside of me yet connected to me. Warmth wrapped around her limbs, and euphoria bloomed in my chest. The darkness behind my eyelids spawned stars and a beautiful full moon wreathed in frosted rings of energy. My fingers and toes tingled as my beast sank back into me, settling, calm and content.

"Cameron?" A female voice cut into my zen space. I peeled my eyes open and looked up at Flora. "There you are."

Around me, everyone else was already on their feet.

"You went deep." Levi sounded impressed. "Did you feel the connection?"

"I'm not sure what I felt, but it felt good."

"Let's see how well you did." Yarrow looked over at Levi.

"If you connected, then you should find it easier to summon your shield," Levi said. "You should be able to reinforce it quicker too." He held up his hands. "But don't be disheartened if you can't. We have time to work on it in the lead-up to the exams, and I'll be on hand after to assist anyone who needs it during initiate training."

He'd be doing classes for initiates too?

"Aziza, you're up first," Yarrow said.

Shar rolled her shoulders and stepped into the clearing.

Yarrow flicked his wrist, and a ball of black smoke appeared in his hand. "This is negative energy in a concentrated form. It will burrow into your mind and draw out your darkest fears and find your pain. If you let it."

"Graynites aren't the only creatures who can get into your head," Levi said. "Some vampires can also do this. The oldest ones. We believe there's a breed of fangs that were born, not made, but we haven't been able to determine for sure."

Born vampires? Vampirism was a curse. At least that was what I'd always known. I guessed there was stuff for me to learn about the hunter world after all. But why had Levi never mentioned this to me?

Yarrow held up the black ball of negative energy. "Ready?" he asked Shar.

"Ready." Shar's gaze was sharp and focused.

Yarrow flicked the dark smoke her way. It surrounded her for a brief moment before being shoved back by an invisible force. The smoke vibrated, pushing against Shar's invisible shield. The shield shoved it farther, and it dissipated.

"Impressive, Miss Aziza," Yarrow said. "Very impressive."

Sharniza exhaled. "Thanks."

Flora jotted something on her clipboard.

"Okay, Lomax, you're next."

Touron took a little longer to shove away the negative smoke, shaking his head as if to dispel unwanted thoughts, but he succeeded. Curi went next and took about as long as Touron. He returned to my side, pale and spooked.

What had he seen when the smoke got in his head?

"Basque? Hello?" Yarrow arched a brow my way.

Shit. I was still getting used to being called Basque. I stepped into the clearing, nerves tightening my abdomen.

My shields were shit. This was going to hurt.

Yarrow lifted his chin, watching me from beneath hooded eyes. "Are you ready?"

"I'm ready." I blew out a breath. "Hit me."

The black smoke rushed at me and ripped me away from the clearing.

I'm in the kitchen at the dorm, surrounded by my friends, but they're all looking at me in disgust, shouting at me, saying awful things that hurt.

They don't want me.

I don't belong.

I'm alone.

"It's all right," Serath says. "You have me. You're not alone."

I run to him, but he backs away, laughing. "You're pathetic. You think I want a halfblood weakling for a mate?"

"No. Please no."

The world fills with light. Romi is standing over me, holding out his hand. Smiling. The pain ebbs, but then a storm cloud appears overhead, and lightning strikes, taking him with it.

He's gone.

I'm alone. So alone.

I'm standing in the hallway, law enforcement on the doorstep. The rain is hammering down. She's gone. Mom is gone.

My chest hurts with the loss. My eyes sting from crying. I'm alone. So alone.

The world is dark, gray, and cold. A voice like glass and gravel fills the gloom.

"There you are, little one. Come here. Let me see you." Dark taloned hands reach for me.

Terror flares in my chest, and ice shards pierce my blood.

"No. Go away. I don't like this place. I want to go home."

The talons reach for me, about to touch me.

"No!"

SHARNIZA

CAM IS ON her knees, her arms up to cover her head, her sobs filling the silence.

Levi takes a step forward, his jaw tense. "I think that's enough."

"No," Yarrow says. "One moment."

"What the fuck?" Curi edges toward Cameron, and I join him.

Palia and Ginia exchange worried glances.

"That's enough," Touron says.

"Stand down!" Yarrow orders. "One more mom—"

A dark form explodes into being behind Cam. Large and looming with silver slitted eyes and sharp chiseled features, it holds out its hands, and light blazes out of its palms, smashing into the smoke and devouring it.

"What the fuck?"

"What is that?"

"Oh fuck..."

The form solidifies into a male shadow, larger than a goyle. It crouches and wraps its arms around Cameron.

"Get away from her." Levi rushes forward, but Yarrow blocks him.

The creature is wholly focused on Cam, its silver slanted eyes somehow filled with concern. "You safe now, my Cameron."

Cameron opens her eyes and looks up at the creature. "Derek?"

Fuck...

CHAPTER 21

Cameron

Derek cradled me against his chest, his frame so large I felt like a child in his arms.

He'd changed. Again. His mournful eyes were now diamond-bright and slanted, set in a slender face with high cheek bones and a pointed chin. His ears were pointed, too, and the razor teeth were gone, replaced by even white teeth and elongated canines.

"You safe now," he said again.

He was speaking real words. "How?"

"Cameron?"

Derek's head whipped up, diamond eyes narrowing on Levi. He relaxed a moment later. "Not hurt you. Safe now." He stroked my cheek. "You be safe now, my Cameron. I sleep."

He misted into nothing, and Levi rushed forward to help me up. "That was Derek?"

I stood, legs like jelly. "He's gone through some changes."

"Derek?" Yarrow said. "You named it?"

"Him. I named *him*. He's my tulpa. A boogeyman I created as a child."

"He protected you in some way back then?" Yarrow asked.

I nodded. "Nightmares. Bad ones."

"And since?"

"Not till recently. I mean, I hunted, but he never showed up. Something has changed."

Everyone gathered around.

"You expected something to happen, didn't you?" Levi asked Yarrow. "It's why you kept pushing."

Yarrow shrugged a shoulder. "I had a strong suspicion."

Around us, the other cadets were murmuring among themselves and looking over at me like I was a freak. It hit too close to home. Felt too much like the strange dreamlike state the negative energy had thrown me into, and anger flickered to life in my chest.

I fixed a glare on my face. "What? You have something to say, then say it to my face." Curi put his hand on my shoulder, and it took everything I had not to shrug him off. "Go on. Just say it. You think I'm a freak, right? I don't give a shit."

"No, that's not it at all," a cadet who I'd never spoken to said. "I think that was fucking awesome." He looked over at Yarrow. "How do we get a Derek?"

"Yeah, I want one too," Waxen said.

Everyone started talking at once.

"Silence!" Yarrow ordered. "As much as I'd like to take credit for Miss Basque's humanoid shield, unfortunately, I cannot. I fear Derek is unique to Miss Basque. A fortunate anomaly. However, there is nothing stopping you from creating shields just as powerful, even though they may not be sentient."

Wait—what... "Shield?"

"Yes, Miss Basque. Derek is your shield."

CLASS DISMISSED, YARROW invited me back to the Arcana classroom for a "chat." Naturally, our whole group went. We came as a package deal, after all. Levi didn't leave my side, so I found myself flanked by him and Curi.

My blue-haired fake boyfriend made sure to hold my hand,

staking his imaginary claim all the way to our destination, and the tic in Levi's jaw told me it bothered the heck out of him.

Back in class, we all took seats while Yarrow paced, hands on hips. Flora watched him, almost warily, while Levi perched on the edge of a desk, arms crossed over his powerful chest.

"This is truly amazing," Yarrow said finally. "When I tested your shields the first time, I sensed their power, but they were dormant. My psychic attack didn't rouse them. I did some research and discovered that in some cases, shields can be activated by a gargoyle's emotional state, appearing only when the goyle truly believes themselves to be in mortal danger. You didn't perceive me as a threat, and that's why your shield...why Derek didn't appear to protect you."

"And when hunting, we were in a team," Levi said. "You had the security of backup."

"But not when Ignus attacked," Shar said. "That time, you must have been terrified."

"And just now," Levi continued. "In the clearing, whatever memories or fears the negative energy dredged up were enough to make you feel threatened."

It all fit. It all made sense. "You're saying I somehow turned my shields into a tulpa?"

"Yes," Yarrow said. "Tulpas are manifestations born of imagination and will. Most remain trapped in the creator's mind, but some, like the ones the goyles fight, develop form and substance. When you created Derek, you gave your protective shields a form. As a child, it may have been the only way you could understand your own power and wield it. You created a formidable being that serves to protect you. But in doing so, you also separated your shields from yourself."

"He's still a part of you," Flora said quickly. "Born from your true nature."

But he was also his own person, and he was changing. "He used to be smaller, unable to speak our language, but his whole form has changed, along with his speech."

"Maybe being here is changing him?" Flora looked to Blake for confirmation.

Blake shook his head. "No. He's part of you, Cameron. If he's changing, it's because something inside of you is changing."

"What could that be?" Levi asked Yarrow.

Yarrow shrugged. "I don't know. Halfbloods vary in their abilities. It could be that Cameron is reaching goyle maturity..." He sighed, exasperated. "I can't say."

"How old are you?" Flora asked.

"Twenty...twenty-one in...well, a few weeks."

"It could be the age thing," Yarrow agreed.

Was that the reason for the granite talons and the weird flushes? I needed to let Willowman know about this.

"I can, however, work directly with Derek to help him master your power...his power," Yarrow said. "Your connection, however, doesn't need any work. As long as you truly feel you need him, he will find you."

He was a shield, but he was a being in his own right. "He shouldn't be living in a closet. Is he doing that because of me? Because I made him think that's what he *needed* to do?"

"He's living off a blueprint a child created," Yarrow said. "So, yes."

"He has his own feelings and wants. He never conformed to frightening people, even though he believed he was a boogeyman. Because I made him think that..." His whole identity was messed up because of me.

"May I?" Flora asked tentatively.

Blake gave her an encouraging smile. "Go on..."

"The tulpas that goyles extinguish are created out of fear. They are monsters. But there are some tulpas who are created from love. We don't usually come across them because they don't make themselves known, but I believe Derek is such a tulpa. I believe that he's sentient, and whatever growth Cameron is experiencing is allowing him to become his own person."

Derek was a person. *My* person. "I'll speak to him. Explain it all."

Yarrow chewed on his cheeks. "I've never had a sentient shield as a pupil before. This will be...interesting."

His golden eyes flashed, and for a moment, it felt as if an age of wisdom was looking out at me, but then he blinked, and the impression was gone.

"I'll speak to Carter," Flora said.

"It's settled then," Yarrow said. "Derek's training can start next week. It's important he not only understand his connection to you but also grow as an independent entity if he is to maintain control of his abilities."

My tulpa was my shield. He was a part of me. And now I needed to explain that to him.

CHAPTER 22

CAMERON

Derek sat on the bed in my old room, his large shadowy form hunched over, head bowed. He looked up slowly as I entered.

"My Cam, I can't fit." He pointed at the wardrobe, which now looked tiny in comparison to his form. "I can't..."—he patted his chest—"shrink."

Sharniza entered the room, and Derek's gleaming diamond eyes settled on her.

"Hello, Derek," she said. "It's nice to meet you. Again."

He smiled tentatively, flashing the edge of fangs. "To meet you nice also." He looked back at the wardrobe mournfully. "I sorry, Cam. I think I broken."

My heart squeezed painfully in my chest with love. "Hey." I crossed the room to stand in front of him and block his view of that goddamn wooden prison he'd been confined to for all these years. "You're not broken. You're perfect. You're my best friend, and I'm sorry, so sorry for not understanding what...who you were."

He peered at me quizzically. "What you mean?"

"Derek, you're not a boogeyman."

He blinked slowly. "I'm not?"

"No. You're my shield. I somehow gave you form, and now you're a person." I cupped his cheek. His shadowed skin was warm against my palm. "You didn't want to hurt anyone or scare anyone because that isn't who you are. You're a protector."

"Like you?"

"Yes. Like me. You and I are connected."

"Best friends."

I hadn't been a good friend. In fact, I'd been a terrible friend to him all these years. Guilt gnawed at me. "You've been an amazing friend, Derek, but *I* haven't. I grew up and neglected you. I thought I didn't need you anymore. But you were *always* there. Waiting. You deserve better. You deserve to be free."

His eyes widened. "My Cam, you telling me to leave you?" His panic stained the air, palpable and real. "You want me to go?"

"No!" I clutched his huge hands. "No, Derek. I want you to have a life. Here. With me." I looked over at Shar. "With us."

"You don't have to hide anymore," Sharniza said.

"I don't?"

"No." I squeezed his hands. "We may be connected, but that doesn't mean you have to live for me. You can have your own life."

"But...you my Cam. I protect you."

"Yes, I am, and I'd love you to protect me when I need it, but other than that, you can do what you want."

"And also train," Shar added quickly. "Mr. Yarrow can help you become even stronger."

"So I protect my Cam?"

"Yes."

I squeezed his fingers. "And you can stay here, in the dorm. This room can be yours now."

He looked over his shoulder at the bed. "I sleep here?"

"Yep."

"And train with Mr. Yarrow?"

"Right."

"Will Cam be there?" He looked up at me hopefully.

"I'll try, but I might have other lessons."

"I'll come with you if Cam can't," Shar said. "Consider me your orientation buddy for the next few weeks."

Derek tensed, then leaned in toward me to whisper, "She too pretty." Only problem was, his whisper was more a stage whisper, but when I looked over at Shar, I found her studiously looking out the window, the twin spots of color on her cheeks the only evidence that she'd heard.

I patted Derek's shoulder. "Maybe, when you feel braver, you can tell her that. I'm sure she'll be flattered."

"We'll need sheets for the bed," Shar said quickly. "And do you eat?"

"I need no sustenance," Derek said almost regretfully.

"Okay, but you can still come hang out at mealtimes with us."

Derek looked to me for permission. I shrugged. "Your choice, Derek."

"My choice..." He smiled. "I would like that."

"How about I show you around the dorm house while Cam goes to training?" Shar said.

Once again, Derek looked to me for permission. I guessed it would take time for him to break away from needing my say-so and instruction. "Would you like that, Derek?"

He seemed to consider it for a moment. "Yes. Yes, I would."

"Okay, so I'll see you guys for supper."

"You're not eating with the elite tonight?" Shar asked.

"They eat late, so I can come and nibble with you guys first."

"We'll see you later, then," Shar said.

I dropped a kiss on Derek's shadowy head, then headed out, leaving him in Shar's capable hands.

THIS TIME, WHEN I walked into the gym, I was ready for Serath's presence, but my mate wasn't there. Instead, Selas and Orix stood chatting on the mats, but they broke off their conversation as soon as they noticed me.

I guessed they didn't want me overhearing their business. Fine by me. I wasn't officially elite yet. "Where's Serath?"

"He'll be along shortly," Orix said. "But we should get started."

I rolled my shoulders. "I am so ready. Let's do this."

Orix's smile was undoubtedly wicked. "Don't you want to know what we'll be doing today?"

"Not when you say it like that, I don't."

Selas bit back a smile. "Just ask him already."

I smiled sweetly at Orix. "Orix, what are we doing today?"

He rubbed his hands together. "Today we play cat and mouse."

"I'm assuming I'm the mouse in this scenario?"

"You assume correctly," he said. "Now go stand back behind the red line."

Red line? Yep, there was indeed a red line that ran around the room. The mats and workout equipment were all on the other side of that line, leaving the center of the room clear.

I crossed the line, and Selas followed, aiming for a panel on the wall. "Stay put," she warned me. "The ground is about to shift."

"Huh?"

She pulled the lever on the panel, and a grinding noise filled the room. The floor beyond the red line broke free and slid down so that I was looking into a whole new room, which extended two levels below us. The floor then split and flipped to reveal new equipment and thick metal poles pushed out of the walls. Each pole had rope or rings fixed to it. The lower level was a gloomy network of obstacles made up of ledges, stairs that went nowhere, and beams. The only way out or in seemed to be via one of the ladders that clung to the walls.

"This is what we call the chase," Orix said.

Selas rolled her eyes. "It's an evasive exercise. Sometimes it isn't wise to stand your ground and fight. Sometimes you need to run away."

"Or lead the enemy into a trap," Orix added.

"Which means employing evasive maneuvers," Selas continued. "You can't shift, and you don't have wings, so this exercise is all the more important for you."

"You want me to play your decoy, your...bait." Was that how

useless I was?

"You have no idea how important this role can be." Orix was all seriousness now. "A graynite will home in on the kill it views as the easiest. Your perceived weakness will be the team's strength."

I could live with that. "Okay. Let's get started."

CHAPTER 23

CAMERON

The sublevel was filled with deep pockets of shadow. Selas peered down from above, her face a pale smudge.

"Just do your best," she said. "This is to gauge your abilities and identify areas we need to work on."

"Where's Orix?" My skin prickled in warning. "Never mind." He was down here with me, but he hadn't taken the ladders like me, which meant there was another exit somewhere. One they didn't want me to use for this exercise.

Around me were pillars and hurdles, steps that led nowhere and platforms that ended in nothing. This arena was designed with wings in mind. For goyles to leap, fly, and latch on to things.

Navigating it and evading Orix wouldn't be easy for me, but the outside world would be no different. As a guardian...as an elite, I needed to learn how to use the environment to my advantage.

I was smaller and faster than the average goyle, and those attributes would be my strength. They had to be.

The air shifted to my right, and I broke into a sprint toward the nearest platform. The flap of wings behind spurred my pulse into a gallop. I launched myself onto the platform, then scrambled onto the next. There was a rail above it that I could use to swing myself onto a higher platform. I could reach a ladder from that perch. All I needed—

Orix grabbed my ankle and hauled me down, slamming me to the ground so fast I barely had breath to yelp.

"Gotcha!" His eyes gleamed with wicked triumph, wings flaring and catching the air on either side of him. He was large and imposing in his goyle form, frightening even. At least, he would have been if not for the rush of annoyance coursing through me. I'd barely had a chance to get warmed up.

I shoved him away and scrambled to my feet. "Again."

He melted into the shadows once more, leaving me unsure of where he was or where he'd attack from.

I opened my senses to the room around me and closed my eyes, feeling for his presence. It took a moment, but then I sensed him on the other side of the platform that was in front of me.

He thought I'd go for the same exit, and he could cut me off.

Not happening.

This time, I didn't wait for him to attack. I made to dash forward, feinted left but went right, taking a set of steps two at a time before launching myself at a set of rings.

Orix's growl of annoyance cut the air behind me, but I was already swinging toward the bar that would propel me to a ladder out of here.

I let go of the rings, boldly sailing toward the bar but smashed into Orix instead. He hugged me to his chest, chuckling softly.

"Nice try."

My cry of frustration was smothered by his pecs. "Put me down!"

He flew us down and set me on my feet. "You did well. You almost got to the ladder."

Almost wasn't good enough. "Again!"

Twenty minutes later, I'd been snagged out of the air, tackled to the ground, smothered by Orix's chest, and pinned so many times

I was beginning to feel like a stress ball.

"Maybe we should call it for the evening," Selas said, her face an anxious blur above us.

Did I look that frazzled?

"Agreed," Orix said, dropping me on my feet. Again. "We can pick this up next session."

Like hell was I quitting so easily. "No. One more try." It was unrealistic to think I'd make it all the way to the top of a ladder and out of this space, but if I could just make it *onto* a ladder, then I'd call it a win for the day.

"Fine, one more round," Selas said.

We took our starting positions again—Orix in the darkness somewhere, and me in the center of the room.

Pinpointing his location was easy now, not that I was going to share that with him. It gave me an edge that I wasn't willing to lose.

He rushed me almost immediately this time.

Fuck!

I turned and ran, using my speed to put distance between us. A ramp loomed, and I picked up momentum toward it, veering off at the last moment, leaving Orix to rush up it without me while I raced up a flight of steps instead. I hit the platform at the top, then threw myself at the thick rope dangling from the beams that jutted out above us. I swung hard, whizzing through the air, aimed at a ladder.

Behind me, the ground shook.

A gust of wind hit my back.

Orix was coming for me, but I was almost there. This time I was going to make it. I let go of the rope and flew toward the ladder.

Fingers grazed my neck, a low growl of frustration rattling the air, spurring the triumph inside me.

"No!" Serath materialized as if out of nowhere, snatching me away from Orix.

Away from the ladder.

Away from my victory.

No...No, no, no! "Get off me!" I twisted in his grip as he set me on my feet. "Let go!" He released me and stared at me in stunned silence. "What was that, huh? What the fuck was that?" Black dots of rage danced on the edge of my vision.

"I...I was..."

"You were what? Trying to protect me from training? I almost had it. I was almost at the ladder." Tears of frustration pricked my eyes. "Dammit, Serath. Stop fucking coddling me and let me fucking train." I headed for the door. I needed air. A break. I needed to scream.

STUPID, POSSESSIVE, PROTECTIVE, obstinate, ladder-blocking stone wall of male. Argh. I had it. I fucking had it, and he ruined it.

The anger rolled over me, through me, and then it was gone. Just gone, leaving me cold and confused.

I was annoyed, yes. I'd almost had the ladder, but the rage was totally out of character and proportion.

"Cameron!" Selas joined me outside the training room. "What was that?"

"I don't know."

"He's fighting his instincts to protect you. This isn't easy for him, especially since his beast is very aware that there was a time, not too long ago, when Orix tried to kill you."

I knew this, of course I did. "I'm sorry. I'm not sure what happened."

Selas studied me for a beat—not my face, but the air around me.

"This is just like the moment when you part-shifted. Like when you breached the wards on Greenwood Forest on the omega moon."

"How can you know that?"

"The colors that surround you...the vibrations...they're the same. The sooner Willowman has your blood tested, the better. I'll speak to him today."

"You might want to tell him about Derek."

"What about him?"

"We know what he is now." I filled her in on how Derek had materialized during Supernatural Defense. "He's my shield."

"Well, that certainly explains a lot. I'll let Willowman know. In the meantime..." She glanced back at the training room.

Crap. "Yeah. I'll speak to him. I know how hard this must be for him, what with Levi here and Curi playing fake boyfriend."

"And how has Curi been with you? Respectful?"

"He has. He was an ass to begin with, but he saved me a couple of times, actually, and...well he's kinda a part of the group now." The strange look on her face, almost one of longing, had me asking, "What is the deal between you two? I know something happened. Dayn was blackmailing Curi over it."

Her eyes snapped wide. "What?"

"Yeah. Curi won't say, but I can tell he's cut up over it... Whatever *it* is."

Her delicate jaw hardened. "It was a long time ago. It doesn't matter anymore."

I needed to shut up now, but the words wouldn't stop. "I think it matters to Curi."

"*Hmmm.* We still have the room for another hour if you want to continue training."

Change of subject. Message received. "Sure."

"I'll pop over to Stone Comfort and grab us some coffee and cakes. We can try the evasion a few more times with Serath in the room once you're fueled up." She gave my shoulder a squeeze and left.

Orix was speaking to Serath in a low voice when I entered, but Serath's gaze snapped up to meet mine immediately. "Cameron, I didn't mean to—"

"I know. I'm sorry I got so mad."

"You went all red in the face," Orix said.

"Yeah, well, you have chest hairs, and they're abrasive."

Orix looked down at his chest covered in lastonflex now that he wasn't in goyle form.

Serath frowned. "You felt his chest hairs?"

"It's hard not to while being smothered by his epic pecs."

Orix shot Serath a wary look. "Not helping, Cameron."

Serath pinched the bridge of his nose and exhaled. "No...no, I'm fine. This is normal. This is what happens during training. I can handle this." He sounded like he was desperately trying to convince himself of the fact.

"What about you?" Orix asked me. "Are you okay?"

"I'm fine. Selas thinks that the rage was a result of whatever changes are happening to me."

"Your late puberty?" Orix said with a smirk. "The late bloom into full goyle femalehood?"

"Orix..." Serath's tone held warning.

Orix strode over to the window and parked his butt on the sill. "Willowman will figure it out."

I hoped so because being hormonal once a month was one thing, but this unpredictable swing of emotions and bodily sensations could be dangerous, especially around Serath. I needed to be in control of my faculties and emotional highs and lows.

Serath stepped closer and lightly touched my cheek. "I'll be fine. We will figure this out."

The anxiety bled out of my pores. "Why do I always believe it when you say it?"

"Because he's so convincing," Orix drawled. "Now stop touching each other and step away from the temptation."

Fuck. When had my hands come up to press against his chest, and when had he threaded his fingers through my hair?

We parted hastily and put distance between us.

"Better," Orix said. "Now how about you run some laps while we wait for Selas to get back." He smiled faux-sweet in my direction. "Can't have you cooling down too much."

Laps sounded like a good way to expel the sudden excess of

energy in my body and put distance between me and the object of my desire.

Yep, Orix knew what he was doing, and I was grateful for that.

CHAPTER 24

CURI

If I focus, I can still smell Cameron on my T-shirt. Heck, who am I kidding? We haven't spent enough time up close and personal for that. One stint at the gym and her scent is all but gone.

And why the fuck do I care?

Stone Comfort looms with the promise of my favorite beverage. Enough to lighten the mood and dispel any thoughts of a petite halfblood nuisance. Play fake boyfriend...Like I don't have better things to do than hold her hand and nuzzle her ear and—

"Mason!"

Ah, fuck, Cam's ex is on my tail. I consider ignoring him and making a dash for the doors to the coffee shop, but fuck that. I don't run from anything or anyone.

I stop and wait for him to catch up to me.

He shoots me a smile, which I'm sure he considers charming, and then fixes his assessing peepers on me. "Can we talk?"

I shrug. "Sure."

His shoulders relax slightly, as if he's relieved.

I need my latte. "What do you want to talk about?"

"Cameron."

My Cameron, as far as he's concerned. She would have told me about him because we're serious. He needs to know that. "Look,

I know you two had a thing, but she's with me now."

Levi gives me a closed-lipped smile. "You see, that's just it. I don't quite believe that."

What the fuck? "I don't care what you believe." I make to turn away, but he moves to block me. Hell no. "Get out of my way, *Master* Halle."

The reminder of his tutor status seems to have an effect, and his puffed-up chest deflates. "Look, Mason, I'm not trying to be a dick. I just need to know the truth."

Heck, I almost feel sorry for the guy. Almost, but I don't have any sympathy for stalker assholes who can't take no for an answer. "The truth? The truth is that Cameron's my woman. The truth is that you need to move on."

He shakes his head, almost as if he's disappointed. "You see, I might believe that if I could smell her on you, or you on her. But aside from the usual level of scent, there is nothing to indicate an intimate relationship."

What is this guy? A bloodhound? "It's called showering. Maybe you haven't heard of it?"

"You know what I mean, Curi." Ah, he's using my first name, trying to force intimacy and encourage disclosure. "I know Cameron is hiding something. I know you two aren't a couple, not in the intimate sense. What I don't understand is why she's doing this. Why are you pretending to have feelings for her?"

For some reason, this whole sentence pisses me off. "What the fuck is wrong with you? Cameron's right, you're delusional." He flinches as if I've hit a nerve. Good. "I don't need to explain anything to you. Cameron and I are in love. We're happy. Back off. You're a fucking teacher here. Act like one instead of a lovesick youngling."

Levi sighs. "You're a loyal friend, Mason. I'll give you that." He smiles wryly. "But be careful. It's all too easy for that friendship to turn into something else. All too easy to fall for her, and if this *is* a ploy, if she doesn't truly feel the same way about you..." He shrugs. "Get ready for pain."

He tucks his hands into his pockets and walks off.

Pah. What the fuck does he know? Cam and I are barely friends let alone...Yeah, right. Whatever.

I need my latte.

CARAMEL LATTES ARE my weakness. I need two a day at least, and Stone Comfort makes them with the perfect balance of caramel and cream. Coupled with a slice or two of shortbread and it's tastebud heaven.

I need to get the recipe for the shortbread. Mother will love that. We can make some together maybe.

I indulge the fantasy for a moment before letting it slide.

It isn't acceptable for grown goyle males to spend time with their birth mothers. We can stay with them until puberty, and then our sires take over our rearing. The thought of my father brings conflicting emotions that I'd rather not dwell on.

Another sip of my latte and my worries melt away; that is, until the bell above the door tinkles and Selas walks in.

Her milky eyes scan the room and settle on me, and for a moment, I can't breathe. She nods her head at me, acknowledging me before heading to the counter to pick up an order. Some bagged goods and four takeout cups in a holder.

She heads toward the exit but adjusts her trajectory at the last minute, veering toward my window table instead.

Gods, she's coming over.

"Is that a caramel latte?" she asks.

I nod mutely because my tongue refuses to help me form words, and my pulse is pounding so hard I'm sure she can hear it.

"You always did love them."

The backs of my eyes heat, and I nod like a fool again.

"There's something I've been meaning to say to you since you got here." She presses her lips together. "Something I should have reached out and said a long time ago, but...I didn't think it would matter back then. I see now that it might need to be said."

I'm frozen. Waiting for the words that I deserve. The harsh words that I've earned from her but she never delivered. Not once. Even though everyone else was quick to tear into me, Selas never said a word. But now...She's ready now.

She sets the paper bag down on the table and puts a hand on my shoulder, her white eyes somehow soft with emotion. "I forgive you, Curi. It was an accident. A terrible, awful accident, but you were just a youngling. I should have said it sooner. I was just..." She sighs. "I was healing. But it's obvious you have some healing to do too. I hope this helps." She gives my shoulder a squeeze, picks up her bag, and leaves.

Leaves me pulse racing, stunned, and grateful. So fucking grateful. The dam inside my chest holding back the twisted dark guilt cracks, and I tuck my chin in and breathe raggedly.

I forgive you.

The words echo in my head, and the awful leaden weight that's lived inside me for years lessens just a fraction.

Around me, the world continues as normal. Goyles laughing and bantering, unaware of the momentous thing that's just happened to me.

Selas forgives me. Now I need to work on forgiving myself.

CHAPTER 25

CAMERON

Everyone was gathered for supper by the time I made it back to the dorm. Touron and Curi were working the stove together in some strange tandem dance, and the air was filled with the delicious aroma of spices.

"You eating with us?" Shar asked, plate in hand.

"I'm not missing whatever's making that yummy smell." I took my usual seat, and Shar popped a plate in front of me. "How's Derek?"

"Tired, I think. I showed him 'round the dorm, but when I tried to take him outside, he balked."

"Do you think he's afraid of the outside?" Palia asked.

"I don't think it's fear," Shar said. "Just...wariness. Severe wariness."

It made sense that he'd be wary. The outside was relatively unexplored and new to him. "The only time I've seen him outside was when he materialized to protect me."

"I'll work on it with him," Shar said. "You focus on your training with the elites."

"How was training?" Ginia asked.

"Exhausting. But I managed to reach the ladder." She stared at me blankly, so I explained the task Orix had set for me. "I lost count of how many tries it took me, but I did it. Now I need to work on evading him till I get to the top."

Curi spooned a creamy soup loaded with veggies and hunks of meat onto my plate. "Try this. It's my special recipe."

His recipe? He cooked? I couldn't hide my surprise.

He rolled his eyes. "We're trained to be able to take care of ourselves."

"But this is next level," Ginia said. "If you fail the cadet exams, you should definitely try out for a position as a chef for the Stone Council."

Touron set a tray of fresh bread rolls on the table.

Palia clasped her hands together in delight. "What a treat."

I wasn't about to tell them that I was pretty sure the elites ate like this every night. For me, being here with my friends was the treat.

We ate in silence for a while, and damn, the food was good. Too good not to have seconds.

Curi passed me more bread, and Touron topped up my bowl. They did it almost absently, as if it were reflex and not thought out.

Across the table, Shar arched a brow, a slight smile playing on her lips.

"Levi pulled me aside for a chat today," Curi said.

I quickly swallowed my mouthful. "Oh?"

"He's convinced we're not a real couple."

"No!" Palia set her bread down. "You two have done an amazing job of pretending. If I didn't know better, I would totally believe you two were an item."

Curi smiled dryly. "Master Halle's nose says different."

"Shit," Shar said. "We didn't think of that."

I looked between them. "Think of what?"

Ginia leaned forward, a wicked gleam in her eyes. "Pheromones."

I winced. "Please..."

"It makes sense," Palia said. "Lovers would exude a certain scent around each other, or at least carry the other's scent on them." She narrowed her eyes in thought. "Just holding hands and hanging out won't be enough. This scent is a skin-on-skin kinda thing."

Curi choked on his water. "Fuck. No."

"Hell no." My cheeks burned.

"Serath would kill him," Shar said matter-of-factly.

No point telling them that Selas had advocated me having sexual relations with someone other than Serath. That was not an option for me. "There has to be another way."

"Oooh." Palia sat up straighter. "Curi, do you have a sleep tee?"

"No."

"Undershirt?"

"No."

"PJ bottoms, or shorts?"

He gave a weary sigh. "Nope."

"Then what do you sleep in?"

He gave her a flat look, which she returned in confusion.

Ginia groaned. "He means he sleeps naked, Palia. No clothes. Everything hanging free."

She said it with a little too much enthusiasm.

Palia's cheeks went pink. "Oh...Oh right. Um...Okay, what about...the tee you wore to the gym?"

"You want my sweaty gym top?" Curi asked, lip curling slightly in disgust.

"It'll have your scent all over it," Palia said. "Cam can sleep in it, and next time she sees Levi, there'll be no doubt that you two are...together."

"Sweaty pheromones," Ginia said, shooting a wicked look my way.

I narrowed my eyes at her. "Fine. Curi, give me your most recent gym top."

"Whatever. But I still think it'll take more than that to convince your ex. He's like a dog with a bone when it comes to you. I don't think he's going to quit digging."

"We just stick to our guns. He'll back off eventually."

But it was obvious from the expression on everyone's faces that they didn't believe a word I was saying.

Yeah...I didn't believe me either.

BACK AT THE observatory, Prasan let me in.

"Just in time for supper," he said. "Selas was about to go looking for you."

"I ate at the dorm."

"But you'll join us for dessert?"

"Sure. I need to drop my bag in my room, but I'll be down in a few."

I took the elevator to my floor and dumped my stuff. Curi's tee was wrapped in a plastic bag to preserve his scent. I'd wear it to sleep for the next few nights, and hopefully, it would be enough to shut Levi up. I needed to let Serath know, though. My reeking of Curi was going to piss him off, but it was necessary. He'd hopefully understand.

The elites were already at the table, eating spaghetti. No sign of Willowman today, and no Serath either.

"Serath probably won't be back till after dawn," Selas said as I joined them.

"I didn't ask."

"You didn't need to," Orix said. "Your disappointed eyes said it all."

"I'm not disappointed."

"It's all right," Prasan said. "It's natural for you to seek his company and vice versa."

Natural to be mooning over him, they meant. "So...where is he?"

"He and Willowman are visiting one of our outposts to strengthen the wards there. They do it every so often."

"One of the outposts close to graynite territory?" The one

where Serath was almost killed.

"He'll be fine," Selas said. "They're not going to venture into graynite territory, just strengthen the wards, that's all."

"Outpost Ten is our usual base when we're not here," Orix said. "There are two alpha teams located there."

"But you're here because you lost Romi?"

"Yes," Selas replied. "The Stone Council can't risk losing more of the team."

"But they didn't mind you and Serath heading into graynite territory to investigate, did they?"

"We're replaceable," Orix said frankly. "There's a Halle and an Albion who can step into our shoes immediately. They're at Outpost Six. Seasoned guardians who can take the elite exam tomorrow if need be."

"Not so much for Prasan and me," Selas said. "Curi would be my closest replacement, and Sharniza Prasan's, both newbies who'd have to have extensive training."

"Like me?"

"Yeah," Orix said. "It's not ideal, even in your case."

So, the Stone Council put as much value on its elite as how easily they could be replaced. What dicks.

Taz leaped up onto Orix's lap and stretched up to rub the top of his head against the elite's neck.

Orix chuckled and stroked the cat under his chin, then rubbed his ears. He was rewarded with a loud purr. "We'll go for a wander later, I promise."

"When are you taking him to the sanctuary again?" Selas asked with a smile. "You know he can't stay here permanently. We could get called to Outpost Ten at any time. You can't keep a pet."

The cat slow-blinked his peridot eyes and fixed his attention on Selas, and I could have sworn he understood every word she said.

Orix sighed. "I know. I just...He's special." He dropped a kiss on Taz's head, his golden hair falling forward, silver streaks gleaming in the overhead lights.

It was hard not to warm to the elite when he behaved like

this. There was a tenderness about him when he interacted with the feline that was absent from most of his interactions.

The cat obviously loved the gargoyle. "Are cats prohibited at outposts?"

"Not that I'm aware," Prasan said.

I shrugged. "Then we should definitely keep him."

Orix beamed at me. "Thank you."

"Do you regret trying to kill me now?"

"Urgh, woman! Will you ever let that slide?"

"Nope."

Prasan chuckled and pushed back his seat. "On that note, I'll get dessert."

The next hour passed in easy conversation with the elites, but my thoughts kept straying to Serath out at Outpost Ten.

Hanging with the elites was pleasant enough, but I was glad to get away and up to my room. Prasan followed me into the elevator and hit the button for the top floor.

"Get some rest," he said. "I'm sure Serath will be riding you hard tomorrow."

"Nice choice of words."

He looked horrified. "I didn't mean...I mean..."

"I know." The elevator pinged for my floor, and it hit me that I wouldn't get a chance to warn Serath about Curi's T-shirt and scent. I grabbed the door to stop it closing. "Will you see Serath when he gets back at dawn?"

"Probably. Why?"

I filled him in on our plan to get Levi off my tail by using Curi's scent. "Can you warn him for me, please?" I grimaced. "I don't want him going all beast mode if he catches Curi's scent on me during the day."

"Of course."

I headed to my room, bone weary, but I doubted I'd get much sleep tonight. Knowing that Serath was outside the safety of the academy, back at the outpost where he'd almost died...Yeah, sleep wouldn't come easy.

CHAPTER 26

SERATH

The stars look down on the outpost, and the world around me is silent and at peace. From high in the tower, everything seems small and insignificant.

This is my favorite spot when I'm here. Strengthening the wards is Willowman's job; I'm merely an escort. Part of me wishes we could stay here longer. But the larger part loathes being away from Cameron.

We were told only Outpost Ten needed a fix, but once we got here, there was a message informing us of two more that needed looking at. At this rate, we won't be back at the academy till almost midday. Goyles don't need much sleep, but that's cutting it fine, even for me. I'll get maybe three hours before the training classes commence, which means I won't see Cameron before she heads off to the dorms and her friends.

It's stupid how much I crave simply being in her presence. Just to see her smile, to watch her eyes light up at the sight of me and know she feels what I do—that we have a connection that's undeniable, no matter what the world says.

Bootfalls on the steps behind me signal an intrusion. The air spikes with a familiar scent, one that a few weeks ago would have spawned heat in my groin but now spawns unease.

"It's a beautiful night," Jana says, joining me at the window.

"It is indeed."

She turns her body toward me and lifts her chin. It's an invitation that I would usually accept. Beneath her lastonflex, her body is a beautiful connection of planes and dips that I've lost many hours exploring. I've had many lovers in my time, but Jana was the most frequent. We shared a tenderness that bordered on affection, and that affection is still present. The desire, however, is not.

"Serath?" She lightly touches my arm. "Did I do something wrong?"

"Of course not, Jana. It's simply been a long day."

She slips between me and the barrier, her body brushing mine, and places her palms on my chest. My pulse jumps because this is familiar. *She* is familiar, but my beast tenses.

She pushes up on her toes and kisses my jaw, her breath hot on my skin. If I close my eyes, I can imagine she's Cameron. I can have her right here while the fantasy plays in my head. Bury my aching cock in her while Cameron's face fills my mind, and her gasps fill my ears.

I can have this and relieve the tension just as Selas suggested. It will take the edge off my need and make it easier to be around my mate. It will keep her safe.

Jana's breath comes faster, and her hands move to my waistband, fingers skimming my cock, which is hard and thick at the thought of Cameron.

"Oh, yes," she says. "Not *too* tired, then." Her voice is thick with desire, and the base of my spine goes tight. My body needs this. It needs the release.

But my heart.

My heart won't condone it.

My heart belongs to another.

I gently grip her wrists and draw her hands away from my crotch. "Jana..."

Her dark gaze shoots up to meet mine. "Oh...I'm sorry. I..."

There's hurt and shame on her face.

"It's not you."

"There's someone else?" Her eyes narrow, and I catch the edge of suspicion in her dark gaze. Jana may be willing to bend to my will during sex, but as a warrior, as a guardian, she's unyielding. Authority matters. The law matters.

She knows I'm a sigma. If she gets the impression I'm too attached to another female, so attached as to reject her now, then she may start to wonder if I've found a mate and then...

No.

I can't put Cameron at risk like that.

I grip her nape and haul her close.

"There are a few others." I smile, bringing my lips closer to hers. "But none I favor as much as you."

"Then what's stopping you?" Her voice is breathless and hopeful.

"You deserve more than a few moments of my attention. Willowman is almost done."

She strokes my jaw. "A kiss, then..."

Fuck. This is the last thing I need. "Of course." I press my lips to hers in a kiss that's soft and filled with promise. The air spikes with the scent of her arousal, and my beast snarls its displeasure.

She isn't our mate.

She isn't Cameron.

I summon an image of Cameron's face and deepen the kiss, imagining that Jana's moans belong to Cameron. That the body pressed to mine is my mate's.

I kiss her for long minutes, and when I break contact, her expression is dreamy and soft.

I run my thumb along her bottom lip. "Next time..."

She smirks coyly up at me. "Next time."

"Serath?" Willowman calls up the steps. "It's time to go."

I take my time extricating myself from Jana, letting her believe that I'd rather stay, while my duplicity claws at me.

She doesn't deserve to be lied to like this.

At the bottom of the tower, Willowman gives me a knowing look. “You better shower as soon as you get back.”

“I know.”

Jana’s scent is all over me, and I need it gone.

CHAPTER 27

CAMERON

"I want you." Curi's mouth skims up the column of my neck, his lips pressing to the pulse that beats hard and fast there.

"This is mine." Serath's growly voice fills my head as his large, calloused hands part my thighs. "I want to taste it." My hips jerk, pussy pulsing as he claims it with his mouth, kissing me there, devouring me with his lips and tongue.

"Look at me." Levi's sea-green eyes bore into mine. His hand slides into my hair, and he kisses me, soft and tentative, then deeper and harder.

Curi moans, sucking on my pulse, hands sliding over my breasts.

They're all over me.

All three of them tasting me.

Wanting me.

No...This is wrong. This isn't what I want. Serath...Please...I just want Serath.

Curi and Levi melt away, and Serath hovers over me, his naked body slick with perspiration as he moves against me. He's inside me...Oh gods, yes. Please.

My body tightens, the sweet spiral of release leaving me wet and sobbing with the relief.

I rose slowly out of the dream, cracking open my eyes to the gray light of dawn. Something was off.

I looked down at my hands, fingers stiff, curled into claws and pinned to the sheets by long, gray talons.

Fuck.

I sat up fast, pulling my hands free of the shredded sheets. My talons were gone, but the evidence of their destruction remained.

Thank fuck it was herbology class tomorrow. The sooner Willowman took my blood sample and got it looked at, the better.

Despite the weird dream, or maybe because of it, I managed to sleep till almost midday and woke up cocooned in Curi's scent. I'd made sure to shower before getting into bed, dressed in his gym shirt. The lastonflex molded to me, a little uncomfortable to sleep in, but I'd made it work.

But it felt good to take it off and put on a pair of regular joggers and a cotton tee from the selection Selas had provided.

Serath would be back by now. Probably still asleep. I took the stairs to the kitchens and headed for the coffee machine. The elites had a fancy one. There was no harm in grabbing a coffee here before heading to the dorm to breakfast with my buddies.

Remnants of my dream flitted through my mind. Curi, Levi, and then Serath. The stress of keeping Levi at bay coupled with Curi's scent was messing with my head.

My stomach grumbled as my gaze fell on a plate of breakfast muffins covered by a clear plastic dome.

Fuck it. One muffin wouldn't hurt.

But one turned into two, and damn I was hungry. They were so good, moist, flavorsome...

"Are you always up this early?" Prasan entered via the stairwell.

I hastily swallowed my mouthful of muffin. "I go to bed

earlier than regular goyles."

"Ah, yes, you need more sleep."

"And you?"

"I haven't slept yet." He shrugged. "I'll grab a couple of hours in the afternoon."

"Is Serath back?"

"Yes, I just spoke to him in the observatory when he—"

The elevator pinged open, and Serath strode into the room. His eyes lit up at the sight of me, but then his nostrils flared, and his beautiful eyes narrowed. A low, menacing growl fell from his lips.

Then he rushed me.

I managed a squeak before I was lifted off my feet and crushed against his chest while he ran his nose up my neck and down to my cleavage, bending me backward till my spine ached.

What the—

Oh fuck.

"Serath, no. I—"

"*Mine*!"

My back hit the table, and he was on me. Fabric tore, and pain raked hot lines across my skin. He pushed between my thighs, face contorted in a mixture of rage and desire, his irises bleeding to black.

He crushed his lips to mine hard enough to bruise and draw blood, and a scent hit me, sharp and syrupy.

Feminine arousal.

But not mine.

My beast surged to the surface with a snarl that vibrated my throat.

Another female had touched him.

A red haze clouded my vision, stealing all logic and thought. There was only his body and mine, only our beasts desperate to be one, to claim and consummate. To solidify our bond.

"Stop! Dammit, stop!" Pain sliced across my senses and dragged me out of the red haze. I surfaced, body on fire, mouth swollen from kisses and tasting of iron. Serath was over me, his cock pressed to my pussy with only my panties between us. My knees were hooked over his arms, so I was spread wide ready for...

"Oh gods..."

Serath growled and pushed against me, and my body shuddered with release from the friction.

"Stop them!" Selas yelled.

"Serath!" Orix's voice was a boom. "Snap out of it."

Another wave of energy washed over us. Serath let out a bellow of pain, back bending, hips crushing against mine and sending me into another spasm of release.

He slumped forward, his huge frame eclipsing mine, then slowly, carefully, he extricated himself from me.

Someone dropped a shirt over my head because my clothes were torn to shreds, and I was practically naked.

"I'm sorry if I hurt you," Willowman said to Serath. "It was the only way to make you stop."

My arms were covered in welts that were slowly healing. Marks from his talons. My skin hadn't turned to stone because my beast didn't see him as a threat.

He was my mate, but he'd been with someone else.

I blinked back the heat that gathered behind my eyes.

"If you were going to fuck him, you should have showered after," Serath said coldly.

What the... "I didn't *fuck* anyone." I looked to Prasan. "Didn't you tell him?"

Prasan cursed. "I forgot."

Serath growled at him. "Forgot what?"

"Cameron slept in Curi's shirt to get his scent on her to convince Levi that they're a true couple." Prasan shook his head, clearly mortified. "Cam asked me to warn you."

Serath's shoulders slumped. "You didn't...didn't have sex with him?"

"No. I didn't." I stood tall and lifted my chin. "But who did *you* fuck?"

My heart sank at the shadow of guilt in his eyes. I'd hoped I was wrong, that maybe my beast had misinterpreted the scent, but no.

He'd been with someone else.

I swallowed the lump in my throat. "I have to go get changed. My friends will be waiting. I'll have supper at the dorms tonight."

I had to get away from him, away from the scent of the other female that clung to him, away from this feeling of betrayal that was totally unjustified because he wasn't mine. Could never be mine. And yet...Yet he lived in every fiber of my being, and that... that fucking hurt.

SERATH

"WHY DIDN'T YOU tell her the truth?" Willowman asks. "Why didn't you tell her you only kissed Jana so that she wouldn't suspect you had someone else and start digging?"

I'd been so close to telling Cameron. To defending myself but... "It's better this way."

"You think this will keep her away from you?" Orix asks.

"If she's hurt...If she hates me, she'll steer clear."

"And fall into someone else's arms?" Prasan says.

I bite back a snarl and force my beast down. "Whatever it takes to keep her safe. To keep her alive. Jana was a blessing in disguise. This works. This can work."

"Cameron won't take a lover," Selas says. "Not yet, maybe not for a very long time. All you've done is hurt her."

"Hurt is better than dead."

"Oh, Serath..." Selas says softly. "And what happens when she *does* take a lover? How will you control yourself then?"

"When that happens, I'll make sure I'm long gone. Once we have Romi back, I'll step down as elite and get reposted."

Stunned silence greets my declaration.

I can't believe I've voiced the plan that's been flitting around in my head ever since my interlude with Cameron in the observatory.

The pull between us is too strong.

It'll get worse the longer we're together.

"Once we have Romi back, *she* can leave," Orix says. "There's no need for you to go."

"No. I won't reunite them just to force them to part."

"You might not need to," Selas says. "Romi may not be capable of taking back his elite spot."

There are too many unknowns right now. "The only thing I can be certain of is that if a distance isn't enforced between us, then we will fail. The pull between us is too strong, and our will to resist too weak. Hate will keep her from me."

"Dammit," Orix says softly.

I'm suddenly bone weary. "Can you two handle her training for the next week? Lionel put me in charge, but he won't know any better if we don't tell him."

"Of course," Selas says.

"I'll help too," Prasan says. "I'm so sorry, I should have remembered to pass on Cameron's message."

I pat his shoulder as I walk past. "Get some rest."

The image of Cam's distraught face plays over and over in my mind's eye. I'll never forgive myself for hurting her.

But at least this way I won't be the cause of her demise.

CHAPTER 28

SHARNIZA

"And you have to keep stirring like this," Touron says to Derek, moving the spatula in figure eights in the pan to scramble the eggs.

Derek looms over Touron, his diamond eyes watching every move carefully. He's a head taller than Touron, his shoulders wide and powerful, taking up so much space at the stove that Touron has to stand to one side.

"Here, you try." Touron hands over the spatula.

Derek begins to stir.

"Perfect," Touron says. "Now you don't want them to dry out, so when you take the pan off the heat, don't let the eggs sit in it. They'll continue to cook and go rubbery."

"Cameron will eat this?" Derek asks in a voice that is deeper and gruffer than a few hours ago.

"Yep. She's joining us for breakfast. Should be here soon."

He nods. "And you will tell her that I made them for her?"

"Yep." Touron butters some toast and pops it onto a plate. "Eggs can go here."

Derek slides the eggs onto the spot beside the toast. "I did it." He slides a glance my way, and our gazes lock. My pulse flutters, but I keep my expression neutral because, what the fuck?

"Now pop it on the table next to her coffee," Touron says.

"Those eggs look amazing!" Ginia says with genuine enthusiasm.

Derek beams at her, and knots form in my belly.

"You okay?" Palia asks, handing me a cup of coffee.

"I'm fine. Why?"

"You just had a weird look on your face."

"Oh?" I take a sip of the coffee, reveling in the burn of it on my tongue.

"Yeah. Kinda like you licked a lime."

"I'm fine."

She shrugs and takes a seat at the table, but I settle against the counter, needing a moment to sort my head out.

I've been spending too much time with Cameron's shield; that's what it is. He's sweet and charming without realizing it, and it's messing with my head.

I need to focus on the tangible achievements we've made.

He's quickly assimilating to being outside his wardrobe and developing a sense of self. Teaching him how to do basic life skill things will help with that, and once Yarrow gets stuck into training him, Derek will have the confidence to stand alone, if need be. It's as if his growth was stunted for a long time, but now he's flourishing.

I'm proud of him.

Pleased that I could help him.

That's all.

He looks up sharply. "Cameron is here." His eyes narrow. "She is upset."

Cameron enters the room a moment later, eyes red-rimmed, hair windblown. She looks like shit, and smells...Oh fuck. Why does she smell like arousal and...Serath?

"What happened?" Derek demands. "I sensed no danger."

She yanks out a chair and sits, elbows on table, head in hands. "Arghhh, I am such a fucking idiot."

Derek takes the chair beside her and puts his hand on her

back. "Breathe, my Cameron."

"Tell us what happened," Touron says.

I CAN'T BELIEVE Serath would hurt Cameron this way. It makes no sense because it doesn't fit with the picture of the male I've built in my head. Derek strokes her back, his diamond eyes dulled by her sorrow.

"I'll be okay," she says. "I just...I need some time."

"What you need is to get laid," Ginia says.

Cameron's jaw tenses. "I don't want that. I'm not...I'm not ready."

"You don't have to do anything but heal," Palia says softly. "He did what he felt he needed to. Now you do what you need to."

Cameron sighs heavily, then fixes a smile on her face. "I need to pass the cadet exams. That's what I need to do. If I can do that, then I may just be good enough to be the elite the team needs to save my brother."

"Your brother?" Curi says from the doorway.

"Mother!" Touron says quickly. "She said mother."

Curi pays him no attention. "Cameron, what's going on?"

Cameron looks to me. I know she doesn't need my approval. This is her story to tell, but reassurance is another thing.

I nod.

Cameron smiles faintly at Curi. "You'd best sit down."

Over the next few minutes, she fills Curi in on the truth about Romi's "death." When she's done, Curi is silent for several beats.

He now knows that the Stone Council is desperate to keep something under wraps. So desperate that they may have tampered with a ghost's memories and messed with Flora Yarrow's mind too.

Curi's smile is bitter. "Typical Stone Council bullshit. Liars, every one of them. I can't imagine the pain of not knowing. Of wondering what he's going through right now."

"It sucks," Cameron says. "I just want to make elite so I can help get him back."

"And you will," Curi says. "I know things got off to a bad start between us. I acted...terribly. I treated you as if you were lesser, but you're not. Cameron, you're one of the strongest females I know. You can't shift, you don't have the same strength as us, but you're here, and you're surviving. That's no easy feat."

"I have help." Cameron's gaze sweeps over us. "I'd be lost without it."

"Why?" Palia asks Curi. "Why were you so awful to us all?"

If he's thrown by the blunt question, he doesn't show it. "It's easier to be a monster and rule with fear than to care and risk getting hurt."

I can empathize with that sentiment. All my life, I've stifled my feminine side and nurtured my masculine traits to please my father. I've denied myself the tiny things that give me pleasure. I'm still hiding who I truly am from the world.

I can understand why Curi came here wearing a façade, but Cameron has found her way beneath it, just like she found her way beneath mine.

This female has somehow brought us all together, and for the first time in my life, I have a family who accepts me.

I'll do whatever it takes to preserve and protect that.

"You can trust me," Curi continues. "Your secret is safe with me, always."

Cameron looks deep into his eyes. This is the moment to tell him about Serath, to reveal all and bring him completely into the circle of trust.

She smiles warmly. "Thank you."

The moment is gone.

I don't need to ask her why she's decided to keep him on the edge of the circle of trust. Telling him that Romi is alive puts no one in danger but herself. Telling him that Serath is her mate puts Serath's life at risk. She had no choice when it came to telling us... Heck, we're the ones who figured it out for her, but with Curi, she has a choice.

Curi leans in and sniffs her, his nose wrinkling slightly. "I thought you were going to wear my shirt last night?"

Cameron's cheeks go pink. Curi doesn't know about her interlude with Serath this morning.

"I did," Cameron says. "But then I was hanging with all the elites so..."

Curi frowns. "That shouldn't mask my scent when it's been against your skin all night." He sniffs her again. "You smell like..." His eyes flare. "Arousal."

"I had a sexy dream, okay?" Cameron blurts out.

Curi smirks. "Oh..."

Cameron's cheeks go red. "It wasn't about you. Just...no one. Faceless males."

"Males? More than one?"

"Shut up." Cameron slaps his arm. "I had a dream, and then I was with the elites at breakfast so..."

"Those elite have potent aromas," Touron says with a chuckle that sounds forced, even to me.

Curi doesn't look convinced, but he doesn't press the issue. Instead, he reaches over his shoulder, tugs his shirt over his head, and hands it to Cameron. "Wear this for a little while before class." He pushes back his chair. "I've got a few errands to run, but I'll meet you there. Save me a seat." He heads out, and for a moment, there's nothing but silence.

Palia is the first to break it. "I think we can trust him about... you know."

Cameron slips on Curi's shirt. "I know I can, but is it fair to put that weight on him? You guys kinda stumbled onto it all. But honestly, if you had a choice, would you rather be clueless about it? Knowing has made you an accessory to whatever crime hiding this mated bond falls under."

"I'm glad I know," Palia says.

"Me too," Ginia adds.

"Me three," Touron says, then looks at me expectantly.

I roll my eyes. "I'm glad too."

Touron rolls his eyes. “You need to say, *me four.*”

I stare at him flatly. “No.”

“Spoilsport.”

I take the seat opposite Cameron. “But you’re right to keep him out of it. You’re keeping him guilt free.”

“Now Cameron eat food.” Derek pushes the plate of egg and toast toward Cameron. “I made it.”

“You did?” Cameron looks up at him in surprise.

“Yes.” He watches her expectantly.

The eggs are stone cold now, but Cameron picks up her fork and digs in anyway.

Derek beams at her, showcasing his fangs and even white teeth. My pulse jumps slightly, and I look away.

Nope. I do not have a thing for Cameron’s shield.

Do I?

CHAPTER 29

CAMERON

Everyone pooled into Arcana class. The seats had been arranged in a circle, and Yarrow stood in the center of the space with his sister.

He caught my eye as I entered and waved me over. "There's no need for you to take the class," he said. "I'll be working with Derek after this session."

"I don't need to do anything when it comes to shield work?"

It was Flora who replied. "As your shield is an independent entity, it's him that we need to train. But we can certainly work on how you can summon him even if you don't feel threatened or are in danger for your life."

"We'll work with Derek first," Yarrow said. "Once he's able to wield his power effectively, then we'll bring you in."

"You don't want me at his sessions?"

They exchanged glances, and once again it was Flora who answered. "Derek has spent all his existence believing that he was a boogeyman. A minor construct, created to serve you. If he's to self-actualize, he needs to do it away from your shadow."

In other words, they needed me to back off because my being around would stifle his growth. "Ouch."

Yarrow put his hand on my shoulder. "This is not a dig, Cam.

You created an amazing being, and now all we want to do is help him flourish so that he can fight alongside you in the war against the graynites."

"I understand. I'll hit the gym and warm up for my back-to-back training with the elites."

I joined the others. "Yarrow says I don't need this class."

Curi looked over at Yarrow with a frown. "Is everything okay?"

"Yeah, fine. He's going to work with Derek later. Shar, will you stay with him?"

Shar looked confused. "You're not coming?"

I swallowed the lump in my throat. "Yarrow thinks it would be best if Derek had that time to himself, away from my influence so he can...grow."

Shar pressed her lips together. "I don't think you're the reason he hasn't grown."

"Agreed," Touron said. "That's bullshit."

"He adores you," Palia added.

The soft spot Yarrow's words had left in my chest throbbed. "I know he does, and I love him, too, but Yarrow seems to know what he's talking about. I want Derek to get the most out of the training. If it means my stepping back, then so be it."

"And how does Derek feel about all this?" Ginia asked. "Or isn't Yarrow going to bother asking?"

"Good point," Touron said.

"Everyone, please take your seats," Yarrow called out.

"I have to go. Shar, will you—"

"I'll stay with Derek," Shar said, her attention on Yarrow.

"Thanks. I'll catch you guys at supper then."

I'D DRESSED IN training clothes in preparation for my later session with the elites, but I hadn't brought my gym bag that carried my water bottle and towel. The thought of going back to the observatory to get it made my stomach hurt. I didn't want to see Serath. Not yet. I needed time away from him before I was forced to be in his vicinity again.

Logically, I had no right to feel so betrayed. We weren't together. But my instincts, my beast, everything primitive in me was wounded by his actions.

I couldn't see him again yet.

I'd make do without a towel. They had paper towels at the gym anyway and a water dispenser.

That would do.

At this time of the afternoon, the gym would probably be empty. Most goyles would be in class, which suited me fine. I'd put on some tunes and rage out with some weights.

I shoved open the doors, already in an iron-pumping mood, to find Levi doing chin-ups.

He froze for a moment before dropping to his feet, hands loose at his sides, expression earnest. The kind that said, *We need to talk*.

Nope.

I made to duck out.

"Cameron, don't!"

Dammit. "What? I have places to be."

"Um...didn't you mean to come in here?"

"Whatever." I turned to go.

"Wait. I'm sorry. Please. Let's not make this awkward. Stay."

The rage toward Serath that had nowhere to go sat up and peered at its new target. "Awkward? You mean like how awkward it was for my boyfriend to get questioned by a tutor on his relationship with me?"

Levi growled softly in exasperation. It was the first time I'd heard him make such a sound, a sound that was totally gargoyle, because he was goyle. He was one of us, and he'd hidden it just like I had. There was common ground between us. Memories. Love. But because of who he was, because of his relation to Ulrickson, we couldn't even be friends.

"Look, Cameron. I'm sorry," Levi said. "I've been thinking, and I'm going to back off."

What the... "Really?"

He looked sincere. Sad almost. "Yeah, really."

Dammit. Now I couldn't even be mad at him. "Thank you."

"But I don't want us to be strangers," he continued. "I miss our friendship."

I couldn't give him even that level of intimacy. "You're a tutor here, Levi. It's hardly appropriate."

"Yet you're friends with the elites."

"I'll be one of them soon enough." What was that in his eyes, a flash of doubt? Fear? "You don't think I can do it, do you?" The spark of rage that had been dimming flared again. "You think I'm too weak."

"No, Cameron. I've never thought of you as weak, but the elite test...It's something else."

"How can you know that? No one remembers those trials. They have their memory wiped."

He looked away. "Yes. I suppose they do."

"What the...What aren't you telling me?"

He fixed me with a challenging glare. "I could ask you the same question."

Fucksake. "I thought you were going to let it go."

He pinched the bridge of his nose. "Dammit, Cameron. Dammit." He exhaled. "Look. Fuck everything else. You want to be with the Mason boy, then so be it. But let me help you prepare for the elite trial."

He knew...He knew what it would entail. "Why don't you just tell me what you know?"

"I...I can't."

"Can't or won't?"

He gritted his teeth. "Can't. But I can help train you in preparation. Trust me."

I'd trusted the old Levi with my life. We'd been a team against the monsters that roamed Old Town, but this Levi was someone else, with allegiances that could get me killed.

Insight into the elite trials would bring him into the elite circle, close to Serath and me...together. I couldn't risk him noticing that there was something between us. But if I simply shut Levi down, it might make him suspicious.

"I'll have to speak to the elite about it. Lionel has put them in charge of my training."

"I can speak to them if you agree," Levi said. "I've been meaning to speak to my cousin since I got here." His mouth turned down in displeasure. "This is as good an excuse as any. Although, my father warned me to steer clear. He's still hurt by Serath's rejection."

Rejection? What the... "Your father told you Serath rejected him?"

Levi picked up his towel and dabbed at his face. "After my uncle and aunt were killed, my father offered Serath a home, but he ran away. My father searched for him for years and finally found that he'd been adopted by another gargoyle."

Was he serious? "Do you hear yourself? A tiny boy ran away, and a grown-ass gargoyle, who had fuck knows how many contacts, couldn't find him? Do you think that sounds realistic?"

He frowned. "Why are you getting so angry?"

"Because you're so far up your father's asshole, all you can see is his shit."

Levi's jaw hardened. "You know *nothing* about my father."

"And you know *nothing* about Serath!" I spun on my heel and strode out the door.

"Cameron! Cameron, wait! Let's talk about thi—"

I slammed the outer door on his words and then broke into a sprint toward the dorms. I'd wait there until it was time for training. It was safe there. No Levi. No Serath. No stress.

I was so done with males right now.

CHAPTER 30

Derek

Cameron isn't here. She didn't come, and this golden-eyed man is ordering me to dispense our power. To waste it on an empty room.

This makes no sense to me. "There is no threat here. Cameron is safe."

"I know," he says. "But we need to exercise your ability so that you can harness your power better to protect her."

"But she isn't here." I'm confused. "Why isn't she here?"

"Cameron is training with the elites, and this is *your* training."

They want me to waste our power simply to show them that I can. I look to Sharniza. "I don't want to waste our power."

"Derek," the golden-eyed man says. "Listen to me. The power is *yours* to wield. Cameron gifted it to you when she created you. You can use it to protect her if you want, but you can also use it at will. I'm here to teach you how."

"There is no need to use the power if Cameron is not in danger."

"But what if she is and doesn't realize it?"

"But how would she not know?" He makes no sense. "Cameron *always* knows."

The man looks annoyed with me. I don't care about his

feelings, though. I only care about Cameron's and now Sharniza's, a little. I can't stop looking at her. She is so pretty and kind. She shines with goodness and—

"Derek, are you listening to me?" the man asks.

"No. I was thinking."

"What were you thinking?"

My neck feels warmer as an unfamiliar emotion fills me. Wait...is this annoyance? Am I annoyed? Yes. Yes, I am. I can feel the heat coming out of my eyes when I look at him, and my voice also comes out deeper. "My thoughts are private."

He takes a step back. I've scared him. I didn't mean to, but if it stops him pushing me, then so be it.

"Derek, you're a being in your own right," he says. "You can protect Cameron, but you can also have control over the power you wield and use it whenever you feel necessary."

"I use it to protect Cameron. We can train when she gets here." I wish she was here. I miss her. The warm annoyance is replaced by the slightly hollow feeling that being away from Cameron spawns.

"Yarrow, can I have a word please?" Sharniza says.

"Of course," the golden-eyed, bossy man says.

Yarrow, like Marrow, or Barrow. Hmmmm...

SHARNIZA

"YOU'RE WRONG, YOU know."

"About what?" Yarrow asks.

"About Cam and Derek. She doesn't stifle his growth. She never has. She makes him happy." Yarrow looks over at Derek sitting on the bench with his head bowed, deep in thought. "Right now, Derek thinks Cameron doesn't care about him. That he isn't important enough for her to be here."

"Maybe she's right, Blake," Flora says. "I can feel his power, but he's holding back."

"Because he feels that he needs Cameron's permission," Yarrow says heatedly. "It's *his* power, and he should be able to wield it however *he* sees fit."

Flora grabs hold of Blake's arm, her expression filled with concern. "Blake..."

Yarrow sucks on his cheek. "I'm sorry, but...I feel strongly about this."

The witch has issues. "Reality check, this isn't about you. Whatever demons you have in your past, you need to leave them out of this. Derek isn't you, okay? And his power is also Cameron's power. He's her shield. They're connected. It seems to me that you should be nurturing the connection, not trying to sever it."

"I'm not...I wasn't..." He presses his lips together. "I'm the tutor here. I don't have to explain myself to you."

Wow, defensive much? "Then maybe you should explain yourself to Lionel Basque."

Flora's eyes go wide with shock. "There's no need for that, is there, Blake?" She looks over at Derek. "Derek is obviously not thriving without Cameron present. They're two halves of a whole, like us." She smiles up at her brother. "We'll have to rethink our strategy."

Yarrow's tight expression softens as he looks down at his sister. "You're right, of course. Please ask Cameron to join us for the next session."

He isn't happy about it, but fuck him. Cameron and Derek are a team, and he has no right to split them up because of his own deep-seated issues.

"I'll let her know. Hey, Derek, let's get back to the dorm. I'll teach you how to fry steaks."

CAMERON

GOING BACK TO the dorm was a bad idea. All it did was give me time to procrastinate before my training session with the elites. I practiced how I would act around Serath—aloof and unaffected maybe. I wanted to show I didn't give a shit, even if it was a lie. I'd keep the conversation with him to the minimum and engage with Selas and Orix instead.

I paced my old dorm room, hoping that Melanie or Derek would show up. Talking to Derek always helped. His presence calmed me. But he was probably still at training with Yarrow.

Melanie was a no-show, although there was a cold spot by the window.

In the end, I headed for a walk around campus to clear my head. My feet took me around the back of the training building and toward Willowman's cottage.

Was he home?

Would he mind a visitor?

We were due to begin herbology tomorrow, but maybe he could take my blood sample now. It would certainly kill time until my training with the elites.

Varsa, the caretaker that lived here with Willowman, was crouching by a flower bed. He looked up as I pushed open the gate.

"Hey, is Willowman in?"

He shook his head and went back to the flowers.

The poor goyle had been damaged by the graynites, his mind broken by their attempt to get information out of him. They'd siphoned part of his soul, leaving him broken.

I crouched beside him. "What are you doing?"

He tensed but didn't say anything.

"Are these your flowers? Are they special to you?"

He nodded, the action stilted.

I lightly touched his hand. "They're beautiful."

He beamed at me, and his eyes lit up. "They are. Beautiful and strong." He lightly touched a petal. "They don't like the cold, but they withstand it. They bloom all year round, stubbornly resilient." He turned his head to look at me, and the beam of his smile was now a gentle warmth, but his gaze was probing. "Are you happy here?"

The question threw me, because it was the last thing I'd expected him to ask. "I guess so."

"You want to kill graynites?"

"Of course."

His smile fell, and he looked at the flowers. "They're so beautiful, but did you know that they're poisonous if ingested?"

"Um...No. I didn't."

"Yes. Their beauty is deceptive. They're not as innocuous as they seem..."

"Cameron?" Willowman strode down the path toward me, his gaze flicking from me to Varsa. "Everything okay?"

"Great." I pressed my hands to my thighs and stood. "Varsa was just telling me about the flowers."

"He was?" Willowman looked skeptical.

"Yeah, he said that they're resilient to the cold, even though they don't like it and that they're poisonous when ingested."

"Varsa?" Willowman said. "Varsa, did you tell Cameron those things?" There was hope in his voice and a slight breathlessness that spoke of excitement.

Varsa stared at the flowers mutely.

"Varsa?" Willowman said again.

Nothing.

Willowman frowned. "He really spoke to you?"

"Yes, we had a conversation just now."

Willowman steered me away from Varsa. "He's been nonverbal for the past few days." He eyed me up speculatively.

"I'm not making this up, Willowman."

"I know. I believe you. Maybe you wouldn't mind spending some time with him tomorrow after herbology class? I have a few errands to run."

I shrugged. "Sure, I don't mind."

"Great. But I wager you didn't come here to see Varsa, did you?"

"No. I was hoping you might take that blood sample now."

"Of course. I'll make sure it's stored properly this time." He headed for the door to his cottage. "Follow me."

In the end, there was no more putting it off. It was time for training. Time to see Serath again.

I walked into the basement level with a shield over my heart, chin up, and ready to focus on anything but my mate. Turned out I needn't have bothered.

Serath wasn't there.

"Shall we start?" Selas's smile was overly bright. "Orix is already down there." She indicated the huge hole in the floor.

I glanced at the door. "Shouldn't we wait?"

"He won't be joining us, Cameron. He's gone back to Outpost Ten for a few days."

My throat pinched. Outpost Ten, where the female he'd fucked was. "Right. Okay. Well, I guess we don't have to worry about him needing to acclimatize to my scent during battle. He'll have another female's scent on him to counter mine." My smile was cold and bitter. "It's a win-win."

She looked like she wanted to say something—argue maybe—but she settled for a tight-lipped smile and a nod. "Yes. It is. It's for the best."

After all, what more could she say?

"Whatever. Let's get this over with. I have somewhere else I want to be too."

I MANAGED TO get to the ladder three times and even made it partway up the third time, but the triumph, the pleasure in the achievement, was a dull throb in my chest.

Serath was at Outpost Ten with another goyle. He'd allowed her to touch him. He'd touched her. Kissed her. Fucked her. The thoughts played over and over in my head.

Training over, I took my anxiety-riddled body to the dorm, but its vise-like grip slackened at the sight of my friends sitting around the table and Derek flipping steaks on the grill with Shar. The room was filled with laughter, joy, and love. It washed over me like a magical balm.

The hollow place inside me that Serath's betrayal had left didn't shrink, but the energy in this room filled it somewhat.

Serath and I had been doomed from the start. We couldn't be together, not without hurting each other. Maybe he'd done us both a favor by putting this distance between us. Maybe this was for the best.

From now on, my focus would be on becoming the best guardian I could. I'd use the space from Serath to build a wall around my heart, not just for me, but for him too. I'd get my brother back, and in time, the pain would be less.

It had to be.

I exhaled, fixed a smile on my face, and joined my guardian family for supper.

CHAPTER 31

CAMERON

"Come on!" Curi yelled from his position on all fours a few feet away. He punched the ground. "Cam, come on!"

Touron joined him on the floor, both guys cheering me on. I couldn't see Shar or the twins. They were blocked by Dayn's bulk as he tightened his arm around my neck.

"Tap out," Dayn growled almost in exasperation. "Just fucking tap out."

Like fuck! I'd worked too hard the past two weeks—sweated and trained and pushed my body to the limit too many times to lose at a mere grappling match.

My weight and size were against me when faced with a goyle, and that would always be the case, but I had other assets. Other skills. One in particular that I'd been cultivating over the past couple of weeks.

Time to test it out.

I pressed my fingers to the arm choking me and released my talons.

Dayn's bellow of pain and shock battered my ear drums, and I was free to roll away and come up with a neat kick to the side of his head. He went down, clutching his bleeding arm.

My talons had already retracted. "Oh, shit, Dayn, looks like you cut yourself a little."

"You bitch! You fucking bitch." But his gaze was wary, and he didn't attack. Instead, he backed away, nursing his sliced-up forearm.

I caught Farnell's look of shock a moment before Curi swept me off my feet and into a bear hug.

"Fuck yeah! That's my girl."

I fell into the hug, wrapping my arms around him and relaxing into him. Being around Curi—touching him, hugging him—no longer felt awkward. The more time we spent together, the more our friendship grew.

He set me on my feet and kissed the top of my head.

"That was fucking awesome," Touron said, handing me a water bottle. "Great use of the assets." He wiggled his fingers.

"What was that?" Farnell demanded. "What did you do? I said no weapons. Where's the blade?"

"She doesn't have a blade," Shar said, joining us.

"Bullshit," Farnell spat.

"There is no blade." I held up my hands. "Just these." I willed the talons to appear.

Farnell exhaled sharply. "Partial shift..." His eyes narrowed, then his body relaxed. "Impressive. But you should have informed me of this ability."

"What? And take away the element of surprise? No fun in that."

He sucked on his cheeks. "You did well."

Across the room, Dayn shot me evil glances.

I gave him the finger.

"Class dismissed!" Farnell said. "Get some rest before the field test tomorrow."

Excitement fizzed beneath my skin because tomorrow we'd be going up against real-life threats just as Yarrow and Levi had promised.

Derek had been training almost daily with Yarrow, and I'd made sure to attend as many of his sessions as possible to provide support. But he didn't need me, not really. Derek could create all kinds of protective barriers—domes, shields, lances of energy that could knock back a threat—and he could do it at will. The only thing we had left to work on was getting him to identify when I was under threat in cases where even *I* might not be aware. For example, if I was spelled or drugged and my instincts were compromised.

We were getting there, though. It was about building Derek's confidence in his own ability to read situations and people, and he was coming along in leaps and bounds.

"We should get some food," Ginia said.

"Stone Comfort?" Palia suggested.

"Sounds good to me," Touron said.

"I'll go get Derek." Shar shot off before I could suggest I go instead.

Derek seemed to need to nap quite a bit recently, but according to Yarrow, it was because he was developing both physically and emotionally, and those changes required sleep.

We headed toward Stone Comfort as a group, Curi with his arm slung over my shoulders in the easy manner we'd become accustomed to. Our relationship status was solid across campus now. I was Mason's female as far as all other goyles were concerned, and even Levi had backed off as promised. I was in fit and fighting shape, both in cadet training and elite training.

I'd made it out of the lower level yesterday and even gotten a high five from Orix over it.

The cadet exams were in less than a week, and I was so ready to take that step closer to elite and ultimately getting Romi back.

Everything would have been perfect if not for one large shadow looming over me.

"Isn't Serath back today?" Ginia asked. "You okay about that?"

Palia nudged her hard in the ribs, and Ginia's shoulders tensed as she recognized her faux pas.

Curi was with us, and he had no clue about the Serath saga.

"Is Serath giving you a hard time?" Curi asked.

"Nah, he's just super bossy and uptight. Things are more relaxed with him gone."

"But you don't need relaxed if you're going to pass these elite trials," Curi said. "He should be here training you."

I loved that he was so invested in my success. "Selas and Orix have been amazing."

His stern demeanor softened at the mention of his cousin. "Selas is formidable. If you can't have Serath, then she's the next best thing."

Levi appeared on the path ahead leading to Stone Comfort from the opposite direction.

"It's Levi," Touron said as if we hadn't seen him.

We were at the crossroads that split toward the gates and main study complex. Curi drew me to a halt and pressed his lips to mine. I gasped in surprise, mouth parting against his in an involuntary invitation. His chest rumbled, and his fingers sank into my hair as he deepened the kiss, drawing my tongue into his mouth and sucking on it in a way that made me throb in all the right places. This was bad because it was so good, and I shouldn't be enjoying it so much, but it felt like an age since I'd been touched like this, savored like this, and Curi was an excellent kisser.

He broke the kiss, his dark eyes soft and hazy as they met mine, and when he spoke, his voice was a low and husky vibration. "That should put my scent on you. Enough to keep our ruse alive."

"He's gone inside," Palia said.

Levi was indeed gone.

A gust of wind blew my hair back, bringing with it an achingly familiar scent. My beast woke, pushing against my skin and turning me to face the direction of our obsession.

Serath stood, facing us on the path to the gate. His husky eyes were bright with an emotion I couldn't define, and his expression was closed and unreadable.

He strode toward us, acknowledging us all with a nod. "Cadets." And stepped into Stone Comfort.

"We don't have to go in," Touron said.

"Why not?" Curi looked confused. "Levi won't do anything, not with so many people around, and especially not with an elite present."

But it wasn't Levi we were worried about.

It was Serath.

CHAPTER 32

CAMERON

There was a line for the counter once we got inside. The twins went to grab a table, dragging Curi with them on the pretext of needing muscle to beat back any table competition.

Thank the gods for their foresight. Curi might be clueless to my connection to Serath, but he'd spent enough time with me to know my scent, and if it spiked around Serath and Curi picked up on it, then...

Yeah.

I needed to be careful.

What I needed to do was go with the twins.

Why wasn't I going with them? Oh, yeah, because Serath was here. A mere goyle ahead of me. I could smell him. See him. Stupidly ache for him to look at me and smile that beautiful smile that lit up his brutally handsome face.

He's fucking someone else, Cam. Snap out of it.

But the primal part of me, the part of me created to bond with his, didn't care about that. As far as my beast was concerned, Serath belonged to us.

Touron leaned in and whispered, "Um, Cam, you're breathing a little heavily."

"I'm fine."

"No, you're not. Go sit down and send Curi to help with the drinks."

The line moved forward, and Levi walked past, carrying a takeout cup. His step faltered adjacent to Serath.

"Serath Halle?" He stopped to address the elite.

"Yes?" The deep timbre of Serath's voice did crazy things to the pulse at my groin.

"I was hoping to discuss something with you," Levi said.

The line moved again.

"And you are?" Serath asked.

Like hell he didn't know who Levi was, but he was putting on a good show of being oblivious.

"Levi Halle." The slight hint of amusement in Levi's tone told me he was aware of the pretense but was willing to play along. "I'd like to speak about Miss Basque."

What was he doing?

"What about her?" Serath's tone was lower now, holding a warning I wasn't sure Levi was picking up on.

"If we could speak outside?"

Serath stepped out of the line, drink forgotten. I caught his profile, the tension in his jaw as he strode out of the building without giving me a second glance.

I broke away from Touron. "I'll be right back."

"Cam, don't," Touron said.

"I have to."

I pushed open the door to the sound of Serath's voice. The two males stood on the grass verge, several yards away from the building.

"Miss Basque's training is my responsibility," Serath said.

"Really? You've been away for two weeks. I can't see how you've upheld that responsibility."

Serath's jaw ticked. "The workings of the elite team are none of your concern."

"Maybe not, but Cameron is. She may be just another cadet to you, a stand-in for your lost elite, but she's more than that to me."

"Yes, I'm aware of your *relationship* with Miss Basque. I'm also aware that it's over."

Oh shit. I needed to get over there.

Levi exhaled in frustration. "That doesn't change the fact that I care about her and want to help her succeed. I can do that if you let me. Her life may only mean the difference between a strong elite unit and a compromised one to you, but it means the world to me." He looked right at me then, pinning me to the spot with his beautiful sea-green eyes, now stormy and dark with emotion. "I love her."

His words were like slugs to the heart.

Serath's scent spiked, bitter and laced with destruction.

Fuck. I rushed over and placed myself between them, my back to Serath's chest. "We talked about this, Levi. I told you I didn't need your help."

"No, you said you'd ask the elites." Levi looked over my head at Serath. "I don't see the problem. I can help because I know what the elite trial entails."

Serath moved forward, the heat of his body kissing mine, forcing me to bite back a sigh of pleasure. "How can you know?" he asked Levi.

Levi's nostrils flared. "Because they were created by my druid clan."

It took everything I had not to lean back against Serath. "But he can't tell us what the trials involve."

"I'll think about it," Serath said. "Are we done here?"

"Dammit, Serath, what is there to think about?" Levi demanded. "Is this about my father? Your uncle?"

"I have no uncle." Serath's tone was gravel and pain.

Levi's lip curled. "Of course you don't. You made that clear when you ran from him as a youngling and refused to let him take you in and give you a home. Your anger at the loss of your parents destroyed that relationship. I can't believe you blamed him for your father's death, even after all the evidence proved otherwise."

Serath's chest vibrated, the beast within riled and ready to rumble.

"Don't." I pushed my body against his but addressed Levi. "You have *no* idea what you're talking about, Levi, so just drop it."

Levi's nostrils flared again, and his gaze flicked from me to Serath and back again.

Shit. Could he smell us? Smell our connection somehow? If he figured out that we were mates, Serath would be taken. Executed. Panic rose inside me like a tide because a threat to Serath was a threat to me.

The air in front of me burst into darkness that expanded and became the large shadowy figure of Derek.

"Get away," Derek boomed at Levi.

Levi backed up, his brow furrowed in confusion. "Cameron...I would never...never hurt you. You know that, right?"

But the appearance of Derek screamed otherwise, and the wounded expression on Levi's face was almost enough to make me cave and jump to placate him—to tell him that, of course, I wasn't afraid of him. But that was a bad idea.

This was for the best.

It would put the kind of distance between us that would keep Serath safe.

Levi took a breath and nodded. "I'll leave you be. If you change your mind about the training..." He turned on his heel and walked away.

I sagged against Serath.

His hands closed over my hips, fingers warm brands, hugging me to him.

"Are you all right?" Derek asked.

"I am. Thank you."

Derek fixed his diamond eyes on Serath. "And you? Are you all right?"

Serath's grip on me flexed. "Why does that matter?"

Derek slow-blinked. "Because it matters to my Cameron."

"Derek, let's go inside." Shar beckoned him from the doors to Stone Comfort. How much had she seen and heard?

I was sure we'd discuss it later.

Derek retreated with Shar, leaving me alone with Serath, who quickly let go of me, putting an appropriate amount of space between us.

"How has training been?" he asked gruffly.

"Good. It's been good. And you? How was Outpost Ten?" How was your time with your lover?

"Good." He fixed his gaze on a point over my head. "I think this situation will help us both."

"What? You being with someone else?"

"That's correct. It's for the best."

"You honestly think it changes anything?" I dropped my voice. "We're fated mates. Our beasts don't seem to care about who else we might be fucking."

He looked at me, his gaze cold and biting. "You're fucking the Mason boy now?"

I was tempted to say yes, to cause him the same pain I felt. But petty wasn't a good look on me. "No. I'm not. I'm not a sellout like you. I don't take the easy path."

His scent spiked, reeking of frustration and anger. He wrestled it under control quickly. "You should go join your friends. I'll speak to the elite about Levi and his offer to train you for the elite exams."

"Are you insane? You saw what just happened. He could smell our...pheromones." I shuddered.

"It won't be an issue if I'm not present."

The pit in my belly got wider. "You're...you're leaving again?" Why did I have to sound so lost and forlorn?

Don't cry. Don't you dare fucking cry.

Serath's gaze dipped to meet mine and softened, his mouth parting on a sigh. "Cameron..." His hand drifted up, as if he wanted to touch me, but he curled his fingers against his palm and slowly lowered it.

I blinked back tears. "Serath...please..."

His throat bobbed. "Don't make this any harder, Cameron.

Please."

And then it hit me, the truth of this whole fucked-up situation. He wasn't fucking this other woman because he needed release. He was trying to make me hate him, to build resentment and dislike to protect me and build a distance between us because look at me, leaning in toward him, body all soft and pliant, eager for his touch.

I was a moth to his flame. But if I could stop. Control it... "You don't have to do this, Serath. I understand, and I'll do my part and stay away."

He closed his eyes, and when he opened them, all softness was gone. "This isn't just about you or the mate bond. Jana and I have history. Feelings. Long before you came. I can have a future with her."

He might as well have gut punched me. "Oh."

Oh? Oh? Was that it? Come on, Cam, think of something cutting and snarky to say. But my mind was blank, too focused on rapidly healing my wounded heart.

"Good luck with the training exercise tomorrow, Cameron. I'll see you at supper."

I didn't try to stop him from walking away.

I was done being that woman.

It was time to move on and find my future.

CHAPTER 33

CAMERON

Prasan popped a plate of carbonara in front of me. "My specialty. You'll love it."

I'd usually be all over the delicious dish, but my appetite was gone, and my mind and body too focused on Serath sitting on the other end of the table. I couldn't see him, thank goodness, but his scent was in my head.

Was I in his head too?

Probably. Hence the issue.

This thing between us was getting stronger, and being apart for two weeks only seemed to have made me more acutely aware of his presence.

Selas passed me some garlic bread, but I shook my head. I'd have enough trouble with what was already on my plate.

Willowman entered, bringing the aroma of fresh air with him, and took his favorite spot opposite me. "Prasan's carbonara. Cameron, you're in for a treat." He rubbed his hands together. "I love this dish."

"There's plenty more where that came from," Prasan said.

"Mind if I take some for Varsa?"

"Of course not. I'll pack you some."

"How is Varsa?" I twirled some linguini on my fork. "Looking forward to our next herbology lesson?" We'd been working on healing and rejuvenation tinctures the past couple of weeks—the basic pick-me-ups to use on wounded guardians to speed up healing and get them on their feet faster.

Willowman swallowed a mouthful of pasta and shrugged. "I don't know. He doesn't speak to me. Only you."

"Oh?" Serath leaned forward slightly so I caught the tip of his profile. The straight nose and strong chin. "He's completely non-verbal when Cameron isn't there?"

Willowman nodded. "It's the darndest thing. I can't explain it. He seems almost coherent when she's around."

Varsa was fast becoming a friend. "I like spending time with him. He knows so many interesting facts."

Willowman's golden eyes dimmed. "Varsa was always a bit of a scholar. Being a guardian wasn't his first choice, but the Stone Council..." He sighed. "Well, you know how it is."

Everyone murmured their understanding.

"Eat," Prasan said to me with an exasperated sigh. "It's no good if it's cold."

We ate in silence for a few minutes before Willowman broke it.

"I'll be leaving in the morning. My contact in the rim finally replied."

"The blood sample?" Selas asked.

I sat up straighter. "Is it still viable?"

"Yes, but I brought my kit so we can take another one just in case."

"How long till you return with answers?" Serath asked.

"A few days. Hopefully before the cadet exams, but I can't promise."

I'd waited this long, what did a few more days matter? "I haven't felt any weird flushes recently, and I've mastered my partial shift." I held up my hand and flashed my talons.

Serath hadn't seen this little trick yet, and I couldn't help the pang of pride his soft exclamation evoked.

"I heard you used it on Mr. Lowther in training today," Orix said with a smirk. "Nice."

"Has he bothered you at all since Carter spoke to him?" Selas asked.

I shook my head. "No. He backed off."

"Good."

"Are you looking forward to the field exercise tomorrow?" Prasan asked.

"I'm nervous but excited to see what I can do. You guys have been so amazing training me. I feel ready."

Prasan patted my back. "It's been a pleasure."

"Hey!" Orix said. "You came to what? Three sessions?"

Prasan looked affronted. "I've been providing nutritional support."

Selas chuckled softly. "We've all done our part."

Serath shoved back his chair abruptly. "Excuse me." He left via the stairwell door.

"At least he ate the carbonara," Prasan said. "I hate wasting food." He looked pointedly at my plate.

I rolled my eyes. "It's delicious." I tucked in, ignoring the rolling queasy sensation in my stomach at Serath's sudden departure. If we were going to coexist, then I needed to learn to block him out. I had to be less focused on his presence, his moods, him.

It would take time, but I was determined to master it.

For both our sakes.

WE'D JUST FINISHED cleaning up when the buzzer on the wall lit up, and the sound of a doorbell filled the room.

The elite froze, exchanging confused glances. Visitors were rare. As in, never. The only person that came here was Willowman, and he had a key.

"Are you expecting anyone?" Selas asked Orix.

"You know I don't bring my guests here," Orix said on his way to the stairwell. "I'll see who it is."

Taz appeared, as if out of nowhere, and padded after him, his personal feline shadow.

I finished loading the plates into the dishwasher and wiped the countertop.

"What's your plan for the evening?" Prasan asked.

"Shower, then bed with a book."

"You can join us for a movie if you like." He smiled kindly. "We have a few on tape here."

It had been too long since I'd watched a movie. "What do you have?"

"You can take a look. Romi built quite a collection." He winced.

"It's okay to talk about him. We're going to get him back."

His warm brown eyes shone with an echo of my confidence. "Yes, we are."

"Cameron." Orix stood at the stairwell door. "It's for you."

Huh? "Me?"

Prasan frowned. "Who is it?"

"Come and see," Orix said in a sing-song voice.

I followed him down the stairs to the entrance hall to find it filled with my friends.

"What are you guys doing here?"

"We came to see if you'd like to come to a party," Ginia said with a cheeky smile.

"We have parties here?"

She leaned in and stage-whispered, "A secret pre-exam party to let off some steam."

"La, la, la, can't hear anything," Orix said, turning his back on us.

"Absolutely not," Prasan said, bristling. "Cameron needs her rest before—"

"Chill out, mother hen," Orix said. "Don't you remember how it used to be? This could be the last time they get to blow off some steam before the actual cadet exams." He grinned at me. "Go, have fun."

"I don't think that's a good idea." Prasan looked seriously concerned.

"It's the last time everyone might be together," Selas said from the metal staircase. Touron's head whipped up, his gaze fixing on her in an expression that looked almost like adoration. "After the cadet exams, not everyone will be here to celebrate," she finished.

There was no real choice here. My friends had come to get me, and I was going with them. "Let's do this."

CHAPTER 34

CAMERON

Goyles didn't get intoxicated, but we didn't need to be tipsy to let loose, as I was witnessing right now.

The lower floor of the dorm had been turned into a club. Colorful lights whizzed about the room, and music blared from some unknown origin. Cadets and initiates danced or stood chatting and drinking from gray plastic cups. Several omegas had joined in the fun, each surrounded by males eager to get their attention.

Evelyn stood to one side with Master Raffi, her sharp gaze keeping track of her wards.

The atmosphere was one of celebration. Like Selas had said, this might be the last time we were all together, all alive. In a few days, some of these goyles would be dead.

The thought of losing one of my friends made my stomach hurt. No. We'd get through the exams together because we had one another's backs.

"Drink?" Touron yelled in my ear, passing me a plastic cup.

I peered up at him to see him bopping his head and scanning the room.

I knew him well enough to sense the agitation beneath his relaxed façade. "Looking for someone in particular?"

"Nah. I'm good," he said.

"Seriously? None of the omegas catch your eye?"

"Nope."

The way he'd looked at Selas, though...I was about to ask when a wave of heat rushed up my body, leaving me hot and sticky.

Shit, what was that?

I took a gulp of the raspberry-flavored concoction—refreshing, heavily alcoholic but barely able to give me a buzz.

The heat ebbed a little.

"Look at Derek!" Touron pointed.

Sharniza had Derek on the dancefloor, trying to teach him how to move to the music. He shuffled from side to side, his diamond gaze fixed on Shar. None of the other goyles paid him any attention. He seemed to have been accepted as part of the group now.

"Are *you* having fun?" Touron said in my ear.

"Don't I look like I'm having fun?"

He pressed his lips together. "You looked bummed out earlier, after the Levi and Serath encounter."

"I'm okay now." I plucked at the collar of my shirt. "It's hot in here, right?"

"I suppose. I—"

"Come dance!" Ginia grabbed Touron's hand, and Palia grabbed mine.

We were hauled into the midst of a throng of large frames.

The heat intensified, focused low in my belly. The beat of the music. All the bodies moving together in a way that was almost sensual.

"Hey!" Curi slipped between me and Palia, wrapped his arms around me, and pulled me against his taut body. "Got to act the part, right?" His breath was hot against my ear, sending a delicious shiver straight to my core. I pressed closer to him, winding my arms around his neck and nuzzling his throat. This felt good. Yes. I needed this. This contact. This closeness. My breasts swelled, nipples aching for touch.

Curi's grip on me tightened, his hands sliding down to cup my ass and haul me closer.

My pussy throbbed as I parted my mouth to taste his skin. I could have this. I *should* have it. I *needed* it. If Serath could find his release, then so could I. I deserved it.

Curi pulled away. "Cam?" His dark eyes locked with mine. "What are you—"

I kissed him hard on the mouth, and he melted against me with a groan, his hands sinking into my hair, fingers raking my scalp.

We kissed deep and long, until my body was on fire with need, my pussy clenching painfully around nothing.

Curi broke the kiss, his eyes wild as they clashed with mine. He grabbed my hand and steered me out of the room and up the stairs.

My body was one throbbing flame of need, and I barely registered the journey to his room.

He closed the door, and I launched myself at him, tearing at his lastonflex, hungry for the sensation of skin on skin. "Curi, please."

"Cameron." My name was a pained groan falling from his lips. Good. He wanted this too.

We could have it. We could be together, and Serath could have his female, and it wouldn't hurt...It wouldn't hurt so badly anymore.

Curi grabbed my wrists. "You're burning up. We need to cool you down."

A sob clawed at my throat. What was this? What was happening?

A wave of need raced through me, painful, twisted, stealing all thought. "Cut the chivalry and fuck me."

CHAPTER 35

SERATH

She's gone for the evening, and I'm still hiding in the observatory. This is pathetic.

"Here." Selas passes me a cup of tea. "It's herbal."

"Great."

She laughs softly. "Trust me, it will help you relax."

"I could do with some of that." I set the cup down to let the beverage cool.

"She should have stayed in," Prasan says from his spot by the computer setup.

"You are such a mother hen," Selas says. "Let her have a little fun before..."

I can't stop the wry smile that paints my lips. "Before her life becomes a series of duties and lethal engagements?"

"You have such a way with words," Selas says.

Willowman enters the room, carrying a mug of something. "I love the view up here."

"You should just move in," Selas says.

"I would, but Varsa needs me."

A rush of heat washes over me, coming out of nowhere.

Alarm bells fill my head as my gut tightens and my cock hardens.

"Serath? What's wrong?" Selas asks.

"I'm not sure." I swallow against a dry mouth. "Is it hot in here?"

Willowman shoots me a strange glance. "No. It's not." He looks down at my ankle. "You're glowing."

I finally register the constriction. The effect that only happens when my beast is being suppressed in Cameron's presence. She isn't here, so how is this possible?

"Willowman?"

He shakes his head. "The sigma mate bond is uncharted territory, and Cameron is halfblood. I don't know what to tell you."

"You should check on her," Prasan says. "She could be in trouble. For all we know, your bond has grown despite not consummating."

Another rush of heat is followed by a deep pulsing sensation low in my belly, the kind that comes when I'm inside a female. Oh...fuck.

"Where is this party?"

CHAPTER 36

CURI

"Cut the chivalry and fuck me," Cameron demands.

She has no idea how badly I want to do that right now. Her scent...her fucking scent is tugging on all the places inside of me that drive my beast wild, and if I believed she meant it, if I believed she was in her right mind right now, we'd be naked and joined at the fucking crotch already.

But this isn't her.

There's something wrong with her.

She makes a grab for me, her pupils dark and too large. I haul her close and pin her hands behind her back. "Stop! Cameron, you need to focus."

"Please...please. Curi, I need it. I need you to..." She rubs against me, her mouth soft and pliant against my collarbone, moving up to my throat—tongue lapping at my skin.

Fuck, I'm gonna need a sainthood after this. I steer her toward the bathroom. If I can get her into a cold shower, then—

The door to my room bursts open with a splintering of wood.

"What the—"

Serath grabs hold of me and yanks me away from Cameron, throwing me against the wall. My back cracks, head banging to leave me momentarily stunned.

Cameron lets out a soft cry of protest, then falls into Serath's arms.

She slowly raises her head and looks up at him as if he's some kind of god. As if he's the center of the world. Her scent spikes, and another joins it. They mingle and explode into a new intoxicating aroma.

I've read about this, and witnessing it now...everything suddenly makes perfect sense.

CHAPTER 37

SERATH

Cameron is putty in my arms, rubbing against me as if she wants to sink into my skin. Was she like this with the Mason boy? Was he about to take advantage of her?

A red haze tinges my vision as I lock gazes with him. "I will kill you."

He stands slowly, hands up in a placating gesture. "I was trying to get her cooled off. Trust me. I don't take what isn't freely given. She's not herself right now."

His words reek of sincerity, and my beast stands down.

"I believe him," Selas says from the doorway. "Can you control your beast?"

It shoves against my skin, egged on by Cameron's arousal, but I push back, using the anklet to ground me.

If I lose control, she'll die.

I can't *ever* lose control. "I'm fine."

"Then go. I'm right behind you," Selas says.

The window is open, so I wrap Cameron's hot, tight body in my arms and leap through it, morphing and taking to the air.

"Please," she whimpers. "I need it. I need it now."

"I know, my heart, I know, and I'll do what I can to give it to you."

"WHAT HAPPENED?" ORIX follows me into my room and then into the bathroom.

My hands are full of a writhing, needy halfblood. "Turn on the shower. Cold. Now."

Orix flips the lever and adjusts the temperature. "It's one of her weird episodes, isn't it? I can smell her." His tone is lower than usual. He's turned on by her scent.

"Get out!"

"Serath, you can't be alone—"

"I said, get the fuck out."

He steps outside but doesn't close the door.

I set Cameron on her feet, but she clings to me, running her hot hands over my shoulders, my biceps, then up to cup my face. Her lips search for mine, and I turn my head away, afraid that if I allow her that much, then I'll lose control.

"Serath, please. It hurts. It hurts so bad."

My cock is painfully hard, my body attuned to her need. I steer her into the stall fully clothed and push her under the spray.

She cries out, a sound that is part pleasure, part pain. Mist rises off her skin where the cold water hits it.

Desperate sobs rack her body, but she continues to rock against me, as if losing contact is too painful.

The water isn't enough.

I need to relieve her. I'll have to touch her. Gods help me. I turn her away from me, push her against the tiles, then reach around and slip my hands down her pants to cup her bare pussy.

She tilts her hips toward my hand, whimpering *please* over and over.

Her skin is fire, her pussy swollen and weeping with need. I part her, sliding a digit over her clit and sliding down to push in and out of her.

"Ah...Yes. Please." She opens her thighs wider. "More. I need more."

Two fingers, three. Fuck she's so tight, sucking on me hungrily. I give her what she needs, upping the tempo and depth of my thrusts. "Imagine that it's my cock inside you. So fucking deep. Take it, take all of me."

"Yes. Mine. This is mine." She rides my hand, head thrown back, mouth parted, emitting guttural sounds that inflame me and make it almost impossible to hold back my beast.

She tenses, then her body shudders, her pussy squeezing me in rippling motions as she comes.

"Yes...yes." She sucks on her bottom lip. "Please don't...don't stop."

I couldn't even if I wanted to. I'm lost in her. Slave to her body.

I keep fucking her with my fingers, hips pressed to the small of her back, the base of my cock nestled between her ass cheeks with just the wet fabric between us. I can't help but chase my own release as she continues to come, gripping my fingers so tightly that I become a part of her. My cock jerks, weeks of pent-up release sinking into the fabric of my lastonflex.

I'm not sure how long we remain joined this way, but eventually, her sobs cease, and her body relaxes against mine. I slowly withdraw my hand and resist the urge to suck my fingers clean.

"Serath..." She presses her palms to the tiles and drops her chin to her chest. "I don't...I'm sorry. I know you didn't want...I know—"

"Hush." I turn her to face me and step into her space, peering down at her through the veil of water that crashes down between us. "Never mistake my distance for disregard, Cameron. You have my heart, even though I cannot openly give it to you."

Her eyes mist, glistening with tears. "Then stop seeing the other goyle. You don't need to give your body to her. We can do this. We can control our beasts without you having to find release elsewhere." Her lips tremble with emotion. "I can give you release just like you did for me."

I want to tell her the truth. Admit that I'm merely using Jana as a boundary, but if I do that, there will be no barrier between us. Nothing to keep her safe from me. "And you think we'll be able to stop every time?" My tone is gruff as frustration seeps into it. "You think it's safe to take risk after risk? I *need* Jana. I need what she can give me. What *you* can't."

She squeezes her eyes closed, and tears track down her cheeks.

I hate myself.

I fucking hate hurting her like this. But this is the point I should leave her. Just walk away and leave her wounded and wary. But instead, I bridge the final distance between us and claim her trembling lips. Her sob breaks against my mouth, and she sinks into me, giving herself to me in a kiss that slices a path across my aching heart.

I don't want this moment to end.

I don't want to let her go.

But I have to.

My eyes burn as I break contact and step away.

Her chin quivers, and she wraps her arms around her body, dropping her gaze to the tiles.

She looks broken, and it's my fault. "I'll give you some time to gather yourself and go to your room. I need to let Willowman know what just happened here."

I step outside to find Orix standing to one side of the door, his back to the wall. His eyes flash with anger. "I don't understand how nature can be so cruel."

Neither do I. Neither do I.

CHAPTER 38

CURI

"Are you all right?" Selas asks.

Me? I'm fucking peachy. But Cameron... "Will *she* be all right?"

"We'll make sure of it." She's watching me shrewdly, her milky gaze probing.

"What?"

She shakes her head. "Nothing."

Touron rushes into my room and comes to a sharp halt at the sight of Selas.

An emotion I can't define flits across her face. "Mr. Lomax..."

"Miss Mason," Touron says.

There's a strange tension in the room that has nothing to do with what just happened.

What did just happen?

Serath took Cam.

He took her because she's his mate.

He's a sigma.

This is bad.

Do they know? They must know. But I need to be careful because what if they don't know?

"I saw Serath come up here," Touron says. "But Cam came up

with you," he says to me.

"Serath has Cam. She'll be fine," Selas says.

"Is she..." He clears his throat. "Is everything okay?"

Fuck...He knows. He fucking knows. And of course Selas would know. How could she not, being around the two of them... together.

Selas's eyes narrow. "What did you see, Curi?"

"I didn't see anything."

She takes a step closer. "What did you smell?"

"Fuck," Touron says softly.

She knows that I know. "I care about Cameron. I would never do anything to hurt her."

Selas nods. "Good." She looks to Touron. "I'll leave you to explain things." She strides out of the door, leaving me stunned and aching with a weird sense of loss that I can't understand.

Touron puts his hand on my shoulder. "Let's take a walk."

CAMERON

WILLOWMAN EXAMINED ME by shining a light in my eyes and checking my pulse while the elite stood around the sofa waiting for a verdict.

"What did you eat and drink tonight?" Willowman asked.

"What? Um...just supper with you guys, then maybe a couple of drinks at the party."

"Anything else?"

"No."

"Why does that matter?" Orix asked.

"I'm not sure it does, but the symptoms are consistent with being drugged."

Serath stepped forward with a menacing growl. "Someone drugged her?"

My skin zinged at the sound of his voice.

"I can't say for sure," Willowman said. "This could simply be an acceleration of whatever maturing developments are happening to Cameron, or..."

"Or what?"

"Or a result of denying the mate bond."

My shoulders sagged. "You mean this could get worse?"

"I honestly don't know." Willowman stood and straightened, looking down at me with a sigh. "You're a halfblood, and this is new territory."

I hated not knowing, but one thing I was certain of. "It can't be drugs. I only took food and drink from people I trust."

"Someone could have injected you," Prasan said. "Your stone skin wouldn't activate if you weren't aware of the threat on some level, but any wound would have healed by now." He ran his hands through his hair in obvious agitation.

"I don't think it's drugs either," Orix said. "Unless someone wanted to take advantage of you, there would be no point of using such a drug."

"Weren't you with the Mason boy?" Prasan asked.

I didn't like what he was implying. "Mason didn't do anything to me. He wouldn't...I...I begged him to, and he wouldn't." Damn, I sounded lame.

"She's right. He had no such intention," Serath said. "He was keeping her safe."

I wish that those moments with Curi were a blur, and that I could claim I didn't remember what I'd said or how I'd acted, but that would be a lie. I recalled every moment of it, and there was no expressing how grateful I was that it was Curi who'd been with me when the heat hit and not some random goyle who might have taken advantage.

"We need answers," Selas said to Willowman.

"I'll do my best to get them for you. I leave at dawn, and I'll do my best to be back before the cadet exams. In the meantime, you need to stay close to the people you trust and do what needs to be done to assuage any flares." He gave me a pointed look.

Any flares? He meant any bouts of intense arousal. My cheeks heated, and I dropped my gaze as the room went silent.

Great, now everyone was thinking about me getting off.

"It's getting late," Selas said. "The sun will be up soon, and Cameron needs her sleep before the field test tomorrow."

The field test I'd been looking forward to suddenly felt like a chore. I needed to recharge and get my oomph back.

Serath took a step toward me, but Selas moved to block him and held a hand out to me. "Come on. I'll tuck you in."

I allowed her to haul me to my feet and made sure to hold my breath as I passed Serath. The last thing I needed was his scent in my head when I fell asleep.

If I couldn't have him in real life, then he needed to stay out of my dreams.

CHAPTER 39

CAMERON

Everyone looked up from their breakfast when I walked into the dorm kitchen. My neck grew hot beneath all the scrutiny. Curi wasn't here yet, thank the gods. It gave me time to prepare myself to face him after I'd tried to rip his clothes off. Urgh.

"Hey." I raised a hand, feeling suddenly awkward. How much of my wanton behavior had everyone here seen? Fuck, this was uncomfortable, and I still had explanations to do.

Derek crossed the room and put his arms around me, pulling me against his shadowy yet solid chest.

"You okay now, my Cameron," he said. "You okay. You not hurt. You safe."

He was right. I was okay. I was safe. These were my friends, and they didn't give a shit how I'd acted. I was being a dick.

"Thank you." I closed my eyes and allowed him to hold me for a few moments longer.

"Now you eat breakfast and be strong for the test." He pulled away and looked down at me with his bright diamond eyes. "Today we work together."

I smiled up at him. "Yes, we will. Are you excited to get out there and test your power?"

He grinned, flashing fang. "I'm excited to protect my

Cameron."

"And kick some ass?"

"And kick some ass."

I joined the others at the table, taking the only vacant seat next to Sharniza. Touron passed me a mug of coffee. I grabbed some bacon and toast.

"Feeling better?" Palia asked from across the table.

"Yeah. I...We're not sure what happened." I filled them in on what Willowman had said and how we'd ruled out the possibility of a drug, leaving the explanation to strange developments.

"Do you think it might happen again?" Touron looked worried.

"I don't know. But I *do* know that as long as I stay with you guys, I'll be safe."

"You should speak to Curi," Sharniza said.

My stomach quivered. "Yeah, I owe him a huge thank you. He could have taken advantage, and he didn't, and believe me, I begged him to. Urgh." I covered my face with my hands. "I can't even..." I took a breath and sat up. "I'll just tell him the truth about my weird episodes and that Willowman is looking into it and—"

"He knows," Shar said.

"Oh, you guys told him. I guess he must have had questions. Okay, good then—"

"No, Cam, he knows about Serath."

My pulse skipped. "What?"

"He figured it out," Touron said. "Serath came to get you and...well, you two together, with you in that state..."

"Pheromones," Palia said, her tone grave.

"Then Selas questioned him and...well, she asked us to fill him in."

"We can trust him," Sharniza said.

Yes...yes, we could. He'd proven that, but I'd wanted to keep him out of this. I'd hoped to keep his conscience clear, but now...

I pushed back my chair. "I'll meet you guys at class."

Curi let me into his room without a word. His blue hair was loose and fell around his face in messy waves that highlighted the slight puffiness around his eyes that said he hadn't slept well.

The drapes were still closed, so the room was gloomy and gray. The bed was rumpled and unmade, and when I inhaled, I got a lungful of Curi's scent and something else...Me. This room smelled like me.

My stomach hollowed. "Hey."

"You feeling better?" His voice was gruff and gravelly from sleep.

"Yeah. I wanted to thank you."

He snorted softly, the sound almost angry. "For what? Not fucking you when you begged me to?"

"Basically, yes."

"Trust me, it wasn't easy."

He scraped back his hair and used a tie from around his thick wrist to pull it into a knot at his nape, the motions jerky and yep, angry. He was pissed at me.

We'd gotten close the past two weeks. Become friends, and he probably felt betrayed that I'd kept this from him. "I wanted to tell you about...everything, but I didn't want to bring you into this mess if I could avoid it."

"Oh, I get it. You needed a decoy. Someone who'd play the part well. Be believable." His lip curled self-deprecatingly. "I understand, Cameron. Trust me, I get it. That isn't the issue."

"Then why are you so mad?"

He let out a harsh laugh. "You really are oblivious, aren't you?" He moved closer, his body pressing up against my personal space but not invading it. "You have no idea the things I've been fantasizing about doing to you, and if last night I could have convinced myself that you wanted me for real, I would have acted out every single one of those fantasies."

My mouth went dry. "What?"

His throat bobbed. "But you belong to someone else, and I'm not into pining over things I can't have. Things that can never belong to me."

Pining? He... "Curi, what the fuck?"

His dark eyes were bright. "I was falling for you."

My stomach dropped. "Curi...I—"

"Don't. It's fine. I'm glad this happened, and I found out."

My eyes heated. I'd hurt him. "I'm so sorry, Curi. I...I care about you, and maybe...if things were different—"

"Stop. I know how fated matings work. There is no one else for you. Not when it comes to your heart. But, Cameron, you need to be careful. If you slip and consummate with him..."

"I know. I won't. *We* won't."

He dropped his chin to his chest. "But you'll want to. You'll have needs."

My cheeks heated. "I can handle it."

"Like you handled it last night?"

"That was...that was an episode."

"Which could happen again. Did he get you off? You think it's safe for him to do that?"

He was right: Serath and I had taken a huge risk last night by being together like that. If he'd lost control... "We're doing the best we can."

He nodded. "I believe it. But please, don't take risks like that. If you need release, then come to me. I'll give you what you need, no strings."

"You just said you were falling for me."

"*Was.* Not anymore."

His gaze was cool and flat, and damn, I believed him. But I doubted I'd ever take him up on his offer. When in my right mind, the thought of being with anyone but Serath made my stomach hurt.

What if you're not in your right mind? What if Serath isn't here the next time this happens? I wanted to ignore the voice in my head, but it had a point.

I might not want to take Curi up on his offer, but knowing it was on the table helped.

He was offering me a lifeline, and there was no harm in accepting, even if I had no intention of using it. "Thank you."

He gave me a wry smile. "You have no intention of taking me up on my offer, do you?"

I returned his smile. "I'm going to make sure I never have to. I value our friendship too much."

He sighed, his expression softening. "Me too, Basque. Me too." He reached over his shoulder and tugged off his shirt. "Now get out of here unless you want to watch me dress for class."

We were back on even footing, and it felt good.

CHAPTER 40

CAMERON

"Everybody, gather 'round!" Yarrow called from the academy gates.

Levi stood next to him with his arms crossed, sleeves rolled up to expose his strong forearms. A backpack hung off his shoulder.

"Willowman has set up a warp zone outside the walls, which we'll be using to get to our destination today," he said.

"Why am I so nervous?" Palia muttered.

"Because bad things happen every time we leave campus," Ginia replied.

I couldn't deny the moths in my belly.

The last time I'd gone through these gates I'd been with Bax, and I'd come back alone. "We'll be okay. We'll be together."

"You'll need to work together to get to the extraction point," Levi said. "There will be threats along the way, and each will have a metallic plate on its body fixed to an area that represents its weak spot. You'll need to strike the plate to disable the creature. Sometimes more than once. The threats are real. They can, and will, hurt you. I'll be on hand to step in, if need be, but if I intervene, then that'll be marks off to the goyles that needed assistance."

He was coming with us?

He didn't look at me, not once, and I should be glad, but it bothered me. I'd have to get over that.

He couldn't be a friend.

He was merely a tutor now.

The gates swung open, and we filed into the mid-afternoon sun, gravel crunching beneath our lastonflex shoes.

Yarrow and Levi led us onto a stretch of grass occupied by a stone circle.

I'd seen pictures of similar stone circles in books from the past. There were sites like this all over the rim.

"Everyone inside," Yarrow said.

Levi led us into the circle.

There were twenty of us, ten from my dorm, including Derek and me, and the rest from the other dorm—faces that were familiar. But I was still working on remembering names.

"I protect you, my Cameron," Derek said to me.

"It's okay for some," one of the gargoyles from the other dorm muttered.

"You have something to share with the class, Hamlin?" Yarrow asked, his tone cold.

"How is it fair that she gets...*that* as protection?"

"Aw." Ginia tracked an invisible tear down her cheek. "You need someone to hold your hand?"

"Shut up, Hamlin," a goyle from his dorm said. "That's her shield. We all have one, just not like him."

"I'm just saying, it isn't fair."

"Life isn't fair," Curi snapped. "Get over it."

Hamlin flinched.

"I'm going to activate the warp now," Yarrow said, pressing his hand to the stone pillar in front of him. "Good luck."

"Hold tight," Levi said from somewhere close behind me.

I was tempted to look over my shoulder and find him but resisted. He was doing his part. I needed to do mine.

The world tipped and shattered as the warp ripped us out of the circle and away.

I CAME TO on all fours with bile shooting up my throat. I gagged and swallowed, wincing as it burned a path back down my throat. "Bleurgh."

"You're okay." Derek helped me to my feet.

Around me, several of the other goyles were also busy dry-heaving. I guess I wasn't the only one who had issues with warping.

Sharniza stood with her back to me, hands on hips, surveying the terrain—an abandoned parking lot with rusted vehicles and several boarded-up buildings to our right. There was a road beyond the broken barriers and an ominously silent settlement beyond that.

"Where are we?" Ginia asked.

"Test Zone Thirty-three" Levi said. "The Stone Council uses it for training exercises for the alpha teams. They agreed to let us borrow it today."

Touron and I locked gazes, and he arched a brow, probably thinking what I was—that Levi had used his connections to get this zone.

"And what are we up against?" Sharniza asked him.

"Out there, in a real-world situation, you'd never know for sure."

"In other words, you're not gonna tell us," Curi said. "Fine." He rolled his shoulders. "I like surprises."

Levi walked to the parking lot barrier. "Beyond this point, there is danger. Navigate it, reach the other side of this settlement, and you pass the test. The exit warp is due northeast."

He shrugged the pack off his back. "I have compasses. Take one as you pass."

Hamlin went first, trailed by a couple of the goyles from his dorm. Levi handed them each a compass, and as they stepped past the barrier, the air rippled. It looked like this was a protected zone.

Shar and the twins passed through, followed by Touron, then

Curi. Then it was me and Derek.

A breeze kissed my face, cold enough to make me squint. "I thought you were coming with us."

"I'll be on hand if needed."

He'd be watching somehow. Monitoring us?

He handed me the compass but didn't let go of it. The tips of his fingers grazed mine, and gentle warmth bloomed between us along with words unspoken. "Be safe," he said finally, letting go of the compass.

I dropped a nod and joined the others outside of the safe zone.

"This way!" Hamlin held up his compass and strode off down the road.

"Someone's overcompensating for his earlier cowardly comment," Shar said.

"Who put you in charge?" Dayn demanded.

"Fuck you, Lowther," Hamlin said.

"Fuck you."

"Why don't you both fuck each other?" a goyle with a square jaw and angry eyes growled. "Or shut the fuck up. This is a training exercise. There's danger out here, and we need to be stealthy."

"Who's that?" Ginia whispered.

"His name's Hawke. He's a Foxe," Palia said.

"He certainly is." Ginia caught her bottom lip between her teeth. "How did I not notice him before?"

"He's one of Farnell's cadets so isn't in our regular classes."

Now that I thought about it, there were a couple more faces that I'd never seen in any of our classes. "Farnell has special cadets?"

"It would seem so. But from what I gather, this is his first year doing it."

I made a note to ask Serath about it. He was close to Farnell. He'd know.

Hawke's admonishment seemed to have shut Hamlin and Dayn up. We trudged down the road and into the town in silent vigilance.

The world here was gloomy, the sky heavy with rain clouds. The sun broke through here and there, lancing down to dapple the earth with golden light. The buildings were worn but patched up. You could see that someone had gone to the effort to put in a new door here or fit a new window there. The Stone Council took care of this settlement because they needed it.

Had there been people living here before the council commandeered it?

The sky darkened as the sun was obscured by a cloud.

A clatter and scraping sound brought us all to a halt, drawing our attention to the rooftops of the nearby buildings.

"There's something up there," Curi said under his breath.

"No shit," Dayn muttered.

"Whatever it is, this is a test," Palia reminded us. "So, it has to be something we might come across as guardians."

"Well, that narrows it down," Hamlin said dryly.

"Shut up," Hawke said. "Listen."

Over the past two weeks, we'd learned about shifters, vamps, graynites, grotesques, and a host of minor tulpa, like boogeymen, the men in hats, shadowmen, and sandmen. But we'd also learned about creatures I hadn't known existed, like wraiths and ghouls. Levi had gone over the properties of each and how they could be bested. The information scrolled through my mind now.

Another clatter above broke my concentration.

"How long till sunset?" Shar asked.

"Two hours," Palia said.

They expected us to fight the threats here in human form *not* goyle. Not that it mattered to me.

All I had was my talons if needed, but flight would have been a bonus to our team right now. "We keep moving and stay alert. We can't do anything while the threat is above us. It'll have to come down for us to deal with it."

"No shit," Dayn sneered.

"Shut your mouth, Lowther," Curi growled.

"Or what?"

"Or I'll break your face," Hawke said before Curi could reply.

Dayn snapped his mouth closed, his jaw so tight I was sure he would grind his teeth to powder.

"What's your name?" Hawke asked Derek.

"Derek, and this is my Cameron," he said proudly.

"Yeah, I've heard." Hawke dropped his gaze to me. "Impressive."

His eyes were like chips of ice, his demeanor not much better. "You're on a special team with Farnell?"

He blinked sharply as if surprised by my direct question. "Yes."

"What's it for?"

Now he looked mildly amused. "Private things."

My scalp tightened, gut twisting in warning a moment before dark gray shapes leaped off the buildings and landed on the street ahead of us.

I'd seen these creatures before, hunched and taloned with wings that looked too small to take them into the air but that, through some mystical power, could carry them anyway.

Grotesque, once our allies, now our enemies, growled and snapped, pawing at the ground. I caught the glint of metal on their ankles. Cuffs of some kind. And in the middle of their chest was a contact point—a diamond-shaped metallic plate. It covered the area where the stone would be soft enough to break through, the spot where their hearts could be torn from their chests.

We had to strike them there to disable them. Or evade. Whichever worked.

"Grotesque..." Touron said softly. "They have grotesque?"

He looked pale, his eyes darker than usual. Shit, his brother had been killed by one of these creatures.

"I count ten on the ground and maybe seven above," Curi said.

"Agreed," Hawke replied.

The creatures waited for us to approach, waiting for *us* to come to *them*. "Why aren't they attacking?"

"I think there's an attack zone," Palia said. "Look at the ground. There's a black painted line up ahead."

"You mean they won't attack unless we pass that line?" Dayn asked.

"I think so."

"What are these things? *Trained* grotesque?"

Not trained. Maybe restrained. "Look at the cuffs on their ankles."

"A restraint of some kind." Hawke's assessment matched mine.

"Cameron, what you want to do?" Derek asked. "We go through, or we take a new route?"

"I don't think it matters," Palia said, answering for me. "I think whichever route we take will have a threat on it."

"I say we take these fuckers out," Touron growled. His body rippled with tension, eager to do some damage.

I hadn't seen him like this before, with such a desire for violence emanating off him. He needed this fight.

But if we were going to do this, then we needed to work together. "Once we cross that line, those things will attack. Not just the ones on the ground, but those above as well, and who knows how many more are up there?"

Hawke's stocky frame blocked my path as he scanned the rooftops. "We need three units. One to focus on disabling the ground attack and two for dealing with the threat that falls from the sky."

"Agreed," Curi said. "Touron, Cameron, Shar, Palia, Ginia, Waxen, and Saffe will take the ground forces."

Hawke nodded. "The rest of you are with me." He rattled off names, splitting his team into two. "We watch the ground team's six."

"Shields at the ready," Shar said. "We're going to need them."

Derek's feet left the ground, and he loomed above me, my own personal cloud.

"Let's do this!" Touron let out a battle cry and burst into motion. We followed at a jog, crossing the dark line to meet the threat head on.

The grotesque let out a collective scream and attacked.

CHAPTER 41

CAMERON

All the hours training, all the time in the gym, the katas, the grappling, everything came together as we fought the stone menace. My body was fluid as I ducked and evaded the swipe of talons, strong as I shoulder-slammed and punched metal plates. My stone skin activated easily, protecting me from the worst of the blows, and Derek remained close but didn't intervene. He knew I had this because *I* knew I had this.

Shar and Touron flanked me, taking down grotesque after grotesque. Someone let out a bellow of pain somewhere, and snarls broke the air.

Hawke shouted instructions to his teams as more grotesque fell into the street. But we continued to move forward, knocking them down and taking them out.

"Another wave on the roof!" someone yelled.

I leaped back to avoid a swipe to my abdomen, then attacked with my talons, raking a line across the creature's stony face to distract it so I could follow up with a left-fisted punch to its chest plate.

It crumpled in a heap.

"I see a black line up ahead!" Palia yelled. "I think it's a safe zone."

"Then let's move it!" Touron said.

We broke into a jog as Hawke bellowed a warning from behind us.

The world rumbled and the ground shook as a hoard of grotesque spilled into the street, blocking us off from the exit.

"Fuck!" Sharniza ground to a halt beside me, her body in a crouch, eyes narrow slits. "There are too many. We won't make it through."

She was right. We'd be crushed—forced to our knees by the sheer number of these creatures. How had the Stone Council managed to capture so many?

"We need to turn back," Dayn said.

"There are more of those things up there," Hawke replied. "They'll block us off if we retreat, and we'll end up trapped."

The grotesque held the line, no longer attacking, knowing that we had no choice but to move forward. To move toward them.

Levi had said they weren't the most intelligent of creatures, so this maneuver had to be engineered somehow.

But why? Why lock us in like this...Wait...

All this time Yarrow and Levi had been training us on how to use our shields. How to draw on nature to strengthen them.

The sky was dark and gray with the threat of a storm. There was power in a storm.

Power at our fingertips.

"I know what we have to do." I turned to the others. "We use our shields. We use the impending storm."

At first, all I got were confused expressions, but then Curi cursed softly. "Of course. We push back with our shields and force a path through."

"Genius!" Touron said.

"Good call." Hawke looked almost impressed. Hard to tell for sure because the guy was rocking a poker face.

I looked up at Derek. "You ready to do this, buddy? We got to help clear a path. There are too many of them. It's too dangerous to fight our way through." I allowed myself to feel the fear, to acknowledge the threat of being pulled to the ground and ripped to shreds.

Derek's form grew larger, his diamond eyes brighter. "I won't let them touch you."

Perfect. "We ready?"

A chorus of yeses filled the air.

I put my head down and charged at the stone wall of creatures. My skin tingled, hardening at the perceived threat. Then a blinding light seared my eyes, and they were knocked on their asses as Derek blasted a hole through the mass.

"Mother fucker!" Waxen cried. "Get behind Basque. We can use her as a battering ram!"

My boots pounded the ground, arms pumping as Derek blasted the creatures out of the way. The air cracked with charged particles. The sharp scent of the storm was heavy on the air as everyone drew from the elements, creating a bubble of protection around them as we ran.

Grotesque attacked in my periphery, but they hit our shields and were flung back.

Their screams of rage and frustration rent the air, then died abruptly.

Derek materialized ahead and came to a stop, his shadowy form hunched over, shoulders heaving.

"We did it!" Ginia let out a whoop and punched the air. "We fucking did it."

"They've stopped," Shar said. "I can't hear them, but they're screaming."

"Must be some kind of ward between those lines," Touron said.

But my attention was on Derek. "Hey..." I hurried over to him. "Are you okay?"

He nodded and looked up at me with a smile. But his eyes were dull, and his frame looked smaller than usual.

"Is he okay?" Shar joined us. "Derek?"

"I will be fine."

But he didn't look fine. "I think you used too much juice too quickly."

"Then he needs to recharge," Shar said.

Derek held out his hand, and I took it, noting the tingle that passed between our palms. "Stay close."

"Always," Derek said.

"We should keep moving." Sharniza waved everyone forward. "Move. The extraction point shouldn't be too far."

"About a mile and a half," Palia said. "We can make that in half an hour."

"Easily," Hawke agreed.

We set off with Palia and Ginia as our navigators.

"Anyone hurt?" Shar asked Hawke.

"Not seriously."

I looked back, searching for Curi to find him helping Waxen along. The goyle had a wound on his abdomen, which was slowly healing.

Curi locked gazes with me for a beat and gave me a short nod, letting me know he was all good.

"Takes longer than usual for grotesque-inflicted wounds to heal," Hawke explained. "He'll be fine in a few minutes."

"We did good," Touron said. "Real good."

"That shield move was genius," Saffe said.

But it had taken a chunk out of Derek's energy levels. "How is everyone feeling after using their shields?"

"I'm good," Shar said.

"Me too," Touron added.

But Derek wasn't. "Do your shields feel...depleted?"

Touron shook his head. "I don't think so. I feel energized. Drawing from the elements helped."

Hmmm...maybe this was the downside of having a sentient shield that existed outside of my body. Maybe it took longer for him to recharge because he was a separate entity. Maybe *he* needed to draw from the elements.

"Derek, can you recharge by drawing from the air? From the storm that's coming in?"

Derek looked up at the rapidly darkening storm clouds. "I don't feel a connection to the storm. My connection is to you."

And I'd fed off the storm like Yarrow and Levi had taught us, but it seemed it would take longer for that to filter to Derek.

Sharniza's lips tightened. "Let's hope that whatever we go up against next doesn't require heavy shield use."

"I think that was the shield test back there," Palia said. "I'm pretty sure we all passed."

The sky rumbled, and a flash of lightning lit up the clouds in the distance. "Great, I think it's about to—" The heavens opened, dropping a sheet of water on our heads. "Great."

We picked up speed, vigilant of the buildings around us—of the alleys and dark spaces. The sun hid, leaving us in gloom, our vision compromised by the heavy rain, auditory perception muted by the thundering sound of the rainstorm.

"Left at the intersection!" Palia called out.

We made the turn onto a wider street lined with stores. It opened out into a larger space with a raised pergola in the center. This must have been the center of this settlement where markets were held and functions were hosted. Maybe the pergola had once held a band of musicians. It might even have been hung with pretty lanterns.

Damn, I'd watched too many olden-time movies.

The rain fell harder, lightning flashes coming closer together as the storm drew near.

We ran in formation, ground-battle unit in the center with Hawke's teams falling back slightly to flank us.

We were ready for whatever came our way.

We were halfway across the square when the twins came to a halt.

"Incoming!" Ginia pulled her sister to the ground as something inky and viscous whizzed over their heads.

"Incoming wraiths. One o'clock!" Hawke confirmed.

They had wraiths here?

What had Levi told us about these creatures? They fed on

life force through touch, but goyles had some resistance, and it would take more than one touch to debilitate one of us. More of the creatures flooded the square until the air was filled with them.

"I can't see the punch plates on them," Shar called out.

"Me either," Touron said.

"Run!" Curi grabbed my hand and yanked me forward. We managed to get a few yards before we were forced to swerve and turn back. We ran around the pergola, then through it, with two wraiths on our tail. Then three. I feinted left while Curi feinted right, and all three turned toward me.

Curi yanked me toward him, and their hooded heads turned, still focused on me.

"What the fuck?" Curi said.

Another blocked our path, and suddenly we were surrounded by cloaked shapes floating a couple of feet off the ground.

They closed in on us.

"Cameron!" Touron shouted from outside the circle.

Curi's grip on my hand tightened. "I can't see any punch plates, Cam. This is wrong. Something's gone fucking wrong."

They were focused on us...No...not on us, on *me*. They were all looking at me. What the actual fuck?

"Cameron..." Curi hugged me to his chest protectively. He'd picked up on it too.

The wraiths let out a collective mournful wail, then rushed us.

Derek materialized in front of us, letting out a roar that sent a blast of light outward, forcing them back.

It was impossible to tell whether their screams were of pain or anger at being thwarted.

Derek cried out and dropped to his knees. "Cameron, run," he pleaded, looking up at me with dull gray eyes.

He was depleted. His energy was too low to fight these fuckers off, but he'd beaten them back and created an opening for my escape.

They were after me, and if Curi was with me, he was in

danger. But his grip on my hand was so tight there would be no getting away.

I'm sorry, Curi. I let loose my talons and stabbed his hand.

He yelped and released me on reflex.

I ran.

CHAPTER 42

CAMERON

"Cameron, no!"

With the hammer of rain and the pounding of blood in my ears, it was impossible to tell who shouted my name.

I had to get these wraiths away from my friends. There had to be a black line somewhere. An end to this zone. We'd obviously missed the start of it.

But my gut trembled and tightened because there was no way Palia would have missed it, and I couldn't help but believe that these creatures weren't part of this exercise.

If that was true, then what would happen?

I exited the square and ran down a street, a quick glance behind me confirming the fuckers were still on my tail. I needed to—

My boot caught on a loose brick, and I went flying, landing on my front with enough force to knock the wind out of me.

Shit. I scrambled to my feet, then hit the ground as a wraith rushed me, but I was too slow to stop its charred, elongated fingers from grazing my scalp.

They snagged in my hair, but I yanked free and turned to run.

My knees buckled and gave way.

No...

A chill spread through me as the wraiths circled. I dropped to the wet ground, rain pounding my frame. Shit...I couldn't move.

The fucker had paralyzed me with one touch.

The world above me was a mass of swirling black robes and hooded faces. They circled closer and closer, and there was nothing I could do.

Panic twisted and writhed inside me, impotent and useless. Romi. I'm sorry. So fucking sorry.

"Get away!" Derek materialized over me, his feet bracketing my hips, arms up to ward off the wraiths. "You won't hurt my Cameron!" White light radiated from his body.

The wraiths reared back for a moment before attacking again. Another blast of light hit them, weaker than the first.

This time, the wraiths pushed past the fading rays.

"No, no, no!" Derek cried. "Cameron, now. Cameron, I need more. Cameron!"

There was a tugging deep in my solar plexus, an unfurling awakening that was both frightening and familiar.

"Yes!" Derek said. "Let me have that. Let go!"

My back arched off the ground, spine bending almost painfully as the strange energy inside me snapped free.

Derek let out a roar, and crimson power spilled out of his hands and wrapped around the wraiths in deadly ribbons that squeezed and squeezed.

The wraiths twisted and screamed, and this time, there was no doubt that they were in pain. Two of the wraiths dispersed, leaving black ash in the air.

What was this? What were we doing?

My vision darkened at the edges, and the crimson ribbons holding the remaining wraith melted away.

We were depleted.

Nothing more to give.

I wanted to tell him that he'd done great. That it was okay to stop, but my mouth wouldn't move. I could barely swallow.

The wraith flew at me.

"No." Derek threw himself over me and gathered me to his chest. "No one hurt my Cameron."

His frame shuddered under the attack of the wraith, his grunts and gasps of pain tearing at my soul.

They were hurting him.

Killing him.

No. No! Please, stop. Please leave him. Derek, get off me. Please get off me and run. My eyes burned with the need to communicate, impotent rage clawing at my insides, hot tears spilling down the side of my face.

Derek...

"My Cameron..."

The world went silent and dark.

Like nothingness.

Like death.

Long seconds passed, then a spear of light cut across my vision, the darkness rushed away, and the world bloomed back to life.

Hawke swung a golden sword back and forth, slicing through the wraiths while, beside me, Levi was creating a domed shield over Derek and me.

The wraiths screamed as the light incinerated them.

Blood rushed through my limbs, bringing them slowly back to life. "Derek..." I reached up to hug him to me. He was smaller now, curled against my body. Still and silent.

"No, Derek, please." My voice was a hoarse whisper. "Wake up. Say something, please."

"Cameron, shit..." Shar fell to a crouch beside me. "Derek...Is he..." Her voice cracked.

"No." I held him tighter. "He'll be fine. He just...He needs to recharge."

"Move out of the way," Levi ordered.

Shar's jaw hardened, and she slowly turned her head to look up at him. "What the fuck was that?"

"We'll talk when we get back to the academy," Levi snapped. "It's no longer safe here."

Sharniza moved back reluctantly, and Curi and Touron moved closer, but Levi blocked them, scooping me and Derek into his arms.

"I've got you, Cam," he said. "You can pass out now."

So, I did just that.

CHAPTER 43

CAMERON

"Cameron, hey, can you hear me?" Levi asked.

Why was it so dark? Where was I?

"Open your eyes, Cam."

I cracked open my eyelids to find Chlobe hovering over me. The omega medic had a pinched look about her as she studied me for several seconds while I struggled to fully wake up.

"Hello, sleepyhead." Her warm smile held an edge of relief. "Good to have you back with us."

"What happened..." My brain felt like cotton wool. "I was...I... Oh shit. Derek! Where's Derek?" I tried to sit up, but my body was like a noodle. "Fuck!"

Levi stepped into view. "Derek is fine."

"No, they hurt him. The wraiths, they...Oh gods, he was protecting me, and they were tearing into him and—"

"He's alive." Levi pressed his hand to my shoulder. "But he'll be much better once *you're* up on your feet. You need to calm down. Breathe."

I closed my eyes, but all I could see was Derek's devastated face, all I could hear were the sounds of the attack and his grunts and cries of pain. "He's alive?"

"Yes."

"He'll be okay?"

"Yes, Cameron."

Derek had given all of himself to ward off the wraiths, but it hadn't been enough. *We* hadn't been enough. But Levi had shown up and... "Hawke has a golden sword?"

Levi's mouth tightened. "Not important. What's important is that you're safe." He had a look on his face, the barely restrained anger look. He was fucking pissed, and it wasn't difficult to guess why.

"The wraith attack wasn't planned, was it?"

"No," Levi said tightly. "It was not. The elite are investigating."

My pulse spiked. Serath was out there? Back in that settlement? "No. It's too dangerous."

"The wraiths are dead," Levi said. "The settlement has been cleared. The elite are sweeping for a breach. The area is warded. The wraiths shouldn't have been able to get in."

"But they did. And they were after me."

Levi frowned but didn't argue.

"The others told you, didn't they? They ignored everyone else and targeted me."

"Yes, Curi told me. But it makes no sense why they'd target you."

He had no idea how much sense it made. "We have a fucking traitor here in our midst, and I'll bet my ass that he or she set me up. Sent the wraiths to kill me and leave us without a fully functioning elite team."

"But that would mean the traitor can control wraiths *and* somehow bypass Stone Council security."

I was beginning to think our biggest weakness was underestimating my wannabe murderer. "Then that's what it means."

He gave a curt nod. "I'll file a report with the council. We will find the culprit. You're safe. That's all that matters."

"Yeah? How safe am I without my shield?" An awful thought occurred to me. "What if this *wasn't* about killing me? What if this was about disabling me? Take away Derek, and I have no protection. Take away Derek, and I might not make it through the cadet exams, let alone the elite trials."

"Then you don't take the cadet exams," Levi said. "You can skip them. Derek should be back on his feet for the elite exams."

But he didn't sound so sure, and my heart sank.

"Levi, how bad is he?"

Levi's throat bobbed. "He hasn't regained consciousness. It's hard to tell. Yarrow is with him doing what he can."

"But if I get to full strength, then so will he, right? We're connected."

"You are. He's your shield, and his power comes from you, but it isn't just his power that's depleted. The wraiths wounded his body. It's his body that we need to heal now. Willowman is the only one that can do that, but he's not here."

But I was. I was here, and I was Willowman's student. I knew the basic rejuvenation tinctures.

I tried to sit up again and failed. Again. "Gah!" Tears of frustration burned my eyes. I looked to Chlobe. "I know some concoctions. Willowman showed me. I just need the right herbs to get me on my feet, then I can help Derek."

Levi's eyes lit up with hope, and it fueled my determination. "What herbs do you need? I can—"

There was a sharp rap on the door. "Hey! Open up."

"Touron?" I struggled to sit up and managed to brace myself on my elbows this time.

Another knock. "Cameron?"

Levi sighed in exasperation and let them in.

Touron and Curi pushed past him into the room.

"You had no right to run off with her like that," Curi growled at Levi.

"And you locked the door!" Touron said in disgust. "Are you that desperate for alone time with her that you'd use her injury to get it?"

Twin spots of color bloomed high on Levi's cheeks, his lips

pressing into a thin line.

"Actually, Mr. Halle was following protocol," Chlobe said. "Wraith touch can, in some goyles, act like a mystical infection and be passed on to others. We had to isolate Miss Basque and test her saliva. She's clean for infection."

But Levi had touched me. "You could have been infected."

"Yes. But as your tutor for this exercise, it was my responsibility to make sure not only you, but everyone else was safe."

"Well, that explains why you yelled at us not to touch her," Curi muttered before turning his attention to me. "And you...What the fuck were you thinking running off like that?"

"They wanted me, I was trying to—"

"Sacrifice yourself. Yeah, we get it, but we're a team. We protect each other." His dark eyes gleamed with passion. "We could have held them off together somehow until Levi got there."

"Or until Hawke decided to pull out his golden sword," Touron said. "What was that?"

"None of our concern," Levi said.

Touron looked like he was about to argue but thought better of it. "I'm just glad you're okay. Those wraiths..." He shook his head. "That was bad."

My mind whirred, going over the final moments of the wraith attack. There'd been something different. Something strange. Oh gods. "Red stuff!"

"What?" Levi asked.

"Red stuff came out of me. Like...red power, and it went through Derek and attacked the wraiths."

Levi looked over to Curi and Touron, who both shook their heads, seemingly confused.

"You didn't see it?"

"No," Curi said. "I was there the whole time, trying to get close to you. I didn't see any red power."

"You were under attack," Levi said. "The mind can play tricks."

"No, I felt it...saw it. I was tapped out, and then this other power..."

The skepticism on their faces spawned shadows of doubt in my mind. Maybe I had imagined it. The wraith's touch could have fucked with my head. "How's Derek now? Did you see him?"

"Don't know," Curi said. "We left him with Yarrow at the dorm. Shar and the twins are with him."

"It looked...bad," Touron said.

"But we can help," Levi said. "Cameron, what herbs do you need?"

My legs were still shaky, my body achy from the aftereffects of the wraith touch, but I was on my feet.

Thank the gods I'd paid attention in herbology sessions.

I stumbled on the dorm stairs.

"Take it easy." Levi braced me, taking my weight. "You're still weak. I can take the tincture to him."

"No. I need to do this. I have to see him."

He swung me into his arms and carried me the rest of the way.

Touron and Curi had gone ahead to let Yarrow know we were en route. My old dorm room door was open, and the twins and the guys stood outside.

Shar was inside the room, kneeling by the bed while Yarrow knelt on the opposite side, holding Derek's slender wrist.

My shield was shriveled and smaller than ever, barely taking up a third of the bed. The imperceptible rise and fall of his chest was the only sign that he was alive.

Yarrow looked over expectantly. "You have it?"

Levi set me down.

"I think I got it right." I passed him the vial.

"Rejuvenation?"

"Yes. Willowman said it heals and restores."

"We might need more than one dose."

"I can make more."

"Good." He slid his hand beneath Derek's head and gently tipped it back to pour the tincture into his mouth.

Some of it trickled out, but most went in, and his throat bobbed as he swallowed on reflex.

"Good," Yarrow said. "That's good."

"Now what?" Shar asked. "What happens? How long will it take to—"

Derek's form shimmered and began to grow, unfurling from its fetal position until he was the size he'd been before his great expansion.

"It's working," Yarrow said.

Derek groaned. "Cameron..."

I exhaled in relief. "I'm here. Buddy, I'm here."

"Hurts..." he groaned again.

No. I didn't want him to be in pain. "I need more herbs. I need to make more tincture."

"I'll gather more," Touron said from outside the room.

"I'll come with you," Curi said.

"I'll head back to the infirmary and get Willowman's appliances," Levi said.

They quickly left, and the twins ventured into the room. "We should all eat something. We'll make some pasta."

They left too.

Everyone needed to be doing something, I guess.

"He's going to be all right, right?" Shar asked Yarrow. "Now we have this tincture?"

"Yes," Yarrow said. "It will heal him, but it'll be slow. I doubt he'll be strong enough to assist in your cadet exams."

Fuck the exams. "I don't care about that. I just want him to be okay."

Shar grabbed my hand from across the bed and squeezed. "He will be. He's strong. Just like you."

"If Willowman makes it back before the exams, he might have a stronger tincture we can use to speed things up," Yarrow said. "But if not...I don't think you should take the exams."

"If I don't take the exams, I'll never be accepted by the initiates. I need to move forward either way. I hunted for years without a shield. I can pass the exam without one. All that matters is Derek heals up in his own time."

"I want to get my hands on the bastard responsible for the wraiths," Shar ground out.

"The elite are looking into it," Yarrow said. "They set off as soon as we got back."

The thought I'd avoided dwelling on since I woke in the infirmary pushed to the front of my mind. I'd been injured. Badly. And Serath hadn't come to see me. He hadn't even tried. He'd gone straight to the settlement instead.

It was his job. I got that, but...fuck, it hurt that he hadn't cared enough to check on me.

"Never mistake my distance for disregard, Cameron. You have my heart, even though I cannot openly give it to you."

I wanted to believe that. I really did.

But the more he pushed me away, the harder it was getting to believe that the distance didn't matter.

CHAPTER 44

SERATH

It's been four hours. We've searched every inch of this place. There is no breach. I need to go back. I need to be with Cameron. Dammit, I should never have listened to Selas and come here.

I should be with my mate. "There's nothing here. We need to go back."

"One more sweep," Selas says. "To be sure." A growl of frustration rattles my chest, and she turns to me, her expression all hard lines and annoyance. "Pull your shit together. You can't be with her. Not in the way you want. She's alive. She's being taken care of. She. Will. Be. Fine. But not if your cousin finds out the truth about your connection to her."

"I can control myself."

"No," Orix said. "You can't. We all know it. You know it. So, let's cut the bullshit and set the ground rules. You're not allowed around Cameron when she's anywhere near Levi or anyone else that doesn't know the truth and could report you."

I know that he's right, but every fiber of my being wants to rebel, and my beast fights tooth and nail inside me to be free.

It's taking everything I have to force it to comply.

"There's nothing you can do for her right now," Prasan says, the third voice of reason. "But you can help us figure out how the wraiths got past the council wards. You can help find that traitor and stop these attacks on Cameron once and for all."

"Yes. I'm going to find out who's behind this, and I'm going to crush them."

"Great," Selas says. "Now let's do that second sweep."

TWO HOURS LATER and nothing. "There is no breach."

"Either that or it's been sealed," Selas says.

"Or there never was one..." Orix chews on his cheeks, deep in thought.

"What do you mean?" Prasan asks.

"If this was an inside job..."

"As in, inside the council?" Prasan's voice rises an octave. "You think someone at the Stone Council is trying to kill Cameron?"

"That makes no sense," Selas said. "The council wants an elite team. They *need* it."

Orix laces his hands on the top of his head. "The fact we haven't been able to identify the mole despite all the checks. The intact wards...Everything points to someone with high level access."

"A mole at the council," Selas says.

"That's impossible," Prasan says. "They have security protocols, checks like you would not believe." He shakes his head. "No, I can't believe it. There has to be another reason."

Whatever the reason, I'm sure of one thing now. "Cameron can't take the cadet exam. Every attack that's happened has been off campus. It's not safe for her. Not until we find the culprit responsible."

"She won't like that," Orix says. "She's worked so hard these past weeks. She'll be so disappointed."

"Better to be disappointed than dead," Selas says.

"Wait." Prasan's eyes light up. "Maybe we can kill two birds with one stone."

"What? How?" Selas asks.

"This traitor attacks off campus. We know that now, and we know what the cadet exams will involve—the three locations where each part will take place. So...I say we set a trap."

A trap? "Okay, I'm listening."

"Willowman will be back before the exams. I'll go with him to check over the warp zones and add a mystical tracker to the wards around each zone."

"What kind of mystical tracker?" Selas asks.

"You remember the transmitter I was working on? The one that was meant to cut through the graynite shade that protects the wards around their stronghold?"

"Yes, I remember."

"Yeah, well they denied my application to plant the transmitter, said it was too risky. Whatever." He rolls his eyes. "But I kept playing with it, and I came up with another use for the hardware. Mini transmitters that can connect to a ward and monitor it."

"That's...that's impressive," Orix says.

"Thank you. I sent off an application to the council last week to see if we can use it on our outposts and possibly Arcadia, too, as a security measure. I figure we could also use it on the graynite stronghold wards to monitor activity." He grins. "If they let me use the original transmitter to cut through the shade, then we can plant the mini ones. I'm still waiting to hear back from them. But Carter is already using it on the academy wards."

"That's amazing," Selas agrees.

Prasan ducks his head. "Thank you. I'm proud of it. I just wish I'd thought to use it for the field test."

"None of us anticipated what would happen," Selas says. "How does the tracker work exactly?"

"Several uses," Prasan says. "It can account for any exits and entries to a ward, and it can also read biometric signatures that have been programmed into it."

"So, you can add the biometric data of all the cadets and

identify if someone not on that list goes through?"

"Yes," Prasan says, looking more than a little smug. "We can do this. We can catch the traitor."

For the first time since this fiasco started, I feel as if I might be able to take a breath. "Let's head back and tell Cameron."

"No!" Prasan says quickly. "Best to keep this between us. The traitor could be anyone."

"A cadet?" Orix snorts. "No cadet has that much clout."

"Maybe not," Selas says, "but they might be working with or for someone. Prasan is right. We keep this to ourselves and Willowman. No one else."

Anything to keep Cameron safe. "Agreed."

CHAPTER 45

Cameron

Dawn was less than an hour away when we sat down in the kitchen for a bite to eat. Yarrow and Levi were still with Derek. They'd shooed us off with instructions to get some food.

I'd wanted to stay, but Levi reminded me that if I wasn't fueled up and recharged, it would make it harder for Derek to heal.

The dorm was quiet now. The hubbub following the field trip was over, although I doubted the cadets would stop speculating on what had happened. Everyone had seen the wraiths go after me. They'd draw their conclusions.

The mood was tense, and we ate in silence, even though I doubted that any of us felt hungry.

"I wonder if the elite are back," Palia said.

"If not, then you stay with us," Curi said.

Leaving Derek wasn't an option, security be damned. "I'm not going back there tonight anyway. I'm staying here with Derek."

"No," Sharniza said. "You're safest at the observatory. They wanted you there for a reason."

Annoyance pricked at my senses. "I'm not leaving Derek alone overnight. Not when he's like this."

He'd risked his life for me. And, yes, some might say that was his purpose, but he was more than a shield. He was a person. With choices. He could have *chosen* to save himself, but he didn't. He chose me. I wouldn't abandon him now. I couldn't. I loved him. He was home. My first family.

Levi entered the room looking weary. His dark hair was ruffled as if he'd been running his hands through it in agitation. "We're moving Derek to Yarrow's quarters."

"What? Why?" Shar asked before I could. "Has he gotten worse?"

"No. But Yarrow's residences are filled with healing crystals, and he feels the tincture will work better in that environment."

"Fine." I pushed back my chair. "Let's go."

"No, Cameron. You need to go back to the observatory. I'm sure Mason will be happy to walk you."

"What? No. I want to stay with Derek."

"What you want isn't important here. What Derek needs is. The healing crystals need to be focused on his injuries, not yours."

My being there would split their focus? "I understand, but I'm not sure how comfortable Derek is with Yarrow. I mean, I'm not sure if—"

"I'll go with him," Shar said. "I'll stay by his side."

Her offer brought a rush of relief. "Thank you."

"Grab your things then, Aziza, we're leaving now."

Shar followed him out of the room, and I sagged in my seat.

"It'll be okay," Touron said. "Willowman will be back before the cadet exams, and he'll fix Derek, and everything will be okay."

I wanted to believe him, but after everything we'd been through, the whole sentence sounded like a fairy tale.

CURI WALKED ME back to the elite quarters but refused to leave until I confirmed that the elites were back.

I let him into the foyer. "Wait here while I go check."

"Nope," he said. "You might lie to me. I'm coming with you."

"You aren't even supposed to be in here."

"I don't care." He crossed his arms. "So, elevator or stairs?"

I rolled my eyes and headed for the elevator.

It was a tight fit with us both inside, but my body had become attuned to proximity with Curi, so it didn't bother me.

The main lounge was empty.

"Looks like no one's home," Curi said.

"They might be in the observatory watchtower."

"I've always wanted to see the view from up there."

He wasn't supposed to be in the elite quarters, let alone the watchtower, but after the day I'd had, the thought of hanging out by myself wasn't appealing.

We took the stairs this time. I stopped off on Serath's floor, then Orix and Prasan's on the off chance one of them was home. But no.

"I'm sure they won't mind me staying till they get back," Curi said.

The observatory watchtower was bathed in starlight, Prasan's computer running in the background, green lines scrolling across the screen. A shadow shot out from behind Orix's favorite seating spot.

"Taz, hey, boy."

He allowed me to pet him.

"You have a cat?"

"Taz is kinda the house mascot. One of Orix's saves."

"I heard he had a thing for pussy, but I thought..." He shook his head in confusion.

I stifled a laugh. "He has a thing for cats *and* for pussy. The man's a hussy, but he has a heart of gold."

Taz purred as if in agreement.

Curi crouched to pet him, and Taz allowed it.

"His eyes, wow, they're gorgeous," Curi said.

"I know."

"We weren't allowed to keep any animals."

"Pets aren't really a thing in the human world either."

"No, I suppose they're not." Curi gave a heartfelt sigh. "But they are in Arcadia, just not for the male or alpha female goyles."

I could believe it. After what Sharniza had told me about her upbringing, it was obvious that the goyle youth were trained to have very little wants or attachments. I suppose it made it easy for them to be trained to serve a singular cause.

Taz, fed up of being petted, wandered off with a flick of his tail.

We moved to the window and the epic view of campus and the world beyond the walls.

The tight muscles in my shoulders relaxed a little. "Beautiful, isn't it?"

"Yeah...beautiful..."

I glanced at him to find him staring not at the view but at me.

My stomach dipped. "Curi..."

He dipped his gaze. "You can't be with him."

"I know that."

"Then be with me."

"What?"

"I can give you what you need. I can fill the emptiness."

"I'm fine. I don't need—"

"Maybe not now. But you will. I want you to come to me." He turned me to face him and stepped closer so that I had to tip my chin up to look at his face. "Promise me that when the time comes...when you're needing...you'll come to me." His voice was a low rumbling caress that touched a place deep inside me. The part of me that longed for physical connection and the warmth of a lover's touch.

"Curi, you feel this way now, but there is an omega out there for you. Maybe even a fated mate."

"Maybe," he said. "But until then, you have me. If you want me."

I wanted to say no. I wanted to tell him that I'd never get to that point, but I couldn't, because a fated mate bond was forever, and forever, when you could never have it, was an eternity. I wasn't made of stone, and neither was Serath.

He'd proven that with Jana.

I tucked in my chin, unable to look at him when I accepted his offer. "When the time comes...*If* it comes, then I'll come to you."

Curi pulled me in for a hug and kissed my temple. "We'll get through this, Basque. We will."

And just like that, with the use of my surname, he set the boundary back in place.

"Thank you." I hugged him back, but an icy finger slid up my spine, and my scalp tightened in warning just before a gruff male voice broke the companionable silence.

"Enjoying the view?"

I stepped out of Curi's arms. "Curi was waiting with me till you all got back."

Serath lifted his chin slightly, looking down his nose at us. "No need to explain. He can sleep over if you want. I'll be at Outpost Ten with Jana."

His words were a stab to the gut, but I bit back my gasp of pain.

Curi cursed softly. "It's not like that with us. Cameron has a little more willpower than you, it seems." He dropped his gaze to mine, and I blinked back the stupid tears that pressed against the back of my eyes. "Unless you've changed your mind?"

I wanted to hurt Serath. Wanted to say yes to Curi, but that would be a lie. It wouldn't be fair to anyone. "No. Thank you, Curi. I'll see you tomorrow."

Serath smiled coldly at Curi. "I'm sure you can see yourself out."

Curi snorted softly and shook his head. "Fate's a bitch."

He left, closing the door softly behind him.

"You should get some sleep," Serath said.

A tide of indignant rage rose inside me. "What is wrong with you?"

"Excuse me?"

"I get that we have to keep a distance. I get why you're with someone else. But you have no right to push me into fucking other people just to assuage whatever fucked-up guilty complex you have going on."

His jaw ticked. "I'm trying to help you. Help *us*."

But I was done with listening to that excuse. "I almost died today, and your reaction is to suggest I sleep with my fake boyfriend? I can understand why you'd avoid being there when I woke up. I get that you can't be around me when Levi is there, but Curi knows about us. You didn't have to be so cold toward me in front of him. You don't have to act like my life doesn't matter to you."

"Yes. Yes, I do." He ground the words out. Low and tormented. "Because if I don't, then we *will* fail. Don't you get that, Cameron? There can be no softness between us. No comfort or care. The door between us must be closed."

A storm of twisted pain filled me. "That door closed the moment you stuck your cock into Jana." I swallowed past the pinch in my throat. "Don't worry, Serath, you and I are done, and once we get Romi back, I'm out of here. I can get a posting somewhere far away from you. See, I'll resolve this issue without opening my legs for another male."

I swept past him and out the door.

I was done with having my heart battered and bruised. Serath had chosen to deal with our bond by finding release with another female, and that...that told me all I needed to know.

CHAPTER 46

WILLOMAN

The van rattles as I drive over a pothole. It's been a while since I was behind a wheel. A while since I traveled the open road like this. Magic is temperamental this far west in the rims, leaving pockets of land where it simply ceases to work. There is no warping because warping requires a steady flow of magic. The last safe warp zone was from Outpost Two, and I took this ride from there.

The world around me is dull and gray, as if the color has been muted. But this is normal for pockets with no magic. It's in these pockets that many of the humans who failed to get into the mageri-ruled city have settled. Tulpas, shifters, vampires, and graynites aren't a threat here. They lose their power without magic to feed them, and the Stone Council has done its best to encourage humans to move to settlements in mundane pockets, but people are either too stubborn, too scared, or too addicted to magic to make the change.

The air is different here, empty and unsatisfying in comparison to the rest of the world, and people can feel that. The loss is an ache deep in their bones, and not all can live with it.

I know I can't.

A sign rushes up to meet me.

Mistlegate population 550/450

I bite back a smile as I drive into the small town, past the neat gray-brick houses and busy streets filled with people. Humans going about their mundane, safe lives, wrapped up against the frosty elements.

This must be bliss to them, but there is an itch beneath my skin. A longing. A needing that will never be fulfilled here.

I press my foot down on the gas.

It takes less than fifteen minutes before the sky ahead takes on a shimmery quality. The colors seem brighter too.

The mundane pocket is about to end, smack bang in the center of the town. And this is what makes Mistlegate unique. It's a settlement where mundane and magic exist side by side. Where one half of the town has none, and the other is saturated with it.

This is where I'll find my contact.

Calista Bentleby is a well-kept secret. An anomaly who happened to save my life five years ago.

She could be anywhere from her mid-twenties to over a century old, for all I know. She doesn't share her past, and I've learned not to probe. She's made the pocket settlement of Mistlegate her home, and the people here seem to be under her protection.

The gray world blooms with color, and my body is flooded with power once more. It sings in my blood and ripples through my hair.

The ache, the itch, the needing, all gone.

The houses here are tall three-story affairs, built from red brick and decorated in blooming ivy. Summer hangs heavy in the air, defying the frost on the other side of town. This half of the settlement, with its four hundred and fifty inhabitants, enjoys an eternal summer.

Beads of sweat have already broken out on my brow.

I take a left at the intersection and onto a narrow road that leads to the market vista.

It's not hard to find parking. Not many people on this side of the town use cars because there are several port zones to get around.

I shrug off my jacket before grabbing the case containing Cameron's blood from the back seat. The inside is specially designed to keep the sample cold, and hopefully the switches from mundane to magic haven't messed with the structure of the case.

Van locked, I head to the nearest port—an ornate lamppost with a beautiful peacock statue set on top.

It takes one touch of my palm to transport me to the post opposite Calista's bookstore, and there she is, arranging some books in a window display. She looks up and spots me. Is that a sigh?

I grin and raise my hand. She shakes her head and ducks back into the store.

She loves me, really.

The bell above the door tinkles as I enter.

"I had a feeling I was about to get a headache today," Calista says from behind the counter.

"You knew I was coming, Cal. I sent a message."

"Bloody Pollock. Nosy fucker."

Pollock is the resident telegram man for Mistlegate. We keep in touch via magigram, and he let me know that Calista was back from whatever "job" she'd been on.

"No one *invited* you, though," an irritated nasally voice says from somewhere behind her.

I spot the speaker on the shelf behind her—a thick, leather-bound tome with intricate stitchwork that makes up a face.

It scowled at me. "We're busy. Go away."

"Now, now, Augustus," Calista says. "I thought we agreed that you wouldn't scare away the customers."

"He's not a paying customer," Augustus retorts.

"He might be." She arches a slender dark brow at me. "Right?"

"I can pay you in news."

She rolls her eyes. "What do I need with news of the inner rims?"

"Just because the graynites won't come this far west doesn't mean you're safe. The world could change at any time. The rift could open again, the alpha could attack, and—"

"The Stone Council will deal with it. Isn't that what the big bad guardians are for?" She gives me a cheeky kitten grin.

I can't help but smile back. This woman has way too much charm, and if I'm honest, I may be a little in love with the minx. "Yes. That's what they're for."

"We have our own problems," Augustus huffs. "Like just today, we had to—"

"Augustus," Calista snaps quickly. "Remember how we spoke about discretion? Why don't you take a nap?"

The book huffs, and the stitches on its cover melt away.

Calista presses her palms to the counter and looks me up and down, her gaze lingering on the case in my hand before sweeping back up to my face. "I hate how pretty you are." She sighs. "Okay, so what do you need, Marcel?"

I'm so used to being referred to as Willowman that for a moment I'm thrown by her use of my first name. "I need a blood sample analyzed."

"Then go to a lab. I'm sure your council has several."

I hold up the cold case containing the vial. "It's not that kind of analysis."

But she knows this. She knows I wouldn't be here if what I needed didn't require her unique ability.

Her lip curls in disgust. "Urgh. I'm going to curse Pollock." But she lifts the counter and ushers me into the back room.

The books in the store are neatly arranged on shelves and in displays, but back here, there is no visible order, just piles of texts on every available surface.

Calista clears a space on one of the tables, and I pass her the case. She pops it open and carefully retrieves the vial.

"Are you ready to catch me?" she asks.

"You could sit down."

"Do you see a chair?" A hint of annoyance filters into her tone.

"I've got you. Just...please help me, the young wom—"

"Stop. Don't tell me. The less I know, the better the reading. Okay?"

"Fine."

She uncorks the vial and takes a deep breath. "Bottoms up." She tips it back and swallows. "Hmmm, that's kind of sweet and—" Her body goes rigid. "Oh, shit, here it comes."

Her eyes roll, and she collapses.

I catch her and carefully drop to my knees, taking her with me.

The fact that she'll do this with me proves how much she trusts me. Proves that despite her prickly attitude, she believes me to be a friend. I'm not sure what I've done to earn so much trust, aside from almost dying and allowing her to save me, but Calista sees things. She knows things. And those things have allowed me into her inner circle.

Long minutes pass before her eyes snap open. Her gaze is glazed, though. She's not back yet.

Several seconds pass, and finally she blinks and focuses on me. "Well, that was interesting."

"What can you tell me?"

"The blood is a cocktail of elements. I see human and gargoyle." She frowns. "Although the gargoyle element is weak. But that could be because of the fae element."

"Fae?" Cameron has fae blood?

"Yes. The fae element is strong. I saw the moon covered in blood. I'm thinking maybe a luna line or even Baobhan sidhe? Could be both, mingled in a human bloodline and brought forth in the owner of this sample."

If Cameron has fae blood, it would account for her strange behavior during the last omega moon, because the omega moons always coincide with a sidhe moon. "Thank you. This helps."

"Don't thank me just yet." She sits up and sweeps her luscious locks over her shoulders. "There's something else. Something I can't quite put my finger on."

"What do you mean?"

"Another element. But it's hidden. Muted." She wrinkles her nose in that way I recognize to be irritation with herself. "I don't know what to call it. Sometimes this can happen with the blood of someone going through puberty or some kind of developmental change. Or if there's a sickness or disease in the blood." She taps her chin. "It didn't feel like a disease, though. Diseased blood has a specific bitter tang to it, and this blood was sweet." She stands and brushes off her clothes. "And that's all. You can leave now. I have work to do."

This is plenty. The fae aspect gives us something to work on. "What do I owe you?"

Her expression sobers. "Let's leave it as an IOU."

"I don't like IOUs."

"I guess you'll just have to make an exception. Now if that's all—"

"Actually, there's one more thing. I need to know how to restore a ghost's memories."

She stares blankly at me. "I gotta give you credit, Marcel. You never come to me with boring tasks."

"So, you can help me?"

"Nope. But I know a man who can."

CHAPTER 47

CAMERON

"You must be careful not to strip the healthy leaves," Varsa said, gently gripping my wrist. "Here, let me show you."

He meticulously peeled away a shriveled leaf from the ironia bush. "Like this. Nothing that has a hint of green must be removed."

"Got it."

I set to work while he went back to whispering to some roses.

This had become one of my favorite places over the past few weeks. I'd come back several times simply to hang out with Varsa. There was something soothing about his presence, and the fact that I was the only person he chose to speak to left me feeling honored.

But today, even Varsa's presence couldn't take away the pit of darkness inside me.

"You're troubled," he said.

"I don't suppose you heard what happened on the field trip."

"Tell me."

Where to start? "I was attacked by wraiths."

His whole body went still. "Wraiths?"

"Yeah. They somehow breached the secure location we were training at." I filled him in on what happened. "Derek was hurt the worst. He's still recovering."

"Willowman will have something stronger for him, I'm sure."

"Yes. He said he would be back before the cadet exams, but those are the day after tomorrow. I'm not sure he'll be back in time."

Varsa's brows pinched. "Then you mustn't take the exam. Not without your shield."

"I have to. No one will respect me if I move to initiate without having proven myself."

"Surely they'll understand that you have a disadvantage without your shield."

"I think some of them will probably see Derek as an unfair advantage. I hunted without Derek's protection for years. I can do this."

Varsa tutted softly, clearly irritated by this.

I bit back a smile. He was such a mother hen sometimes.

"What did the elite find?" he asked. "I assume they went to the location to check for breaches?"

"Yeah, they did. I spoke to Selas this morning. She says there was no breach, and they have the situation under control."

He huffed in irritation. "And did they tell you *how* they have it under control?"

"Nope. I guess it's on a need-to-know basis, and I'm not on the list."

His brown eyes filled with compassion. "I'm sorry that you don't feel safe."

My throat tightened, and the dull gray feeling that I'd been smothering rose to the surface because he was right. I didn't feel safe. Hadn't felt safe since Ignus had tried to kidnap me, and everything that had happened since had merely been a distraction to hide that truth.

"It's not about me. It's about—" I caught myself before mentioning Romi. Varsa wasn't in the know about that. "It's about making the elite whole and protecting us all from the graynite alpha."

"And about getting your brother back," Varsa said.

It was my turn to freeze. "You know?"

"Willowman talks to me, even though sometimes I'm...away." He frowned. "But I hear him."

Away? "What do you mean, *away*?"

"Sometimes there's a veil between me and the world. I can see it, but I can't seem to interact with it. But when you're here, the veil is gone."

"Do you know why?"

He shook his head.

"Well, it doesn't matter why. I'm glad you're here. I'm glad that we get to hang out."

Varsa's smile lit up his weathered face. "I'm glad too, Cameron. Our gardening sessions are the highlights of my week."

I returned his smile. "Mine too." The gate creaked, letting Willowman onto the path. "You're back!"

"Observant little thing, aren't you?" Willowman said.

There were dark smudges beneath his golden eyes. It was the first time I'd seen him looking worn out.

"Long trip?"

"You have no idea." He stifled a yawn, gaze flicking over my shoulder. "Hello, Varsa."

Varsa didn't reply.

All animation had bled from his features.

My gardening buddy was gone.

I NURSED THE cup of herbal tea in my hands, allowing the warmth to seep into my fingers as I absorbed what Willowman was telling me.

"I'm not sure exactly what kind of fae," he said, "but the genes are in your blood."

"You're sure about this?"

"Positive. My contact doesn't make mistakes."

"But my mother never said anything. She was normal. A regular human."

Willowman yawned and shrugged. "Maybe the attributes skipped her. Maybe your goyle blood activated yours." He picked up the teapot and topped up his cup. "It's impossible to know for sure. But this is good news. It explains your strange omega moon episode. It was a sidhe moon."

"And all the strange...yearnings?"

He gave me half a smile. "The fae are complex and varied creatures. The race of fae you're related to could have certain... yearnings. My contact suggested Baobhan sidhe."

"What are those?"

"I'm not an expert, but from what I know, they're blood drinkers with the ability to sexually beguile their prey." He winked at me over the rim of his cup. "Not a bad skill to have, if you ask me."

"It is when you have no control over it and your fated mate is a sigma."

"Ah...good point."

"And feeding off blood? Am I a monster?"

He set his cup down with a sigh. "You're not a monster. You're not even Baobhan sidhe, you simply have one in your family tree somewhere." He leaned back in his seat. "It may not even be a Baobhan. My contact said it could be a lunar fae type. Honestly, I think we should speak to Mirrowind about it. She's on a short sabbatical but will be back in a week."

"So, my episodes are related to these fae genes coming out?"

"It seems so."

"And that's it? Did she say anything else?"

He yawned again. "She said there was something else that she couldn't identify, but it was probably related to developmental changes." He indicated my hand. "Your partial shift is a prime example. You're obviously hitting goyle puberty late." His gaze dropped to the mug in my hand. "Are you going to drink that?"

"Why? Do you want it?"

"I won't say no. The herbs are rejuvenating, and I'm exhausted."

Guilt gripped me by the throat. He'd traveled goodness knew how far just to get me answers, and I was picking at him, demanding more. "Here." I passed him my mug. "Thank you for going to see your contact. I appreciate it."

He took the mug and waved off my gratitude. "It's fine. I enjoyed the trip. Aside from the stretches outside of magic." He drained the cup.

"You went as far as the pockets?"

He nodded. "It's always a little draining passing through a world without magic. I'll be fine. I'm glad I made it back in time for the exams. Derek's tincture will be ready in a couple more hours. I'll take it over to him when it's done."

Willowman had wasted no time in preparing a stronger remedy for Derek once I'd filled him in on what happened on the field trip. The man was a gem.

He yawned so widely his jaw clicked.

A tired gem.

This was my cue to leave. "I should go. I have training." My stomach dipped because it was an elite session, which meant that Serath would probably be there. I hadn't seen or spoken to him since our conversation in the observatory last night. That interaction had left me feeling hollow, and now I wasn't sure what I was most afraid of—having to train with him watching me or getting to the session to find out he wasn't coming.

There was a knock on the door, and I answered it for Willowman.

Prasan blinked in surprise. "I was looking for Willowman. I assume he's back?"

"I am," Willowman said from behind me.

"I was hoping for a private word," Prasan said.

A sudden wave of protectiveness toward my witch tutor washed over me. "He's exhausted from his trip so don't stay long."

I stepped back to let Prasan into the room, and Varsa shuffled in after him, his gaze vacant. How could he go from being so filled with life to this...this shell of a being?

Prasan sidestepped as Varsa brushed past him.

"It's fine," Willowman said. "We can talk with Varsa here."

I stepped outside. "Don't forget the tincture."

"Wait!" Willowman hurried over and pressed a vial into my hand.

"What's this?"

"A memory spell. For Melanie."

Shit. I'd almost forgotten about my ghostly friend. "How do I use it?"

"Uncork it when she manifests and throw it at her."

"That's it?"

"That's what I was told."

I pocketed the vial, gratitude warming my chest. "Thank you. Truly."

His smile was warm honey. "Anytime."

I hurried up the path. I had a ghost to find.

CHAPTER 48

CAMERON

Melanie was a no-show, so I left the vial in the drawer and headed to training, where Serath was a no-show. Selas and Orix ran me through drills, and then we hit the gym for a workout that left me soaked in sweat.

"You did great," Orix said. "I'm so fucking proud of you."

My eyes heated because this was a huge compliment coming from Orix, who wasn't impressed by anything. "Thank you. You have no idea how much I needed to hear that."

"Serath would say the same if he was here," Selas said.

The warm fuzzy feeling died. "Well, he isn't here, and he didn't train me. You guys did. I owe you."

Selas's mouth tightened. "Just pass the exam, and we're square."

Orix nudged Selas. "Can I ask her now?"

Selas chuckled. "Yes, you can ask her."

"As elites, we get a day off every so often, and ours is tomorrow, but with everything that's happened, we've decided we'll take the evening off tonight instead. We'd like you to join us."

"It's a spontaneous trip, so no one will have had time to prepare an attack," Selas said bluntly.

They were changing their time off so I could go with them?

"I...Thank you. I'd be honored to hang with you."

"Great!" Orix rubbed his hands together. "We leave in an hour."

"Where are we going?"

"Asteria."

I COULDN'T LEAVE for the evening without checking on Derek. I showered quickly and made my way to Yarrow's quarters on the second floor of the main academy building. The tutors lived here, in what they called the residents wing. But there was no access without a swipe card.

I buzzed and waited.

The intercom crackled, and a male voice answered, "Yes?"

"Hi, it's Cameron Basque. I'm here to see Mr. Yarrow?"

"Cam?"

"Levi?"

The door beeped as the lock released, and I pushed through into the corridor beyond to find Levi striding toward me.

"Willowman visited a half hour ago and administered some healing tincture, and Miss Aziza stepped out for a bite to eat," he said.

"Is Derek awake?"

"In and out." He studied me for a beat. "Are you all right?" The question was asked tentatively, almost as if he were no longer sure if he had the right to inquire.

"I'm fine. Just...tired."

His expression softened in sympathy. "I know, Cam. I know." He pressed his lips together for a moment, then exhaled through his nose. "We can still stop this."

Huh? "Stop what?"

"You having to fight for elite."

Bloody hell. Why wouldn't he let it go? "I want to do this. I've made that clear."

"But if I just—"

"Enough." I shook my head and shoved past him. "I'm going to see Derek."

"First room on the right," Levi called after me, but thankfully, he didn't follow.

DEREK WAS PROPPED up on several pillows, taking up most of the sofa bed. Levi hadn't been joking when he said that Yarrow had a room filled with crystals. They were everywhere, in clusters on shelves and tables, and a couple of huge ones sat on the floor. The room buzzed with energy that skimmed over my skin invasively.

"I'll give you two some privacy," Yarrow said before closing the door.

I crossed to Derek and knelt by the bed. "How you doing, buddy?" I covered his hand with mine. "I'm so sorry this happened."

"Cameron?" He opened his eyes, but they were still a dull gray color, telling me he had a long way to go before he was fully healed. "I'm feeling better. No more pain."

I squeezed his hand. "I'm so glad."

"We can pass the exams."

"You don't need to worry about that. You need to focus on regaining your strength."

"*You* are my strength."

"No, Derek. You're mine. You always have been. I just didn't know it. Please, promise me you'll stay here and rest. That you won't try to find me if you sense I'm in danger."

He tried to sit up but groaned and fell back in pain. "I...I have to protect you."

"No. No you don't. Not at the expense of your life."

He turned his hand so that our palms were touching. "*You* are my life, Cameron. I would not exist if not for you."

Is that what he thought? That he owed me? That his life was worth less than mine? I wouldn't allow that. I leaned forward and gently gripped his chin. "You listen to me, and you listen well. You do *not* owe me your life. Your life is yours. It matters. To me. To Shar. To us all. I want you to live, Derek. I want you to find your own happiness, not just cater to mine."

Confusion clouded his gaze. "We are connected. I can't ignore your fear."

"You don't have to ignore it. But you shouldn't sacrifice yourself over it, either. Promise me that you'll practice self-preservation from now on."

He stared at me for long seconds, then smiled. "Don't you get it, Cameron? Saving you *is* self-preservation. You're my tether. My anchor. But more than that...I love you."

My throat constricted. Damn him with his words and his beautiful heart. "I love you too, buddy."

"Then let me be me, the only way I know how."

It wasn't a request. "Fine. But not until you're fully healed. Deal?"

"Deal."

I left him as he was drifting back to sleep and found Yarrow in his small kitchenette, sipping a cup of something.

"I just spoke to Derek, and he said something that I need to ask you about."

Yarrow lowered his cup. "Go on."

"He said that I was his tether. That self-preservation meant keeping me alive."

Yarrow's jaw ticked. "It would seem so."

"I thought he was his own entity. His own person."

"He is, or at least he will be once he believes in himself. Right now, if you die, he might cease to exist simply because he believes his existence is dependent on yours."

"So, he needs to believe it?"

"Belief is a powerful force. Derek was born of belief. Crafted out of need using imagination, and now he must exercise his own if he wishes to be free."

"We have to help him. Can you work with him? Make him

see that I'm not his tether?"

"If I do that, then he'd no longer be obligated to protect you."

"I don't care about obligation. I care about his life."

He set his cup down and tucked in his chin. "It seems I've misjudged you, Miss Basque. I'll do my best to find a solution."

"Thank you."

We were at the main door when a thought occurred to me. "Can you keep him here until after the exam?"

Yarrow looked down his nose at me, his golden eyes bright in his face. "You're worried he'll come to your aid and injure himself further."

"Yes."

"Then I'll do what it takes to keep him safe."

That's all I could hope for.

CHAPTER 49

CAMERON

The elite and I took an orb to Asteria, but unlike the last time when I'd visited with Evelyn and the omegas, we didn't arrive in an alley. We materialized in a room neatly piled with boxes. Orix led us up a flight of stairs and into a dimly lit hallway.

"This is our Asteria residence," Selas said. "This is where we sometimes stay when we have time off."

"If we don't want to go all the way back to Arcadia," Orix added.

"Serath should be here," Prasan said, slipping past us and through a door to my left.

"He'll find us," Orix said.

He was coming? I took a breath to calm my racing pulse.

"You all right?" Selas studied the air around me.

"I'm fine. Eager to get out there and explore."

The house was on a quiet street not far from the center of town. Dusk had fallen, and the temperature had dropped, but people were still out walking the streets, wrapped in coats and hats.

"Asteria is one of the most protected settlements in the inner rim," Selas said.

"Yeah, Evelyn mentioned that."

"The wards here are powerful," Prasan added.

It was impossible not to feel safe surrounded by the elites. They exuded power and authority, and we garnered plenty of looks as we walked into the market square.

"We should get a bite to eat," Orix said. "Viola's has a special on tonight. I promised Taz leftovers."

"You and that feline..." Selas shook her head with a smile.

"Viola's is by booking only," Prasan said.

"I know," Orix replied. "But I have skills. Leave it to me." He dropped us a wink and headed across the street.

I spotted the store where Shar and I had stopped to get accessories. Maybe I should have asked to bring my friends with us? But this was elite time. It would have been an intrusion. I'd have to come back with Shar and the gang soon.

Selas stopped at a stall that sold pretty crystals. "This one exudes cleansing energy." She held it up to admire it, but all I saw was a white chalky stone.

I was curious to know what she saw when *she* looked at it. "What do you see?"

"A rainbow." She smiled and held it out to me. "For you."

I took it, and her smile dipped slightly.

"What?"

She blinked and shook her head. "Nothing." She paid the vendor. "How is Derek now?"

"Getting better. I popped in to see him before meeting up with you guys."

"Will he be healed in time for the exam?" Prasan asked.

"It's doubtful. But I can do the exam without him." Selas and Prasan exchanged a glance, and something unspoken passed between them. "What is it?"

"Nothing," Prasan said firmly.

Orix jogged across the road with a satisfied smirk. "Guess who managed to get us a table at Viola's?"

"You're joking," Prasan said. "They're always booked out."

"Even for elites?" I arched a brow.

"For anyone," Selas said. "Elites don't get special treatment at Viola's."

"But Orix does." Orix waggled his eyebrows.

"Please don't speak about yourself in the third person," Selas said, sweeping past him with a sniff and a flick of her hair. But the smile flirting with her lips was indulgent.

Viola's was what I'd call a classy joint. Not that I'd been in many of those, but I'd seen plenty on-screen in the movies that Romi and I had watched over the years.

Candlelight, napkins, and actual tablecloths. The chairs were wood, not plastic, and they had breadsticks on the table.

We were given a table for six.

"I'll be right back," Prasan said. "I need the washroom."

Selas and Orix took the seats opposite me, leaving the one beside me vacant for Prasan.

"I feel kinda underdressed," Selas said, tugging at her elite uniform. She had a point, because the women in this place were all made up and wearing pretty dresses while the men wore dress shirts and pants.

"Fuck it," Orix said. "We're elite, and this is the only outfit that matters. Besides," he said with a soft smile, "the most beautiful women are sitting at this table."

Selas's eyes widened slightly, and then her cheeks went pink.

I grinned at Orix. "Have you thought about opening a charm school for goyles? Trust me, there are some males that could really do with the lessons."

"If you're referring to a specific grumpy sigma, then trust me, I've tried. Serath is resistant."

"Resistant to what?" Serath said from behind me.

My whole body reacted to his voice by flooding with heat. My breasts swelled, and the pulse between my thighs throbbed dully.

Fuck. Why was he sitting next to me?

I shot Prasan a glare as he returned from the toilets.

He looked sheepish before claiming the free seat at the head of the table.

Serath could have taken that, but he didn't. He'd *chosen* to sit next to me.

Dammit. Why did that make me feel good?

"How was training?" Serath asked me.

I hated how much it pleased me that he was speaking directly to me.

"It was good." I kept my tone light. "Derek is healing. Willowman is back. Everything is good."

"Good."

"Great," Orix said with a slight eye roll. "Let's order."

THE FOOD WAS delicious, and I would have enjoyed it more if I hadn't been so hyperaware of Serath's every move beside me. Every shift of his body, every accidental brush of his taut thigh against mine, every touch of his elbow to my arm as he lifted his cutlery to his mouth.

Urgh.

I needed this meal to be over because this was like some kind of twisted foreplay.

Finally, the main course was done with. Some kind of savory meat and sauce, and fuck it, I barely tasted a thing.

"They do some delicious desserts here," Orix said.

"Actually," Serath said, "there's somewhere I'd like to take Cameron."

"Sounds great." Orix grinned widely. "Let's go."

"No," Serath said. "Just Cameron."

"I don't think that's a great idea," Selas said.

"For goodness sake," Prasan snapped. "We're in the middle of Asteria, surrounded by people. They're not about to fornicate in the square."

Orix snorted. "Fornicate."

"Oh. For the love of..." Selas shook her head.

"What do you say, Cameron?" Serath asked. "Would you like

to take a walk with me?"

He was looking at me. I could feel his regard on the side of my face, and for some reason it pissed me off. What the fuck was this Jekyll and Hyde bullshit?

I turned to him with a stiff smile. "I'd love to." I shoved back my chair and walked out of the restaurant.

He joined me on the street a moment later. "You're angry."

"What gave it away?"

He chuckled softly. "You don't hide your emotions too well."

"I seem to have an issue *reading* them, too, because if I'm not mistaken, the last time we spoke, you made it clear that you didn't want us to spend any time together."

I picked up my pace down the street, wanting to walk off the anger.

"Cameron, wait. Please."

Damn him and that pleading tone. "What?"

"It's not that I don't want to spend time with you. It's just that I know we shouldn't. Sometimes I can uphold that, and others..." His eyes darkened. "Others I can't. I'm not as strong as I'd like to be, not when it comes to you."

The rage bled out of me in the face of his candor. Because how much had I truly helped the situation? Yes, the wanton episodes weren't intentional, but they hadn't helped. I should have taken some responsibility for keeping the boundaries and not left it all on his shoulders.

"Look," he said. "Here, in Asteria, it's a safe zone. No one knows us, and yet we're surrounded. For a little while, we can just...be."

"Just be?"

"Take that walk we once talked about. Eat those scones I promised you."

A lump formed in my throat. "Yeah?"

"Yes. Let's have this moment, Cameron. Something we can take with us. Something to cherish that no one can take away."

I nodded dumbly because if I spoke, I'd unleash the sob that was locked in my throat.

He stepped forward, steering me into the shadows of an awning and cupping my face. "I'm so proud of you. So very proud."

I never thought that being praised would have such a visceral effect on me, but I guess it wasn't the praise, more the person who was delivering it that mattered.

I covered the backs of his hands with mine. "Is this our wish moment?"

"It is."

"Then let's make the most of it."

THE BAKERY WAS an all-night place, tucked down a side street but easy to find because of the wonderful smells drifting from it. We took a table outside, despite the chill.

Serath placed an order of hot chocolate and scones before fixing his pale blue eyes on me. "I've fantasized about this so many times."

To someone else, this scenario might have seemed mundane, but to us, it was a fantasy. Being together like this. Just the two of us. This...date scenario.

"Me too. I'm glad you invited me."

"We can make more of these memories," he said. "If we get a chance before—"

"Don't. Don't spoil it. Tell me something about you. About your time as a cadet or your life with Farnell. Or...what was it like for you as a child before..."

His gaze took on a misty look. "It was happy. I was happy. Innocent. Lucky that my omega mother lived with us. That we had the illusion of a real family. She used to take me for walks every day to feed the birds. She loved birds. There was a garden close to our home filled with them. Every color imaginable. It was as if they were attracted to that place. To her." His smile was soft, his expression faraway as he lost himself in the memories. "We'd sit on the same bench every time, and she'd read to me, surrounded by all the beautiful birds, and she'd say, '*One day you'll be able to fly, just like them*.'"

"Wait...can omegas fly?"

"No. Omega's don't shift. Their bodies are made for procreation."

"And your mother...she went onto the front lines?"

His smile was filled with pride. "Yes. She did." His gaze swept over my face. "Everyone considered her weak, but she proved them wrong, again and again, just like you do, Cameron. I know that she would have loved you."

I would have loved to know the woman who'd sired such an amazing male. Resilient, a survivor. "She sounds wonderful."

"She was. What about you? Tell me about your childhood."

"When I was little, my mother worked six days a week. She'd come home every night exhausted, make supper, then fall asleep on the sofa. But on Sunday..." I sighed, recalling the feeling of a Sunday morning with my mother. "On Sunday, my mother would bake. I'd sit at the table with a plate of cookies and a glass of milk and watch her work. Sometimes I'd help, but mostly I'd listen to her talk. She had a beautiful voice. She'd tell me stories while she cooked. Afterwards, we'd snuggle on the sofa and watch our favorite cartoon tapes. Sunday was the best day because on Sunday, she was all mine." Gods, I missed her.

Serath reached across the table and took my hand. "I would have been honored to know her."

"Here you go." The waitress placed a tray on our table. "Enjoy."

We spent the next half hour drinking hot chocolate, eating scones, and chatting about anything and everything. Being with Serath felt easy. It felt right.

I polished off my final scone with a satisfied groan. "Delicious."

"You have powder on your cheeks," Serath said with a smile. He reached out to brush it away, his fingers lingering at the corner of my mouth.

His touch stole my breath.

"You have powder on your mouth too," he said gruffly.

I licked my lips, and he made a soft sound, part distress, part yearning, because if this were real, we'd be going home to bed. Skin to skin, satiating the need between us. If this were real, there'd be no barrier, and he would kiss me right now.

He exhaled softly, as if reading my thoughts and leaned in.

Oh gods, he was going to do it. He was going to kiss me.

"Serath?" a female voice called out.

Serath sat back in his seat, his expression shuttering.

The goyle strode toward us, another two goyles in tow. They were dressed in alpha team colors of gray and silver. My heart sank because could this be—

"Jana, what are you doing here?" Serath asked warmly.

"Outpost Ten respite. We have an evening off."

"You should have let me know." Serath pushed back his seat and stood.

"Oh?" Jana's smile was flirtatious and pretty. "And what would you have done?"

Serath smiled, the slow burn smile that usually made my panties wet, but now, when aimed at someone else, left me dry as the Sahara.

Jana lifted her chin, eyes lighting up with expectation.

The scones and hot chocolate I'd consumed churned in my belly while my beast pressed against my skin, begging to be let out. Begging to defend what was ours.

"And who is this?" Jana finally looked my way.

"Miss Basque, meet Jana Rune," Serath said.

"Basque?" Jana stood straighter. "Our new elite-to-be. It's so good to meet you. Best of luck with the trials, not that you'll need it with Serath as a mentor."

Had he been her mentor at one time? Had they fucked back then? Oh gods, I needed to get out of here.

I stood up quickly and fixed a warm smile on my face. "Lovely to meet you too." I blasted Serath with the same smile, cheeks aching from holding it. "Thank you for showing me this place. It was kind of you. I should get back to the others."

"I'll walk you," Serath said.

"No need." I waved him off. "I'm sure you have better things to do." I walked away before I could lose my shit and claw out the poor, unsuspecting female's eyes or bawl out my own.

The world blurred, hot tears of anger and frustration stinging my lids.

"Cameron! Hey!" A hand fell on my shoulder, and for one stupid moment I thought it was Serath, but it was Orix looking at me with concern. "Ah, shit." He put his arm around my shoulder and tucked me into his side. "Where's Serath?"

"Jana found us."

"Ah..."

"I'm so fucking pathetic."

"No. No you're not. This situation is pathetic." He gave me a sideways hug.

"Can we..." I swallowed back a sob. "Can we please go home?"

"Sure we can. Let's go find the others."

CHAPTER 50

TOURON

Jogging usually clears my head, but not today. Today, the doubts won't stop circling like vultures.

I know what I'm doing is dangerous because it can never lead to anything, but I can't stop. I don't want to.

She'll have to put a stop to it. Until then, I'm all in.

Dammit. I'm all in.

"Lomax!" Curi jogs to catch up to me. "You seen Basque?"

He sounds relaxed and unfettered, and it pisses me off. "Why do you do that?"

"Do what?"

"Call her Basque when you want to call her Cam?"

"What?" He looks confused, but it's a lie. He knows exactly what I mean.

"Look, I know you have feelings for her."

Curi stops and draws me to halt. "What crawled up your ass and died?"

I'm being a bastard. He doesn't deserve it. "I'm sorry. Bad day." I'm a mess.

Curi studies me through narrow, speculative eyes. "Who is she? One of the omegas? Did you guys hook up after the moon? You know it's allowed. You don't have to hide it."

"It's not...I'm not...Shut up and mind your own business."

He grins. "Same to you."

I can't help but grin back. "Noted."

We head toward the dorms.

"Any plans for tomorrow?" Curi asks.

"No. You?"

"Nope. Procrastination probably."

Yeah, giving us the day off before the cadet exam leaves us plenty of time to procrastinate. "We should all hang out. Make some food, watch some movies."

"Sounds good."

The sounds of pots and pans clashing drift out from the dorm kitchen. I follow Curi inside to find Cameron at the sink, washing dishes. Every surface is covered in pots and pans. It looks like she's pulled everything out of the cupboards.

"Cameron?" Curi says.

She looks over her shoulder. "Oh, hey, sorry, I was just cleaning. I mean this place is a mess, and nothing is where it should be, and there were dishes so..." Her mouth looks all wobbly. Oh, fuck, has she been crying?

"Why are you crying?" Curi demands. "What happened? Is it Derek?"

"No. I'm fine. Derek is fine." Her tone goes up an octave. "I just—I wanted to clean."

Curi backs up a step so he's level with me. "I don't think she's okay."

"I'm fine," she snaps.

"It's Serath, isn't it?" Curi says.

The plate she's cleaning slips from her hand and smashes in the sink. "Fuck!" She throws down the sponge. "Fuck you! Fuck, fuck, fuck!"

Curi crosses the room and pulls her into his arms.

"No." She shoves at him. "I'm fine. I'm fucking fine."

He doesn't let go of her, holding her tightly and stroking her hair until she sags against him and begins to cry.

She's crying. Serath made her cry. Anger washes over me. "What the fuck is his problem?" I turn to the door.

"Don't!" Cameron calls. "Please, don't."

"Dammit, Cameron, why not?"

"Because I'm fine." She says it like she wants to believe it. Like she needs *him* to believe it.

Oh, Cameron. My sweet, sweet, Cameron.

"You are *not* fine," Curi grinds out. "What happened?"

She takes a deep breath and pulls out of his arms. "I met Jana."

"Who?" Curi looks confused. "Wait, the goyle Serath is fucking?"

My heart sinks.

"It's okay," she says. "I just...I wasn't expecting to have to meet her."

"He introduced you to her?" Curi looks like he wants to punch a wall.

Cameron shakes her head. "No, it was an unfortunate coincidence. I don't want to talk about it."

But someone needs to. "Where is he now?"

"I don't know. I came back with the other elite. They took me to Asteria." Her smile is watery. "It was fun until...until it wasn't." She wipes her nose with her sleeve and looks around the kitchen. "Wow, jealousy is not a good look on me."

I hate how this fated bond has reduced my fierce friend to this red-eyed teary mess. "We'll help you clean up."

She looks like she's about to protest, but then her shoulders droop in defeat. "Thanks."

"Then we'll watch a movie," Curi says.

"Something with blood and guts?" Cameron asks.

"My favorite." Curi grins down at her, and she beams up at him.

Why couldn't fate have bound her to someone like him?

Someone, anyone, free to love her would be better than the sigma elite.

It makes no sense in the grand scheme of things that Serath and Cameron can't be together.

None at all.

CHAPTER 51

SELAS

The sun's rays slowly light up the sky as a dark silhouette makes its way across campus and slips into one of the dorms. The figure glows against my monochromatic vision, a soft amber, the color of sexual satisfaction.

"I'm not going to ask where you've been," Orix says, handing me a cup of coffee. "But you should get some sleep soon."

I wrap my hands around its warmth. "Do you think Serath is doing the right thing pushing Cameron away like this?"

"I can respect his decision," Orix says. "But I hated seeing her so upset the other night. Him not coming home made it worse."

"She thought he was with Jana."

"It's what he wanted her to believe. I'm glad she had some quality time with her friends today."

"I don't think he has to rub it in her face. She already believes that he spent two weeks with Jana. She doesn't know he spent them doing the rounds of other outposts."

"He's protecting Cameron."

"Then he shouldn't have taken her on a date in Asteria."

Orix joins me at the window. "It's not always easy to give up the things that we want."

The gentle heat of his gaze kisses the side of my face, then drops to my mouth. If I turn toward him now, he'll step closer and touch me. Will I let him? No. Not any longer. There is another male under my skin now. At least until he too is taken from me.

Orix releases me from his probing gaze. "Cam will be fine. She has a strong support network. She'll help us get Romi back, and then she'll leave. If she thinks Serath is seeing Jana, she'll steer clear of him. Heck, she probably hates him a little now. He just needs to keep up the charade for three more weeks."

But what if we don't get Romi back? Or what if we get him back and he's wrong like Varsa? No. I can't think about that. I must keep a positive mindset.

I look up into the night sky. "It would be better if Serath could stay gone until after the cadet exams."

"I know. But Lionel will expect him to be present."

"If Lionel even shows."

"Carter said he would," Orix reminds me.

The door swings open, and Prasan enters, carrying a ring-bound folder. "What are you two doing awake?"

"Waiting on you," Orix says. "How did it go? All set for tomorrow?"

"Willowman and I have everything set up. If the traitor makes a move, we'll catch him. Willowman even set up a shut-down on the wards if we get a hit."

"So, the traitor won't be able to escape?"

"Exactly." Prasan grins. "I have it all under control." He crosses to the computers and settles in his seat.

"I thought everything was set up?" Orix says.

"It is. I'm going to run a diagnostic on our system, make sure all channels are clear and operational."

"Didn't you do that last week?" Orix asks.

A flash of annoyance crosses Prasan's usually amiable features. "Do I tell you how to do your job?"

Taz hisses at Prasan.

"Hey, I was just asking."

Prasan sighs. "Sorry, I'm just tired. Planting the transmitters took a lot out of me. But Willowman looked about ready to drop." He taps away at the keyboard. "Is Serath back yet?"

"Not yet," Orix says.

Taz wanders over to the door and stares at it.

"It's weird having Serath dropping in and out like this," Prasan says. "I honestly think he should just tell Cameron the truth about what happened at Outpost Ten, that he only kissed Jana so she wouldn't get suspicious and start digging into why he suddenly didn't want to sleep with her any longer. She needs to know he isn't sleeping with anyone."

"We've been over this," Orix says. "It's best if Cam hates Serath."

I snort. "He's her fated mate. She can't hate him."

"Dislike then."

Taz claws at the door and meows.

Orix crosses the room and opens the door for him, but Taz isn't interested in leaving.

Orix and I exchange glances.

"Do you think there was someone there?" Orix whispers.

My heart sinks because the only other person in the tower except us is Cameron.

CHAPTER 52

CAMERON

I wasn't an eavesdropper. Not usually, but this time I was glad I'd snooped.

There was a sense of peace inside me now. The awful clawing was gone. I waited for an hour until I heard Selas come to bed and then an hour after that until the tower was silent, then I took the stairs down to Serath's floor.

My beast sensed that he was back, and we needed to talk.

I knocked softly on his door, and he answered almost immediately, as if he'd been waiting.

He was still dressed in his elite outfit, dark hair windswept, powerful frame silhouetted by the moonlight that filled the room behind him.

He towered over me, solid and safe, and it took every ounce of will not to step closer and wrap my arms around him.

"You shouldn't be down here," he said gruffly.

"I know."

"I'm sorry about Jana. I wasn't planning on you meeting her like that."

"Or ever."

"Sorry?"

"I know, Serath. I know the truth."

His left eye flinched. "I don't understand."

"I overheard the others talking about it earlier. You're not really sleeping with her."

He exhaled through his nose, the corners of his mouth dimpling. "It doesn't change anything."

"Yes. Yes, it does. Because the awful pit inside me is now gone. My beast can focus on the exam tomorrow. I can stop feeling as if my heart is being torn from my chest."

His throat bobbed.

He was wrong. Everything had changed. "I know you thought you were doing the right thing. I understand why you felt you had to. I know that the forces drawing us together are getting stronger every day, and I know that it won't be easy to fight them, but I promise you that I'll do my part. From now on, I'll respect the boundaries too. It's not all on you, Serath. I'm sorry you felt that it was." He took a step toward me, but I backed up. "A few more weeks, and we can go our separate ways. We can do this."

His bright eyes dulled. "Cameron, I—"

"I know." I smiled up at him, taking a moment to soak in his beauty as it shone down on me. "Wish me luck for later?"

His shoulders drooped, the muscles in his body unknitting as he relaxed. "You don't need luck. You have the skill, and I'll be there at the finish line to celebrate with you."

"Thank you." I walked away, every step a shard in my abdomen as I fought my primal instinct to run into his arms.

Knowing that he hadn't betrayed our bond, knowing that he was still mine had removed the pain, but it had also lifted the barrier he'd put between us.

It wouldn't be easy to build and maintain a new one, but I was certain that we could do it. Together.

THE SUN WAS an hour from setting, and the sky was tinged crimson. The iron gates of the academy loomed in front of us, open wide enough to allow us to spill out.

Farnell stood in that aperture, his back to the outside world, his focus on us.

Around me, my fellow cadets murmured and shuffled, eager to get this show on the road.

Today, we were all dressed in lastonflex, blue with yellow cuffs and collars. The colors of a cadet. If we made initiate, we'd graduate to navy. General would be bottle green. For me, it would always be navy, whether I passed with a high score or not, but that fact made me more determined to prove myself. To prove that I deserved the navy colors.

"Cadets, today is a big day," Farnell said. "If you're worthy, you'll make it to the finish line and be allocated either general or initiate. If you scrape through or if you're carried, then you'll be allocated to a spot in administration, and trust me, death is preferable to that fate."

"Wow," Ginia muttered. "Harsh."

My gaze flicked to the elites, standing in a row beside Farnell, hands clasped behind their backs like good soldiers. Orix caught my eye and winked, but Serath kept his gaze straight ahead. Selas had her chin tucked in, and there was no sign of Prasan.

"You will be monitored," Farnell said. "You will be watched, and your performance scored."

How would they watch us? How would they score? I had questions, but there was no time to ask them before we were ushered through the gates to the warp zone between the stones.

Prasan was there, standing by one of the huge stones.

"Where's Willowman?" Farnell asked him.

"He got held up. But everything is set. We're good to go."

"All right, everyone into the circle," Farnell ordered.

I adjusted the pack around my waist and followed the others past the stones.

Curi and Shar flanked me, and Touron and the twins were close behind us.

We ended in a cluster with Hawke and a couple of the goyles

from his dorm.

"What you got in there?" Hawke asked, indicating my pack.

"Healing tinctures. I got permission to bring them." Farnell had allowed it, and Selas had given me three daggers. One was strapped to my arm, the other to my hip, and the final one to my thigh.

The majority of the exam would take place at night, and as I couldn't shift and didn't have a goyle's strength, I was allowed a weapon.

"You make the tinctures yourself?" Hawke asked.

"Yeah."

He looked almost impressed.

"Cameron's a whizz with herbology," Touron said proudly.

"How's your shield now?" Hawke asked. "Derek?"

"He's healing."

"Brave, what he did."

"Yeah. Yeah, it was." I wanted to ask about his golden sword, but it didn't seem like the right time.

"Three tests," Farnell reminded us. "Be aware of your surroundings and work together."

I searched for Serath and locked gazes with him for a moment—the connection fortifying in a way that was impossible to describe. He gave me a nod, his beautiful eyes filled with confidence.

Confidence in me.

I wouldn't let him down.

The world shattered, taking me away.

We materialized in a deep canyon bordered by steep rock face. It stretched into the distance, then curved to the left.

"What do we do?" Ginia said. "Go up or forward?"

"Or back," Palia pointed out.

"Saffe, Touron, with me," Curi said. "Let's go back a ways and check."

"Everyone else stay put," Hawke ordered.

Dayn rolled his eyes but didn't argue.

Curi and the others jogged off into the rapidly gathering gloom and were back a minute later.

"Dead end back there," Touron said. "Rock face will be a bitch to climb."

"Then we wait," Hawke said. "Sun's about to set."

"I'll carry you up," Curi said to me.

The sky turned to blood, and darkness fell. A ripple of electric energy rushed over me, and the goyles growled as they morphed into their beast forms, casting distorted shadows across the dusty valley.

Tails whipped back and forth, and wings stretched to catch the air.

My beast swelled and pushed against my senses, sharpening my vision. I willed my fingers to elongate and release talons.

"Nice." Hawke's voice was a grumble of appreciation.

"Let's get out of here," Touron said.

Curi wrapped his arms around me, and we took to the air. Touron led the charge with Hawke close behind. The rest of us fanned out below them.

The canyon had to be over three thousand feet deep, a bitch of a climb without wings. We were almost at the top when Touron let out a bellow and dropped out of the air.

"Barrier above!" Hawke dove to grab Touron.

Shit, there was indeed a shimmer in the air above us.

Hawke managed to snag Touron's ankle and arrest his fall long enough for him to shake off the effects of the force field and get his wings working again.

The rest of us dropped altitude, aiming for the ground.

Touron landed in a crouch and shook his head as if to clear it. "That hurt." He grimaced. "Thanks for the assist," he said to Hawke.

"Don't mention it."

"What the fuck?" Dayn spat. "What are we supposed to do in this earth crack?"

"There has to be a way out farther along," Palia said.

Curi released me. "We can fly if we have to, but not out of the canyon, it seems."

It was dark, even with the moon hanging like a beacon above us. "The attack will be down here. Something will come for us. We just need to be vigilant."

"Agreed," Shar said. "Let's team up and watch one another's backs."

We split into teams. Shar, Curi, Touron, and the twins were with me. Hawke teamed with Waxen, Saffe, and two guys from his dorm. And Dayn reluctantly joined Hamlin and the other goyles from Hawke's dorm.

The canyon widened, making it possible to walk side by side, but we spread out, making an arrow with my team at the peak.

The shadows grew longer, and the canyon walls seemed to close in.

"It's getting narrower," Palia said.

"Fuck," Curi growled. "Dead end."

There was indeed a dead end ahead of us.

I scanned the walls, noting pockets of darkness here and there. Wait...those were holes. Huge holes in the rock face.

"Guys, there are caves in the walls." I pointed. "You see them?"

"You think one of them could be a way out?" Ginia said.

My gut twisted, scalp tight with foreboding. "I think—" A scrambling sound echoed around us, followed by the clink of falling stones.

Oh shit. The caves weren't a way out...They were a way in.

CHAPTER 53

SERATH

The bank of screens allows us to watch the action from various angles. The canyon is filled with hidden cameras, and the show is riveting. As the canyon is flooded with grotesque, the cadets burst into action, aiming for the punch plates to knock them out. They're careful not to fly too high, but the Mason boy, Hawke, and Lomax soon realize that another way to incapacitate the threat is to throw them up against the electrified wards.

Soon the cadets are working together to eliminate the threat by hammering the shield with them.

"They're working as a team," Farnell says proudly.

"Your protégé seems to be a natural leader," Orix says. "Are you going to tell us what this special team is about?"

Farnell smiles thinly. "Of course. When it's time."

But my gaze skips from screen to screen, searching for one face.

There.

Cameron uses her talons to fend off a grotesque, then delivers a neat swivel kick to its chest, hitting the punch plate squarely and knocking out the grotesque.

That's my girl. "How many more?"

"That's it," Farnell says with a grin. "Now they just need to figure out how to get out of the canyon."

All the caves in the walls close off, leaving the cadets without an exit. They'll have to use their observation skills to find the escape hatch.

"Come on, Cameron," Orix mutters. "You can do this."

On screen, Cameron walks away from the others, her head tipped back as she scans the walls. Good girl.

"That's it, pet," Orix says.

"Prasan, any interference from outside yet?" Selas asks.

Prasan doesn't reply.

"I think he stepped out," Orix says.

On screen, it looks like Cameron has spotted a clue.

CAMERON

THE GROUND WAS littered with unconscious grotesque, but who knew how long they'd stay incapacitated? We needed to get out of this canyon, but the caves had closed. Even if they had remained open, how would we have known which one to take?

There had to be a clue somewhere to the exit. A lever. A depression plate. Something.

Moonlight bathed the walls of the canyon, and several feet from the top something gleamed where the light touched it.

Metallic.

There was something metal up there. Right at the top. "Hey! I see something." I pointed. "There."

Hawke joined me, squinting up at the moon-drenched rock face. "I see it. You want to check it out?"

I grinned up at him. "You bet I do."

He hooked a thick arm around my waist and launched us into the air. The object came into view—a pressure plate built into the wall.

"Get ready to punch it." Hawke flew us toward the wall, and I palm-punched the plate. A soft rumbling sound filled the canyon below along with a series of whoops.

"We have an exit!" Touron shouted up to us.

We joined the others at the mouth of a cavern lit by silvery runes.

"It's a warp," Palia confirmed.

"We just go through?" Ginia looked skeptical.

"Oh, for fucksake." Dayn shoved her out of the way and vanished into the cavern.

"He's such an ass," Ginia said.

Hamlin followed, and the twins went next, followed by the goyles from the other dorm. I trailed after Touron with Curi and Hawke close behind.

The world tipped, then righted itself in a field surrounded by woodland.

My stomach rebelled, begging me to throw up, but I breathed through it. Several of the other goyles didn't have such luck, and the sounds of retching filled the air.

What did this second trial have in store? Farnell had warned us the tests would get harder, so what could—

A shadowy lump lay several feet away from us.

"What is that?" Hawke said.

I started walking toward it, picking up speed because, oh fuck. "It's a body!"

"Cameron, wait," Touron called.

But I couldn't wait because I was close enough to recognize the body and oh no...Oh gods...

SERATH

THE SCREENS GO dark as the final cadet passes through the warp.

"Perfect!" Farnell claps his hands together. "They're through to the next test. This one won't be so easy to pass, though," he says smugly.

"The labyrinth?" Selas says with a smile. "I remember."

This test is about trusting senses and instincts.

"Why are the screens still black?" Farnell asks with a frown. "Prasan?" He looks over his shoulder. "Where is he? What's going on?"

Unease crawls up my spine.

"It must be a tech issue," Orix says. "I'll go find him."

But he's been gone for too long. Something isn't right.

Orix leaves the room, but Selas goes over to the computer. "Serath, can you take a look?"

I have basic tech training, but the screen shows a game of solitaire. "I...I don't understand."

"What's going on?" Farnell demands.

Orix comes back into the room. "He isn't in the washroom. I can't find him."

The screens flick on suddenly, and Prasan looks back at us from each one.

"What is this?" Farnell mutters.

"I'm sorry," Prasan says. "I genuinely like you all. You've been good friends. But there are larger forces at play here. Forces that I believe in and I must be loyal to. You won't see me after today, but you deserve answers. A few months ago, I made the call to tell Cameron her brother was dead. I lured her here. But things haven't gone to plan. She isn't as easy to kill as I hoped, and you refuse to give in to your primal nature despite the tiny pushes I've given."

"What is he talking about?" Farnell asks.

"Hush!" Orix snaps.

"But she has to die. It's the only way. I'm sorry. I know how much she's come to mean to you all, and admittedly, she's grown on me, too, so I'll give you this final gift. I'll permit you to watch her die."

The screens go dark again before flicking to a view of a clearing.

Where is she?

Where's Cameron?

The goyles come into the shot, running across the grass toward a couple of crouched figures. The moon glints off silver-blond hair.

Cameron!

There's someone on the ground.

A man.

"Shit!" Orix points at a screen to the left—a close-up of Cameron and the man in her arms.

It's Willowman.

"There's incoming!" Orix says. "Oh fuck. Oh, fucking hell!"

I zero in on the shot of the sky, of the huge, gray-skinned monsters flying toward the cadets.

I can count on one hand how many times I've come face-to-face with one of these things. The last time I barely survived, so these cadets...

They have no chance against the graynites hurtling toward them.

CAMERON

"WILLOWMAN. OH GODS. What happened? What are you doing here?"

"Prasan," he groaned. "Traitor."

An icy fist formed in my stomach. "No..."

"Cameron, the tincture," Palia urged. "Maybe it can help him."

Yes. I rummaged in my pack for a vial, popped the cap, and pressed it to his lips.

He gulped it down. “Thank you. Oh...” He pressed his fist to the wound at his chest. “He thought I was dead. I faked...but then...the blood loss. I slowed it down, but...” He groaned again.

“You’re healing?” I wanted to pull his hand away to examine the wounds.

“Hey!” Waxen waved his hands in the air, turning this way and that. “Hey, we need to stop the test.”

“He’s communicating with the cameras,” Hawke said.

“They won’t get here in time,” Willowman said. “We’re two hundred miles south of the academy. Prasan shut down the warp to this place. I need to open it again.”

He was too weak, though. “You’re hurt.”

His mouth flattened. “One more of your tinctures should do the trick.”

I gave him another vial.

“We have incoming!” someone shouted.

A dark mass was on the horizon, getting larger by the minute.

“Help me up!” Willowman said. “We don’t have much time.” He grabbed my shoulders. “This is about you. He wants you dead, and he doesn’t care who he takes down with you.”

I wanted to ask why. Why would Prasan want me dead? But the threat was getting closer. “What is it? What’s coming?”

“Graynites!” Hawke bellowed.

“Keep her safe!” Willowman shoved me at Curi and Touron, then broke into a loping jog toward the tree line.

I didn’t need to ask why he wasn’t taking me with him. I was a target, and having me with him would make him one, too, making it impossible to fix the warp.

“They’re after Cameron!” Palia said.

“Close in!” Curi ordered.

The gargoyles closed in around me, hiding me with their huge frames.

“Wait!” Palia said. “I have an idea to buy us some time.”

“Spill it,” Touron said. “These fuckers are coming in fast.”

Palia shifted to her human form. “They can’t possibly know

what Cameron looks like, right?" Murmurs of assent echoed around me. "But they might know she can't shift. So Ginia, Shar, and I, we need to shift to human form."

"They won't know which female to target," Shar said. "Genius."

But they'd target them all. "No. I won't have you put yourself at risk like that."

"If you die, we're all fucked," Hawke growled. "Protect the females!"

I was shoved into a circle of male gargoyles with Shar and the twins.

They were defenseless—no weapons, no partial shift.

I handed them each a dagger.

The graynites landed, and the ground shook with the impact. The goyle cadets closed ranks, creating a barrier between us and them, but I caught a glimpse anyway, and my heart dropped into my stomach.

The fuckers were huge—uglier and meaner-looking than in the pictures Mirrowind had shown us. Spikes jutted up from their backs and shoulders, and their chins were pointed, eyes as black as night fixed on us.

Moonlight rippled over their gray, bumpy skin, highlighting every lethal, muscular dip and plane. They weren't hunched over like in the pictures we'd been shown. They stood tall, broad, and thick-waisted with lashing barbed tails and powerful thighs. I had no doubt that any one of them could crush me without any effort at all.

The cadets were all a head shorter, even in their goyle forms.

We looked like children playing war.

There were five graynites, but there might as well have been fifty.

The odds were against us.

How could they be here? How had they bypassed the wards? None of this made sense, but it was happening, and my body was flooded with adrenaline, my beast alive and ready to fight.

"The girl," a gruff voice demanded. "We take. You live."

"Fuck you," Curi growled. "You want her, you'll have to go through us."

All the males growled and snarled in agreement.

"Then. You. Die." The graynite threw back his head and let out a roar that turned my legs to jelly and my bowels to water. "Attack!"

The world blew up with the sound of battle cries and the thunder of footfalls as the goyles and graynites clashed.

A golden sword cut through the night.

Hawke!

Curi fought alongside him, taking on the same graynite, but a moment later, a swipe of its tail sent Curi flying through the air.

I rushed toward him. "Curi!"

Shar grabbed my arm and dragged me back. "No!"

The wall of cadets was already down to five. How had that happened?

Dark eyes locked on me. "Kill the females."

A graynite leaped over the cadets, his talons aimed for me and Shar but was knocked out of the air by a stony blur.

Touron!

The graynite hit the ground with Touron on top, but my buddy barely had time to land a punch before the beast had him by the throat.

Touron bucked and clawed, attempting to get free. The graynite stood slowly, lifting Touron into the air and squeezing.

He was killing him. The bastard was killing him.

I broke free of Shar and sprinted toward the creature with a blood-curdling scream.

Its head whipped my way in surprise, and I buried my talons in its thigh.

It let out a screech and released Touron.

I yanked my talons free and rolled away, coming up in a run, hoping to the gods that Touron had managed to get clear of the beast.

The ground behind me shook.

It was on my tail.

Fuck, fuck, fuck. I was headed toward Willowman. Shit, shit, shit. "Watch out!"

He turned at the sound of my warning, golden eyes lighting up like flames before he hit the ground.

The tree line behind him ripped open, and a huge gargoyle burst into the clearing, wings spread wide, dark hair whipping back, husky eyes bright with rage.

Serath!

His gaze skimmed over my head, mouth turning down with rage as he flew at the beast.

Selas and Orix were close behind him, followed by several goyles in alpha uniform.

I hit the ground with my knees, a sob of relief clawing at my throat.

"I've got you," Willowman said. "Hurry, get through the—"

He was torn away from me and hit the ground with a large male on top of him.

"Prasan! No!"

Prasan punched Willowman in the head, knocking the witch out cold. "This is your fault," he snarled at me.

I turned to run, but smoke clouded my vision and poured down my throat. My knees buckled, and my head went woozy, and the next moment I was in Prasan's arms, my back to his chest, his forearm pressed to my throat.

"Look!" he hissed. "Look at the death you've caused simply by existing."

Serath fought for his life against two graynites. Selas was on the ground with Curi leaning over her, his hands on her chest as he screamed for help.

"They can't shift to chimera here," Prasan said. "I made sure of that."

"Why are you doing this?"

"You think I'm a fool?" I felt the bite of a blade against my throat. "I'm not about to monologue and waste time."

He was about to kill me. This was it. Oh fuck, this was it.

Derek

"Cameron!" My body is alert and screaming with alarms. Cameron is in danger. I have to go.

I will myself to her side, but nothing happens.

No. This isn't right. I have to get to her. I need to find her.

Yarrow will know...He'll help.

I roll out of the bed and stumble toward the door, but it won't open. "Yarrow!" I hammer on wood. "My Cameron is in danger."

"It's all right," Yarrow says from the other side of the door. "She'll be fine."

"No. I have to go. I can't...Why can't I go?"

"She asked me to keep you here. She needs you to be safe. She cares about you."

Panic claws at my insides. "You...You're doing this? You're keeping me here?"

"I made her a promise."

Another wave of horror washes over me. "No! No, you don't understand. This is bad. The danger is bad. Let me go!" I punch the door over and over. "Let. Me. Go!"

"I'm sorry, my friend. This is for the best."

Cameron

The blade bit into my skin, and fire bloomed where it made contact, but Prasan didn't push it further. Instead, he let out a shrill whistle.

"Serath Halle. I have your mate!" His voice resonated around us, somehow amplified. He was using magic? How was he using magic?

Serath turned, his gaze locking on me. His rage turned to horror. "Don't!" He took a step toward us.

"Stop!" Prasan boomed. "Stop or I will end her. You and your initiates are no match for us."

I counted six cadets still on their feet along with three initiates and two elite. We were fucked.

"We could take the warp back to the academy right now and wipe you all out," Prasan said. "But we don't want that. All we want is her." He pressed the tip of the blade to my throat again.

"I won't let you kill her," Serath said.

"You don't get a choice about that," Prasan replied. "But I made you a promise to let you watch, so you get to wat—"

Dark shapes dropped out of the sky and fell onto the graynites. What the...More graynites?

They attacked the first bunch.

Prasan let out a shocked cry that turned into a gurgle, and the next moment, I was free.

"You should run now," a voice whispered in my ear.

I knew that voice. "Ignus?" But there was no one there but Prasan on the ground, dead-eyed and bleeding from the mouth.

"Cameron!" Serath ran toward me while behind him graynites took to the air, chased by more graynites.

They were leaving.

I broke into a stumbling jog toward my mate, my legs still rubbery from whatever shit Prasan had drugged me with. "Serath... Oh gods..."

He was safe. I was safe. It was going to be okay.

We were mere feet apart when a gray shape landed behind Serath.

The world slowed down as talons punched through Serath's chest. Shock froze the scream in my throat.

He coughed blood, frowning in confusion as he looked down

at the talons protruding from his body.

"No!" I tried to run, but my body refused to cooperate. Refused to move faster. "No, no. no. Serath, no!"

He reached for me, his mouth forming words I could barely catch. *Love you.*

"No!"

"Live free."

His body jerked as the graynite took to the air, taking my mate with it.

Cameron's journey continues in
The Stone Curse.

THE STONE CURSE

USA TODAY BESTSELLING AUTHOR

DEBBIE CASSIDY

The Stone Curse

Gargoyles are meant to be unbreakable.

Until they aren't.

The attack on the cadets shattered everything I knew. Now the academy is under lockdown, and betrayal bleeds through our ranks. With every secret exposed, my circle of trust shrinks to nothing.

The only balm for my grief is vengeance—the promise of bringing down the graynite alpha. But his death will demand more power than I possess. Power that can only be earned by surviving the elite trial.

So I'll seal the fractures in my heart, breathe through the ache in my soul, and fight back.

It's time for retribution.

But the path to justice is paved with lies. As secrets unravel, I'm forced to face the one certainty that remains—nothing will ever be the same again.

ALSO BY DEBBIE CASSIDY

The Veritas Legacy
Wicked Onyx

Gargoyles of Stonehaven
The Stone Initiation
The Stone Secret
The Stone Curse
The Stone Survival

Labyrinth of Gods
Lost and Stolen Gods
Damned and Broken Gods
Restless and Insurgent Gods
Wrathful and Avenging Gods

ABOUT THE AUTHOR

Deviyanee Cassidy is a *USA Today* Bestselling Author of Paranormal and Fantasy Novels. She writes under the pen name Debbie Cassidy. Born in the UK, and raised in a small town, she spent most of her time reading and dreaming up stories. After studying psychology at university, she worked various jobs before finally pursuing her passion for writing full time.

Deviyanee has drawn upon her cultural experiences, and Indian Mythology when creating some of her worlds. Her books are filled with action, vivid descriptions, multi-layered plots, and heart stopping romance. They feature strong female protagonists who find themselves drawn into supernatural worlds filled with magic, danger, and romance.

Deviyanee explores themes of personal growth, redemption, and the struggle between good and evil. She's been praised for her engaging characters, intricate world building, and emotionally resonant storytelling.

Learn more at: debbiecassidyauthor.com

STORIES WITH IMPACT

WWW.PAGEANDVINE.COM